# DIRTY LAUNDRY

Paul Thomas was born in the United Kingdom and grew up in New Zealand. He graduated from the University of Auckland and subsequently worked in journalism and public relations in Auckland, London, Toulouse and Sydney. He has written several books on sport. His novel *Inside Dope* was joint winner of the 1996 Ned Kelly Award for best Australian crime novel.

*Also by Paul Thomas in Vista*

INSIDE DOPE

# PAUL THOMAS
# DIRTY LAUNDRY

VISTA

First published as *Old School Tie* in New Zealand 1994
by Moa Beckett Publishers Limited

This Vista edition published 1997
Vista is an imprint of the Cassell Group
Wellington House, 125 Strand, London WC2R 0BB

A catalogue record for this book is
available from the British Library.

ISBN 0 575 60393 3

Printed and bound in Great Britain by
Cox & Wyman Ltd, Reading, Berks

98 99   10 9 8 7 6 5 4 3 2 1

*For Mum & Dad & Jeni*

## Acknowledgements

I would like to thank my friends Steve Barter,
for providing a piece of the jigsaw, and Pam and Richard
Thom for their boundless hospitality during this and
previous projects.

# CHAPTER *1*

*I*t was entirely appropriate that Wallace Guttle, the private investigator, should have spent the last hour of his life looking at pictures of other people having sex.

Such pictures were both Guttle's stock-in-trade and the basis of what could be termed his sex life. As he studied these particular photographs for the first time, he congratulated himself on a job well done: the definition was superb given that they had been taken from a distance of 10 metres and through a window. The object of the exercise had been accomplished: there was absolutely no doubt as to the pair's identity nor the nature of their relationship.

Mingled with Guttle's self-satisfaction was disdain for the couple's carelessness in not bothering to draw the curtains; it offended his sense of professionalism when his quarry made things too easy. Not that it surprised him in the least. In the course of his long experience of such matters, Guttle had frequently observed that people engaged in illicit love affairs often took infinite pains to conceal the fact from those they lived and worked with in their day-to-day existences only to behave with a remarkable lack of caution as soon as they stepped outside that environment. He supposed it was the pent-up desire. Guttle was seldom affected by desire; for him sex was a solitary activity undertaken under controlled conditions.

He fanned the dozen large colour prints out on the desk in front of him. Six months they'd been at it the wife reckoned. She was probably right; Guttle had built up a very healthy respect for his female clients' ability to sense when their partners' libidos were focused elsewhere.

Guttle was one of those lucky people who love their work. He was a private investigator who specialised in personal and confidential enquiries. The changes in the laws relating to adultery, divorce and matrimonial settlements had driven some practitioners out of the industry and persuaded others to find new niches. Guttle, however, had stayed with what he knew and loved. As long as men and women lusted, lied, coveted, cheated, betrayed, suspected and succumbed to the green-eyed monster, he would make a living. In other words, he had a job for life. Guttle was aware that some of his acquaintances in the industry, particularly those involved in what could be broadly termed industrial espionage and counter-espionage, made more money than he did. But they were forever fiddling around with complicated and expensive equipment. Furthermore, their clients were often high-handed and demanding; those who employed Guttle's singular talents were generally prepared, in their consuming suspicion and fragility, to give him a free hand.

And the work itself! Guttle liked tracking people, spying on them, watching them in their most abandoned moments, figuring out their subterfuges, anticipating their moves, employing his ingenuity to obtain photographic evidence that could not be denied.

An aspect of his work which Guttle particularly enjoyed was reporting to the clients. Even clients who were unwaveringly convinced that their partners were having affairs reacted gratifyingly when presented with the photographic evidence. It tickled Guttle to hesitantly push the manila folder containing the photos towards the client then, leaving his hand on the folder and adopting an expression of solicitous concern, to say 'Maybe you shouldn't look at these.' He knew that once he'd

10

said that, they'd no sooner follow his advice than run naked up Queen Street.

Guttle reshuffled the photos, noting what a fine physical specimen the female participant was. She was at least 20 years younger than his client, the betrayed wife. He thought, life's a bitch then your arse drops, your tits sag, and your husband starts bonking his secretary. When he showed his client the photos, first she'd get angry, then she'd cry; over what? The fact that her husband was porking a 23-year-old with a hot body and a dirty mind? Get real. Only the month before Guttle had handed a young and attractive woman a set of prints showing her husband performing oral sex on a male street kid in the back seat of his car. Now that, said Guttle to himself, is what I call a real kick in the guts.

The private investigator interrupted his reverie to glance at his watch; it was seven o'clock on a Friday evening. He knew he'd be the only person left in the three-storey Newmarket office block, just off Broadway. Under normal circumstances, he would have mixed himself a generous Scotch and water and reviewed the contents of the folder in his wall safe which contained the most salacious photos he'd accumulated in the course of his 20-year career. Tonight, though, he had an appointment with a client at 7.30.

The prospect left Guttle unenthused. It was not his usual type of case; it in no way catered to his perverse inclinations and was, in his opinion, essentially a waste of time. However the client had been insistent and, more to the point, prepared to pay the exorbitant rate Guttle had quoted with the aim of deterring him.

Guttle sighed, gathered up the photos and put them in his briefcase, turned off the lights, and locked his office. In the lift down to the basement carpark, he wondered how much longer this new client would be prepared to throw good money after bad. Not much longer, he supposed.

Guttle exited the lift and headed for his car, the only one

left in the dimly lit basement, mentally rehearsing the speech he would use to put the best gloss on his modest progress. As he fumbled to insert the key in the lock of his car, he was asked:

"Mr Guttle?"

Guttle, simultaneously, dropped the briefcase he was carrying in his left hand, jumped backwards a foot, and exclaimed "Suffering fuck!" in a voice several octaves above its usual timbre.

The speaker was standing in the shadows of a pillar half a dozen metres away, virtually invisible. Guttle was not a particularly brave man and had long feared that one day someone whose life had taken a turn for the worse as a result of his professional efforts would come seeking revenge. The speaker stepped out of the shadows and Guttle relaxed slightly; he'd never set eyes or trained a lens on him before.

"Jesus, I just about shat myself," he said.

The stranger chuckled, brought up his right arm, and shot Guttle three times through the head, which was twice more than was absolutely necessary.

Wallace Guttle had lived alone and, understandably, was largely shunned by his neighbours. Under normal circumstances, therefore, his body would have lain undiscovered in the basement carpark until the following Monday morning.

He was shot at 7.12pm. At 10.25pm Margo Dugdale, who worked as a receptionist for the law firm which occupied the second floor of the building containing Guttle's office, drove her 10-year-old yellow Datsun, at a speed several kilometres per hour above what was sensible, into the carpark and over the recently deceased private investigator.

Ms Dugdale had come from the Iguaçu bar and restaurant in Parnell where she'd just consumed three strawberry daiquiris in the space of 45 minutes. That was on top of the several beers she'd had at the regular Friday night office drinks session, the two Bacardi and Cokes in the bar before dinner, and the half bottle of Hawkes Bay chardonnay with dinner which she'd eaten in the bar's restaurant with two colleagues from the secretarial pool. Back in the bar and halfway through her third daiquiri, she'd decided that the best possible way to complete these celebrations marking the arrival of the weekend was to engage in sexual intercourse, preferably several times.

By the time she drained her third daiquiri, she'd settled on a partner. The gentleman in question, a real estate salesman named Tony Rispoli, was quite amenable to her proposition which was worded in a manner precluding the remotest possibility of misunderstanding. Since he was married, chez Rispoli was out of the question as a venue for the assignation; since Ms Dugdale lived with her parents, staunch members of a particularly irrational branch of fundamentalist Christianity, her residence was equally unsuitable. They therefore settled on Ms Dugdale's office; she hoped that none of her colleagues had had the same idea.

Twenty-four hours after Margo Dugdale's stomach had spasmed horribly as she stepped out of her car into Wallace Guttle's brains, some 20,000 kilometres away in Toulouse, south-west France, Reggie Sparks, remittance man and failed gigolo, sat on the window sill of his sparsely furnished apartment and read the handwritten facsimile from his mother, Mareena. It was short and to the point:

Dear Reggie,
    I was sorry to hear of your trouble with the police or whatever they were. I presume you and your friend Mr Khong were very drunk at the time. You were certainly very silly but that's no excuse for the way the police behaved. I hope Mr Khong's jaw is mending.
    I am sending the money to pay your fine to your account with Banque Populaire and some extra to cover an air ticket home. Whether you decide to use it

for that purpose is up to you but I'm afraid to have to tell you there will be no more money from me should you decide to remain where you are. You've had a good run. How long have you been living in France – is it four years? Living rather well I might add. You seem no more able to pay your own way for any length of time than the day you left. As far as I'm concerned, this is the last straw – 20,000 francs is over 7,000 NZ dollars, which is hardly to be sniffed at.

Reggie, I'm sorry if this seems harsh but I really think it would be for the best if you came home. You can stay with me, just like old times.

Please let me know what you're going to do.

Your brother sends his regards.

Your loving mother.

Sparks re-read the fax, which had been sent to the cafe on the ground floor of his apartment building, with a mounting sense of resignation, grimacing at the reference to his brother. He folded it, slipped it into the back pocket of his jeans, stood up and stared out onto Place Wilson, a circular space in the centre of Toulouse, which is known as the Pink City on account of its ubiquitous rose-coloured terracotta walls and roof tiles. It was a glorious morning and already the outdoor cafes and the expensive boutiques were well patronised. Now that the gendarmes had dispersed the winos and beggars, old men sat reading their newspapers in the little park in the middle of the Place, which was full of life and bustle and steadily circulating traffic.

Goodbye to all this, thought Sparks. There was no question that he was going to have to do as his mother suggested and fly back to Auckland, which he'd left over a decade previously to wander the world. Despite his mother's wounding assertion, he had managed to support himself for the majority of that time; it was true, admittedly, that since settling in Toulouse his income had been a little irregular and had required topping up from time to time. But even leaving aside the ugly matter of money, it had been made abundantly clear to him that he was now a marked man as far as the French forces of law and order were concerned and he was well aware of what that meant. Look at poor old Khong.

The events to which his mother's fax referred, and which would precipitate Sparks' return to New Zealand, had occurred one month earlier. It had started when Sparks, out for a Sunday evening promenade, bumped into Larry Khong in Place du Capitole.

Khong, a fiftyish English-educated Lebanese, was a notorious figure among Toulouse's English-speaking community, virtually all of whom had some connection with the aircraft manufacturing consortium Airbus Industrie which was based on the outskirts of the city. Khong himself worked for Airbus as an aircraft salesman; his patch, broadly speaking, was the Arab world. He had several major deals to his credit which his numerous detractors, who habitually referred to him as "the filthy Arab", attributed to his alleged talent for bribery and corruption and the fact that he supposedly had every high-class call-girl from Paris to Monaco at his beck and call. They insisted that Khong's deals owed more to his willingness to bribe anything that moved when in the field and his ability to arrange the satisfaction of the depraved whims of Middle Eastern government and airline officials on their frequent visits to France, than to any aeronautical expertise or persistent salesmanship.

According to *Radio Couloir*, as the unofficial information system at Airbus headquarters was known, Khong was also in the habit of fiddling his expenses on a colossal scale, a cost ultimately borne by the taxpayers of France, Germany and the United Kingdom who funded Airbus. It was also whispered in the long corridors that he'd been caught red-handed by customs agents at Orly airport trying to smuggle diamonds into the country on his return from a trip to North Africa. In each instance, the gossip went, he had retained not only his freedom but also his job because of the intervention of some Arab princeling with a direct line to President Mitterand. Whereas many in the English-speaking community, whether out of jealousy or fastidiousness, detested Khong heartily, Sparks found him engaging company. Sparks was also intrigued by the talk of Khong's network of call-girls.

Sparks had never intended to stay long in Toulouse. It was a difficult place in which to scratch a living; he was a journalist by trade and, apart from a few pieces for the British rugby magazines, there was precious little scope for it. Eventually, in order to make a few francs before moving on, he'd undertaken some casual work as a translator and tour guide for the local tourism authority. It was there that he met and fell in love with Gisele Bacarat.

Gisele was a 30-year-old administrator in the tourism authority. She had short brown hair, big brown eyes, long brown legs and a slim, firm, flexible brown body. She was by a considerable margin the most uninhibited, inventive and energetic lover Sparks had ever had. She was also married.

That didn't seem to trouble her in the least. Sparks never ceased to be amazed at the way she'd sit up in his bed after a prolonged and fiercely passionate session of love-making and prattle on cheerfully and affectionately about her husband Pierre – what they did last weekend, where they were going for their summer holidays, what he'd given her for her birthday, what they'd had for dinner at her parents-in-law's place the night before and so on. One sultry late afternoon in July, as he lay naked on his back gazing in wonder at the bite marks and streaks of sweat on his torso, half-listening to Gisele complaining about how badly Pierre, who did something in a bank, was paid, he finally raised the subject.

"How do you do it?" he asked. "How can you spend the afternoon in bed with me then go home to Pierre as if nothing's happened?"

Gisele shrugged in that Gallic way which involves eyebrows, mouth, shoulders, arms and hands. "I don't understand. What do you mean, how can I go home to Pierre? He is my husband; it's completely normal that I go home to him, n'est-ce pas?"

"But how can you just switch from me to him? Doesn't what we've been doing affect you, you know, like the way you react to him?"

Gisele sat upright in the bed and waved a finger at Sparks. "Ah oui, now I understand. I didn't think you were so much the Anglo-Saxon, cherie. It is the English way that one has only so much love and to give it to a new man means taking away from the old. C'est vrai, non? You think that if I love you, I cannot love Pierre?"

"I was just asking," said Sparks. "Is that right? You really love me?"

Gisele's eyes flashed. "What do you think – I'd do this if I didn't?" she asked indignantly. "Of course I love you; I've loved every man I've had an affair with. But Pierre is the one I'll love always."

Sparks failed to grasp the significance of this remark and never really understood Gisele's ability to compartmentalise her life and control her emotions. Some 18 months later he discovered what it meant in practice. Early one evening after they'd made love, she got straight out of bed and went to the bathroom. That was unusual but Sparks assumed she was going out for dinner. When she reappeared, she began getting dressed.

Sparks propped himself up on an elbow. "Going out?"

She regarded Sparks solemnly. "Reggie, this was the last time. I can't see you any more. Pierre and I want to have a child so . . ." She shrugged as if further explanation was entirely unnecessary. As her words sunk in, Sparks' heart began thundering; a terrible feeling of nausea was spreading from the pit of his stomach. He vaulted off the bed and went to embrace her. She held up her hands to stop him.

"Please Reggie. You must understand. I must go now."
She smiled a sweet, sad smile. He dropped his head, unable to
look at her. She kissed him tenderly on his bowed forehead,
whispered "Au revoir cherie", and was gone.

Sparks' recovery from heartbreak was slow and difficult.
For several weeks he left his apartment only to go to the market
or the laundromat; after five months he remained resolutely
disinterested in any sort of relationship. The celibate life,
however, was starting to make him fidgety. He found his
thoughts turning in the direction of depersonalised sex. While
the well-used ladies who patrolled certain side streets off Allees
Jean Jaures held no appeal, the prospect of an encounter with
one of Khong's exclusive stable – who were all stunning-looking
and immensely skilled in his imagination, whatever they were
like in fact – increasingly did.

He had attempted to broach the subject with Khong a
few weeks before that fateful Sunday night, at a party in the
English enclave of Pibrac, a village just outside the city.
However Khong, a gregarious fellow at the best of times, was
in social butterfly mode, flitting from one conversational
cluster to another, quite unconcerned as to whether he was
welcome or not. By the time Sparks was finally able to
manoeuvre him far enough away from the other guests to feel
comfortable discussing the topic of prostitution, Khong had
consumed a stupendous quantity of armagnac. Sparks was still
wallowing in euphemisms when Khong cut him short:

"Excuse me old boy, I must have a puke."

Two minutes later a hellish row broke out when the
hostess discovered Khong, on his hands and knees, throwing
up into the bottom of a wardrobe where she kept her
considerable shoe collection. The hostess, a demure and retiring
woman, began ranting obscenely at Khong, betraying a long-
suppressed working-class accent and vocabulary; he affected
not to notice the string of vile names he was being called,
apologised fulsomely, presented her with a signed blank cheque,

18

and made as graceful an exit as was possible with a trail of richly-coloured vomit down the front of his cream cashmere jersey. The encounter in Place du Capitole was the first time Sparks had seen him since.

Khong, dapper as ever in a dark-blue silk shirt and cream chino trousers, had greeted Sparks warmly and insisted on buying him a drink. Once seated in a bar Sparks, conscious of Khong's unpredictability, wasted no time in getting to the point.

"Larry, I hear you're on good terms with some very classy, shall we say, ladies of the night?" he blurted.

The good cheer disappeared from Khong's black eyes.

"You've obviously been talking to some of my admirers," he said.

Sparks went a shade pink. "Shit, it doesn't bother me – in fact, I'd like to meet one."

Khong took a hard pull on his Glenfiddich and water and looked appraisingly at Sparks.

"I don't mean to pry Reggie, but are you liberally endowed with discretionary income?"

"Absolutely," said Sparks glumly. "Loaded."

"I can take that as a 'no'?"

Sparks nodded.

Khong pushed away his empty glass and leant back in his chair. "My dear chap, these ladies of the night, as you so delicately call them, are used to getting five thousand US and a Rolex for licking some sheik's backside. Now given that you're a white man with no visible diseases and" – he sniffed noisily – "no obvious stench, they might give you a discount; a tenner maybe."

Sparks started to protest but Khong gently but firmly interrupted.

"Reggie, even if you could afford it, why waste your money? These bitches are sharks – I'd rather spend the night with Yasser Arafat."

Sparks sipped his beer morosely. "It was a bit of a fantasy I suppose . . ."

Khong, restored to his customary joviality, clapped Sparks on the shoulder.

"Fantasies should remain fantasies Reggie," he boomed. "Reality is always a disappointment. Now where shall we eat?" It was clear that the subject was closed.

They bar-hopped for a while before deciding on L'Entrecote, on the corner of Allees President Roosevelt and Boulevard de Strasbourg where diners have only to decide how they'd like their steak cooked and which house wine they'll drink: red or rosé. Khong simplified things even further by ordering a bottle of each.

Afterwards Khong insisted that they went clubbing. He draped an arm over Sparks' shoulder: "Why a presentable chap like you should be contemplating going to a tart is beyond me. This town's awash with delicious soubrettes. We'll get you fixed up – just leave it to your Uncle Larry."

On the stroke of midnight, they were forcibly ejected from the Ubu Club in Rue Saint-Rome. Khong had taken his vow seriously despite Sparks' protestations. He approached a number of young women to ask, in his flawless French, if they'd like to meet Mickey Rourke, the film star. The offer was accompanied by eye movements and twitches of the head towards Sparks, by then too drunk to be embarrassed. Khong was rebuffed with varying degrees of brusqueness but remained unfazed until an outstandingly pert mademoiselle spat "Va te faire enculer" which amounts to an instruction to go away and submit to sodomy. Khong reacted to the implication by depositing a massive gob of mucus and saliva in her lemon cordial.

After being refused admittance to a couple of other nightclubs, they ended up drinking armagnac in Khong's apartment in an elegantly crumbling old building in Place des Jacobins. Shortly before two o'clock, when both were on the

verge of falling asleep in their chairs, a savage catfight broke
out in the courtyard below. Khong was galvanised. He sprang
cursing from the sofa, rushed out of the room, and returned
with a small black pistol. He flung open the double windows
opening onto the courtyard and loosed off half a dozen shots.
The caterwauling ended abruptly.

Khong returned to the sofa, giggling.

"Only blanks more's the pity," he said. "God, I hate cats."

There the matter may have ended had it not been for an
unfortunate coincidence. Khong's apartment was on the third
level; the apartment directly across the courtyard was occupied
by a Palestinian surgeon, one Abu Fazali, and his family. Fazali
periodically invited Khong over for a cous-cous but they were
not intimate friends; Khong wasn't aware, for instance, that
Fazali's brother, Naim, was a senior figure in the revolutionary
council of the Palestine Liberation Organisation. Naim in fact
happened to be visiting Abu from his base in Tunis that
weekend and, Khong's gunplay notwithstanding, was at that
moment sound sleep in his brother's spare bedroom.

There is a significant Arab community in Toulouse and
most of the various strands of Arab radicalism are represented
there. For reasons of protocol and security, given that several
of the more extreme of these groups regarded the extermination
of the leaders of the PLO as an absolute priority, Naim had
quietly informed the French Foreign Ministry of his private
visit to Toulouse.

The French Government regarded his visit as a major
security issue; over the years it had been embarrassed more
than once by Middle Eastern blood feuds spilling over onto
French soil. As a result, stationed around Place des Jacobins
that night were a dozen or so highly-trained killers from one of
the various shadowy para-military outfits at the disposal of the
French state.

Less than five minutes after the cat-scaring episode, the
door to Khong's apartment was smashed off its hinges and in

21

stormed six heavily-armed, black-clad figures. Luckily for Khong, he had discarded the pistol; if he'd held on to it or kept it within reach, he almost certainly would have been machine-gunned into bloody shreds where he sat. As it was, he was struggling to his feet when the leader of the raiding party hurdled a low coffee table and kicked him with sickening force on the point of the jaw. Khong did a back-flip over the sofa and crashed to the floor where he lay very still. Paralysed by a combination of fear, fatigue and intoxication, Sparks remained sprawled in his armchair, which saved him from similar treatment. He suffered nothing more than a swollen upper lip when the muzzle of a sub-machine gun was rammed under his nose and held there while the intruders proceeded to lay waste to Khong's apartment.

Sparks was taken to an airforce base south of Toulouse and questioned for a day and a half. It was conducted with a minimum of brutality; Khong's firearm, it transpired, was a starting pistol. On the Wednesday morning Sparks was visited in his cell by an urbane civilian who appeared to know every detail of his life since he'd arrived in France. His visitor told him the affair had been "an unfortunate misunderstanding". It would already have been sorted out, he said, were it not for the fact that Monsieur Khong was proving difficult.

It turned out that Khong, speaking in a bubbling hiss through his wired-up jaw, was threatening, amidst repeated references to his friends in high places, to take the matter further. What eventually persuaded him to change his mind was a visit from a prosecuting magistrate who told him bluntly that unless he cooperated, he would be put on trial for firing on members of the security forces; exhibit A, he was promised, would not be his little starting pistol but a 9mm Beretta which ballistic tests showed had been used in the attempted assassination of an Israeli diplomat in Paris some months before. If it came to that, said the magistrate, Airbus would be building flying saucers by the time Khong got out of jail.

They were tried and convicted of unspecified anti-social behaviour and fined 20,000 francs. The day the money from his mother came through, Sparks paid his fine and bought an air ticket home. He then packed his bags, vacated his apartment and caught a train to Lyon where he spent his remaining funds on a gastronomic binge in that city's famed grand restaurants. At the end of a week of relentless self-indulgence and suffering the worst hangover of his life, Reggie Sparks took the fast train to Paris where he boarded a 747 bound for Singapore.

# CHAPTER 2

*T*he police investigation which commenced upon the discovery of Wallace Guttle's body was initially complicated by confusion over the precise cause of death. That he'd been run over was clear; how he came to be lying on the floor of the carpark and what state he was in when Margo Dugdale's Datsun trundled over him were, for the time being, matters of conjecture. Having rung the police from her office, Ms Dugdale was of little assistance to them on their arrival; befuddled by alcohol and convinced that she'd done terminal damage to her employment, her right to drive a car, and whoever it was down below with his head squashed beyond recognition, she was reduced to tearful incoherence.

Tony Rispoli was no help at all since, having assessed the situation as being fraught with the potential to ruin virtually every aspect of his life, he'd departed the scene even before Ms Dugdale had dialled the emergency number. Taking advantage of Ms Dugdale's disorientation, Rispoli slipped quietly away, thanking his lucky stars that the lady had been more interested in exchanging bodily fluids than life stories or even names for that matter.

Constables Crane and Drinkwater from the Newmarket police station responded to Ms Dugdale's call. Their first thought was that the deceased had passed out, either drunk or ill, and, in doing so, had by pure bad luck positioned his head in the spot which Ms Dugdale's front right wheel would later also occupy. A swift perusal of the photographs in Guttle's briefcase suggested other possibilities and persuaded them that the safest and most sensible course of action was to alert higher authority. That arrived on the scene shortly after midnight in the forms of Detective Inspector Finbar McGrail and Detective Sergeant Tito Ihaka.

Constable Crane had been put through to Ihaka when he'd rung Auckland's Central Police Station to report a suspicious death. He informed Ihaka that the contents of the briefcase indicated that the deceased was Wallace Guttle, a licensed private investigator; that said briefcase contained photographs of a highly personal if not scandalous nature; and that a second and closer inspection of the deceased revealed what could be entry wounds. A quick search of the area had failed to turn up any firm evidence of foul play, such as ejected shell casings.

Ihaka listened with growing perplexity. He'd been on the point of going home where he planned to have several beers with his takeaway dinner and, in the unlikely event that he'd managed to programme his VCR correctly, watch a rugby league match. He thought about what Crane had told him for several seconds, then snapped: "Was the fucker shot or not?"

Ihaka considered Constable Crane's answer to be less than satisfactorily concise covering, as it did, an hysterical woman, the partially crushed head, and a mysterious male companion who'd vanished from the scene. He cut Crane short, hung up, alerted forensic, then walked down the corridor to McGrail's office.

Finbar McGrail, 44, had grown up in Belfast, Northern Ireland, and joined the Royal Ulster Constabulary straight from school. By the age of 30 he was regarded as one of the RUC's rising stars. At least that was how he was described in a front-page lead story in *The Belfast Telegraph* relating how he'd led a team of detectives which had tracked down an Irish Republican Army hit squad. All four members of the hit squad had died

25

the previous day in a British Army ambush involving careful planning, clinical execution, and sufficient firepower to have sunk the royal yacht Britannia. As he read the article, McGrail reached two conclusions: firstly, that the so-called troubles in Northern Ireland would more than likely continue for the rest of his career; secondly, that being the case, the odds on his reaching retirement age were no better than even. Finbar McGrail put down the newspaper and rang directory service to obtain the telephone number of the New Zealand High Commission in London. When he got through to the immigration department, he asked whether they were interested in acquiring the services of a trained detective and devout Presbyterian whose hobbies were jogging and military history.

Tito Ihaka was well aware that McGrail was a lay preacher, that he'd run a dozen or so marathons, and that he needed very little encouragement to talk at length about war in general or his favourite practitioner, Field Marshal Montgomery of El Alamein, in particular. In Ihaka's view, none of these things were as close to the Ulsterman's heart as a good murder.

He knocked on McGrail's door and went in; McGrail looked up from his paperwork, his thin, dark face expressionless. McGrail's dourness was a byword among his colleagues; a bold constable had once slipped a tape of the children's song *The Laughing Policeman* into a tape deck when McGrail was expecting to hear the confession of a housewife who'd beaten a vagrant to death with a hockey stick for trampling her daffodils. McGrail had maintained a poker face as the song, punctuated by frequent bursts of braying laughter, filled his office. Those who witnessed it swore that a flicker of a smile did cross his face when he told the constable in question that he was being transferred to Otara, or "Jungleland" as it was known to those who worked there.

This ought to cheer you up, you gloomy prick, thought

26

Ihaka: "Sir, Newmarket just reported a guy run over in a basement carpark. Looks like it's a private investigator, fella called Wallace Guttle. The boys on the scene think he might've been dead already."

McGrail took off his glasses. "I know of Guttle," he said. "He takes dirty pictures."

"That fits," said Ihaka. "He had a briefcase full of fuck photos – not porn, more like shots of someone caught doing a bit of sly rooting by the sound of it." Most junior officers watched their language around McGrail in deference to his churchiness; Ihaka made no effort to temper either the foulness of his speech or the crudity of his observations. He lived in hope of provoking a reaction but thus far not even his most imaginative clusters of obscenity had ruffled McGrail's *sang-froid*.

McGrail's thin-lipped mouth twitched; there was a perceptible stirring of interest in the dark-brown eyes. He stood up, six foot tall and lean as a lifeguard, carefully rolled down his shirtsleeves, and reached for his jacket.

"It looks like we'll be working this weekend, Sergeant," he said, leading the way out of his office.

Yes Deacon, thought Ihaka. Sex, murder, perversion – beats the shit out of family service any day.

Reggie Sparks' usual policy when flying was to drink steadily from take-off to touchdown. He did so not because he was a nervous flyer or found air travel too disagreeable to be undertaken sober. It was simply that he was temperamentally almost incapable of declining free drinks. This time though, to his mild surprise, he found himself sipping his vodka and tonic disinterestedly, having to make a conscious decision to accept the offer of a glass of wine with dinner, and allowing the liqueur trolley to proceed down the aisle. Sparks was preoccupied; he knew he'd reached a watershed and the realisation had prompted some soul-searching, although reviewing his achievements required only a few of the 28 hours it took Singapore Airlines to transport him from Paris to Auckland.

Sparks had been born in Auckland 39 and a half years before, the son of Stanley and Mareena Sparks, née Hazard. His father owned a scrap metal business, the earnings from which he supplemented with income derived from a black market meat racket. Every Thursday night he'd drive an old Bedford van into the carpark at a South Auckland freezing works; his accomplices would then transfer fresh meat, which they'd smuggled out of the works, from the boots of their cars to the van. In the evening Sparks would tour the rugby and rugby league clubs selling the meat at a carefully calculated discount to butcher shops' prices.

The management of the freezing works knew all about the meat smuggling ring. Seeing that it comprised the site representative of the freezing workers' trade union and his entourage of enforcers, management felt that the weekly theft of a few hundred pounds worth of meat was an acceptable price to pay for a quiet life: it ensured comparative industrial relations stability and meant the bosses could stroll around the works without worrying about the possibility of having a meat hook embedded between their shoulder blades. One Thursday night however, Stanley drove his meat-laden van out of the freezing works car park and into a police road block.

By that stage Stanley had profitably off-loaded his scrap metal business so the two years he spent in Mt Eden prison were not a great hardship for his family, although Mareena had to put up with regular unannounced visits from male admirers keen to capitalise on her husband's absence. On his release, Stanley bought into a milk run. The 5am starts left him with plenty of spare time in the afternoons, which he spent fishing, doing odd jobs, and stalking his former accomplice in the meat racket.

He'd learned, via the highly effective intelligence network in Mt Eden Prison, that he'd been sold out by the union representative, who'd since become a Labour Party member of parliament. Although now based in Wellington, the MP returned frequently to Auckland to – in ascending order of priority – see his family, consult with his trade union masters, and visit his mistress who resided in a small block of flats in Epsom.

While in prison Stanley had also learned about the mistress and where she lived. He often spent an hour or two of an afternoon parked across the road from the block of flats in the hope of encountering his betrayer. Eventually his patience was rewarded.

When Stanley saw the MP and his girlfriend pull up in front of the block of flats, he slid out from behind the steering wheel and walked round to the rear of the van, in the back of which his carpentry tools and gardening implements were arranged on a blanket. He selected a mini-crowbar, about a metre long. Head down and holding the crowbar down his leg, he crossed the road and approached the couple. He walked straight up to them and, without a word of warning or introduction, took a good backswing and cracked the man on his right knee. He collapsed on the grass verge, moaning loudly. The woman squealed. Stanley told her to clear off.

Stanley was contemplating where to strike next when the MP spoke urgently through gritted teeth: "Leave it mate, leave it. I'll make it worth your while."

Stanley rapped him crisply on the left ankle. The MP switched his grip from his right knee to the new source of pain and swore feebly.

"No bullshit," he gasped. "Lay off and I'll give you some red-hot bully. Deal?"

Stanley nodded. He fully intended to carry on until he'd broken several bones but thought he might as well hear what the man had to say.

"They're going to build a harbour bridge," groaned the MP. "It'll be announced next month."

Stanley bashed him once more then walked back to his van, threw the crowbar in the back and drove off.

Despite Mareena's protestations, Stanley sold the milk run and sank the receipts, plus most of their savings, ill-gotten and otherwise, into North Shore real estate. The Harbour Bridge was opened in 1959. In mid-1962 Stanley sold one of his several Takapuna Beach waterfront properties at a handsome profit and bought himself a second-hand Jaguar. He sold two more 18 months later and moved the family into a two-storey house with a swimming pool in Victoria Avenue, Remuera, which he regarded as the poshest street in the poshest suburb. They moved in on the hottest day of that summer. After he'd mowed the large front and back lawns, Stanley stood in the shallow end of the pool with a beer in one hand and a cigarette in the other and told his wife he'd never mow another bloody lawn as long as he lived. The following day he rang the headmaster of Prince Albert College to discuss the enrolment of his two sons.

As an ex-jailbird, it tickled Stanley's fancy to send his boys to the most exclusive school in town. Prince Albert College had been founded in Meadowbank 100 years earlier by a group of God-fearing Auckland merchants who profoundly admired Queen Victoria and her German consort. The school had promoted the values associated with their reign – religiosity of the Anglican persuasion, hard work, puritanism, and conformity – ever since.

Despite the pleasure it gave Stanley, the decision to send Reggie and his older – by 18 months – brother Gavin to Prince Albert was not a complete success. Gavin – conscientious, obedient, eager to please – was highly regarded in the college's staff common room. He passed through in the top form and was made head of his house.

If Gavin inherited his mother's social ambitions, Reggie was very much his father's son. He was a schoolmaster's nightmare – lazy, disruptive, always looking for the short cut and, most disconcertingly, apparently blessed with a cast-iron bottom which made him impervious to the threat of the cane, even when wielded by the headmaster, Dr Foster Hogbin. A towering, angular figure who only removed his mortarboard to eat, sleep and worship and who was prone to mood swings of unnerving suddenness, Dr Hogbin could go from a state of beatific serenity into a paroxysm of frothing rage in the blinking of an eye. If he considered the boys were making too much noise as they changed classrooms between periods, he was likely to gallop down corridors with a cane in each hand and his university cloak billowing behind him, howling "Scoundrels! scoundrels!" at the top of his lungs, and flailing indiscriminately at those too slow to take refuge.

At the end of Reggie's fifth form year, Dr Hogbin wrote on his end-of-year report: "To say that Reginald is a disappointment would be an understatement of grotesque proportions. The consensus among those unfortunate enough to teach him is that he is a shiftless lout, devoid of even the slightest redeeming feature. I urge you to consider whether he would be better suited to the state system where, for all I know, those tendencies of his which to us seem thoroughly anti-social might scarcely attract notice."

When Dr Hogbin was in an implacable frame of mind, his comments in reports could be brutally frank. But even by those standards, these were harsh words. They were written in the hope of shaming the Sparks into withdrawing Reggie from the college since he hadn't actually done anything which in itself justified expulsion. Such subtlety was wasted on Stanley. Before long however, the Doctor's prayers were answered.

Early the following year, a few of Reggie's classmates organised a party. Reggie wasn't invited since the venue was the home of a boy who regarded him as insufficiently house-trained. The snub rankled because the boys' parents were overseas and parties without parental supervision were rare events promising unimaginable decadence. In retaliation Reggie anonymously tipped off a gang, the Boot Hill Mob, which drew its membership from the Glen Innes state housing area, about the party. He'd expected that a few gang members would crash the party, swagger about threateningly, commandeer whatever booze they could find, and then go on to something more their speed than a bunch of private school kids playing Beatles records and postman's knock. He seriously underestimated the surge of class resentment felt by the Boot Hill Mob when they barged into what was indeed one of the grander properties in the eastern suburbs.

Things got rapidly out of hand: a motorbike was ridden through the house and out onto the grass tennis court where a series of high-speed manoeuvres involving violent braking were performed; a piano was pushed into the swimming pool; a double bed was heaved through a first floor window onto the street; girls were pawed; boys were punched; a great deal of methodical damage was done.

The anonymous tip-off came to light when the police rounded up the Boot Hill Mob later that night. Under pressure from the owners of the sacked mansion, Dr Hogbin launched a witchhunt to find the culprit; Reggie was a prime suspect. As the enormity of the situation dawned on Reggie, so did the realisation that if he wavered for one second in his denials, he was doomed. Even when Dr Hogbin's interrogation went well outside the most broad-minded view of what constituted acceptable headmasterly behaviour, Reggie stuck to his guns. He was not believed of course and even Stanley accepted that his son's position at Prince Albert had become untenable. It was not to be the last time that Reggie Sparks failed to last the course.

Sparks completed a relatively incident-free schooling in the state system and astonished all who knew him, even given the accreditation system's lack of rigour, by gaining university entrance. He then passed an undistinguished year and a half at Auckland University before being cast out of the grove of academe.

It was not so much his failure to pass any units which annoyed the authorities as his habit of producing ever more elaborate and heart-rending excuses for failing to hand in assignments. In order to mollify and disarm his various tutors, Sparks invented the comprehensive maiming or deaths – lingering in some cases, traumatically unexpected in others – of grandparents, aunts, uncles, sisters and brothers. The hospitalisations, touch-and-go fights for life, or funerals inevitably took place in the remotest parts of the country necessitating his absence from Auckland for periods of a week or more.

Sensing that his English tutor was becoming suspicious, Sparks produced the excuse that brooked no scepticism. He wrote off his parents, claiming they'd been obliterated when their hired car had been crushed like a bug by a 10-ton truck somewhere on the endless highway which crosses the Nullabor Plain from Adelaide to Perth. At a film society wine and cheese that evening, the English tutor mentioned Reggie's orphanhood to a colleague in the history department. The historian was surprised to hear of Mr and Mrs Sparks' fate since Reggie had told him only the week before that they were indefinitely confined to a decompression chamber in Honolulu, having suffered serious attacks of the bends in a diving accident. The English tutor then surveyed Sparks' other tutors and pieced together a chronicle of carnage involving car crashes, plane crashes, rare diseases, hunting accidents, shark attacks, botched operations and acts of God. It was clear that either Reggie was a compulsive, shameless and sick-minded liar or, that when it came to ill-starred families, the Kennedys had had a dream run compared to the Sparks.

Reggie then startled his parents by announcing that he wanted to become a journalist; he subsequently amazed them

33

by gaining a cadetship at *The Auckland Evening Standard* and making of a success of it. He endured the abject existence of a cadet reporter without complaint; he dutifully covered numbingly boring local body meetings; he did little to antagonise his superiors and even managed to ingratiate himself with the chief reporter by happily running down to the TAB to place his bets. Reggie, it seemed, had found his vocation.

By the time he reached his mid-20s and after six years at *The Standard*, Sparks had become a valued member of staff, regarded as a young man with a real future in the game. While his lifestyle was messy, it was quite unremarkable by the standards of the newsroom. His writing, excitable at first, had adapted to the narrow discipline of the news story – the one sentence intro; what, when, where, why and how; arrange the facts in descending order of importance. Hard news was really his forte – no one chased an ambulance with greater zeal or gathered facts more single-mindedly – but his mentor, the chief reporter, decided he should gain experience of politics. Few had attained a senior editorial position at *The Standard* without a stint in the parliamentary press gallery in Wellington, an experience which supposedly imbued one with the wisdom and gravitas to pen weighty leaders on subjects ranging from the crushing of the Prague Spring uprising to the meaning of Easter. To groom Sparks for the gallery, he was promoted over the heads of more senior reporters to cover the Auckland City Council.

At this pivotal point in his career, Sparks discovered the work of the American journalist Dr Hunter S. Thompson. Thompson scorned the principles of detached observation and impartial reporting by which news journalism traditionally operated. He became part of the story; he was aggressively partisan; he frequently attacked those with whom he disagreed in savagely abusive language. He also celebrated in his writings a wild and bohemian lifestyle fuelled by relentless consumption of alcohol and drugs.

Sparks was captivated by Thompson's rebellion, his flouting of convention, his zany insights, his roaring outlaw behaviour, his twisted humour, his thundering, exhilarating, Biblically uncompromising prose. However, New Zealand journalism in the late 1970s was not ready for Hunter Thompson imitators, no matter how pale.

Warning bells sounded when Sparks submitted a feature about the deputy mayor, a large man of forthrightly conservative views, whom he described as being "as piggishly greedy as King Farouk and also sharing the late Egyptian monarch's absolute indifference to the plight of the dispossessed and disadvantaged". The line was sub-edited out. Subsequent stories from the city council roundsman needed pruning to delete unsubstantiated allegations of graft and gratuitous denigration of council officers. The mounting concern about Sparks' copy coincided with a barrage of complaints from councillors and council officials about Sparks' behaviour which had changed from not unpleasant directness to crusading abrasiveness in the space of a few weeks. Within a month of embracing gonzo journalism, Sparks had been removed from the city council round.

He was transferred to a new section of the paper called *City Beat* which had been launched with the aim of attracting a youth readership. Perhaps it was felt that his newly truculent attitude would strike a chord with alienated teenagers but, after a series of corrosive record reviews peppered with comments like "if pus made a noise, this would be it", the feedback from readers indicated that they would prefer a less trenchant approach. His career as a reviewer was terminated when a record distributor filed a writ against the paper claiming damages for loss of sales after Sparks had written that "clinical tests at Harvard University have established that listening to disco music can cause rectal cancer".

By that stage Sparks had precious little support among the paper's hierarchy. He was put on final notice and transferred to the sub-editors' desk where he was kept under constant supervision. Unable to imitate Dr Thompson in his work, Sparks sought to do so in his lifestyle. He stepped up his alcohol intake and began taking whatever drugs he could lay his hands on. However, among the attributes which Thompson possessed but Sparks did not was the Doctor's self-proclaimed "mule shark" constitution. After a month-long spree of whisky, marijuana and LSD, Sparks threw the newsroom into uproar by stabbing the shipping reporter with a copy spike, apparently in the conviction that he was a giant lizard. After being subdued, Sparks lost consciousness for 36 hours; when he woke up, he was unemployed.

CHAPTER *3*

Wallace Guttle was shot on Friday, August 13. Seeing no more than a second separated Guttle's realisation that he was about to die and his demise, he didn't have a chance to reflect on the significance of the date. On the Wednesday of the fifth week after that event, Constable Jarrad Renshaw was working the midnight to 8am shift at the Harbour Bridge police station. It turned out to be an eventful night.

There was the usual paperwork, the distasteful task of cleaning up after an incontinent drunk who'd staggered in looking for somewhere warm to spend the night, and a barney in one of the Fort Street knock shops between an Estonian seaman and the manager over whether the "hostess" or the client bore ultimate responsibility for the achievement of an erection. Then just after 4 o'clock a mate who was working the same shift at the Papatoetoe station rang to tell him about something which had happened on his patch. Renshaw understood why his friend wasn't wasting any time spreading the news. The incident had the two hallmarks of your classic on-the-job story; it was bizarre, even by cops' standards, and it reinforced their basic working premise that most people out there are pretty fucked up: a man who'd been woken up by the barking of the dog next door had beheaded the canine with a chainsaw and flung the severed head through his neighbour's bedroom window. His neighbours' reaction was vociferous rather than violent; although they were mightily upset at having their three-year-old Alsatian's head and a fair amount of broken glass land on their bed in the early hours of the morning, they also had enough sense to keep their distance from someone wielding a blood-stained chainsaw.

What with one thing and another, the duty constable didn't notice the car on the monitor screen until 4.27am. Even as he picked up the phone, the presence of a stationary car on the Auckland Harbour Bridge was being reported by Beryl Baptist, a 20-year-old welfare beneficiary of Whangarei.

When she'd awoken at 1.35am that morning to discover that her live-in boyfriend of two weeks' standing hadn't returned from what he'd promised would be "a quick beer with the boys", Ms Baptist had made a snap decision. She threw some clothes into an overnight bag, strapped her year-old son Axl into the baby chair in the back seat of her heavily rusted Honda, and drove south with the intention of spending a few days in Auckland with her sister Eve.

Driving south across the Harbour Bridge at 4.18am, Beryl noticed the stationary car in the far left north-bound lane at the bridge's highest point. She found it ominous that the driver's door was open but there was no sign of the driver. When Beryl arrived at her sister's flat in Grey Lynn, and following their short but vicious exchange, she rang the emergency number and reported what she'd seen.

At 4.21am Fred "The Freckle" Freckleton left his villa in Herne Bay to drive to the studio in Takapuna from which, each weekday morning, he broadcast the mixture of semi-hysterical gibberish, juvenile smut and pop music which had made him the undisputed king of Auckland's early morning air waves. At 4.28 The Freckle stopped his Porsche behind the newish Saab 9000 parked on the crest of the bridge blocking the far left-hand lane. He peered in the windows, front and back; the car was empty. Shivering a little from the early morning chill and a vague sense of apprehension, he peeped tentatively over the railing; in the darkness, he would have been lucky to spot a school of whales frolicking in the sea 43 metres below. The Freckle was on his car phone explaining to his producer why he was going to be late when the police car arrived.

The Saab belonged to Victor Appleyard. Three hours after Eve Baptist had called her younger sister a "bludging slut" and three and a quarter hours after he'd plummeted into the still, grey waters of Waitemata Harbour at a speed approaching 100 kilometres per hour, Victor Appleyard's body bumped ashore at the Chelsea sugar refinery in Birkenhead.

In the following 48 hours policemen and women shuffled, for the most part apologetically, through the existence out of which Victor Appleyard had, seemingly, opted although neglecting to formally announce the fact in a farewell note.

Appleyard had been the 41-year-old director of sales and business development for Berkeley Enterprises, a substantial property and construction company. The small police team which arrived at Berkeley's five-storey Onehunga headquarters at 11am was led by Senior Sergeant Ted Worsp who, over the course of his three decades in the police force, had gained a reputation for sensitive handling of such situations.

Worsp's experience had taught him that when men like Appleyard went off the rails in some shape or form, their secretaries were invariably excellent sources of information and insight. The late sales director's secretary was Janet Gabites, 49. On meeting her, Worsp noted her age, homeliness and the absence of a wedding ring. When she volunteered that she'd served Appleyard for eight years, his satisfaction was complete. He dispatched his underlings to interview Appleyard's fellow executives and settled down with Miss Gabites and a cup of tea.

After half an hour of Miss Gabites, who turned out to be every bit as infatuated with her ex-boss as he'd guessed, Worsp felt he knew as much about the saintly Appleyard as he wanted to know.

"You know what it's like Sergeant," said Miss Gabites, dabbing away with what Worsp estimated was the tenth tissue she'd immersed in her moist eyes since the interview began. "I'm sure it's the same in the police; the people who care, who can't simply shrug their shoulders and switch off, just get taken advantage of. As if Victor didn't have enough on his plate, they" – her eyes swivelled like anti-aircraft guns across the office to the boardroom – "dumped Australia in his lap, so he was spending a lot of his time over there trying to sort out the mess they've got themselves into. No wonder the poor man hadn't been on top of the world lately – he was working himself into the ground."

Miss Gabites nudged her chair slightly closer to Worsp's, lowered her voice, and continued: "I'm not a gossip Sergeant – I'd like to think I haven't got a malicious bone in my body – but I have to say that Victor could've done with more support at home. Maybe I'm speaking out of turn but Louise – that's Mrs Appleyard – never seemed to accept the hours Victor had to work, the travel, the stress, or the importance of being the corporate wife from time to time. Mind you, on the other hand, she certainly gave the impression that she was only too happy to have the rewards – the lovely house, the skiing holidays, the clothes. It's not for me to say so but there are people here who'd tell you that she enjoyed the benefits of being Mrs Victor Appleyard but resented the sacrifices and, as you know Sergeant, you don't have one without the other."

The picture of Victor Appleyard which emerged when the police team held their de-briefing session late that afternoon was of a good bloke, solid citizen and dedicated company man. Some of his colleagues had commented that he'd seemed preoccupied and somewhat withdrawn in recent weeks but put it down to the extra pressure that went with being given responsibility for Berkeley's troubled Australian subsidiary. There were hints of tensions on the home front. A check of his diary had revealed nothing untoward. He'd appeared to be okay

40

the previous evening, ruefully resigned to working until past midnight. No one at Berkeley had ever entertained the idea of him committing suicide.

"That proves bugger all," pronounced Worsp. "People who go round saying they're going to top themselves either end up in loony bins or dying in bed at the age of 90."

Louise Appleyard did not conform to Senior Sergeant Worsp's expectations or experience of widows.

Slim, elegant, darkly attractive, and seven years younger than her late husband, she sat at the jarrah table on the deck overlooking Lake Pupuke smoking a Dunhill and drinking coffee. There was a mobile phone on the table. Every few minutes it would ring and Mrs Appleyard would pick it up and listen for a while. Then she'd murmur a thank you and say she'd better go, she was being interviewed by the police and no doubt they were anxious to get back to catching criminals.

Constable Beth Greendale admired the fact that little more than 24 hours after learning of her husband's death, Louise Appleyard's only visible concession to the situation was dark glasses, which were really unnecessary in the weak early spring sunshine. Senior Sergeant Worsp felt otherwise. Sure it's black he thought, but the skirt could be a bit longer, for Christ's sake. It wasn't that Worsp was averse to long legs in black stockings but he was used to grieving women responding more favourably to his snowy hair and breezy personality and what, in his frequent moments of conceit, he thought of as his reassuring, even comforting manner. When, on their way out to the deck, Worsp had laid a solicitous hand on Mrs Appleyard's elbow, she'd reacted with a slight but perceptible recoil and a tense little smile which together amounted to an injunction to keep his hands to himself.

Constable Greendale who, after a day's exposure, was starting to tire of Senior Sergeant Worsp, had picked up on the body language immediately. She was looking forward to the interview.

Worsp began by asking Louise Appleyard if her marriage had been a happy one. She lit another cigarette and exhaled luxuriantly causing the sergeant, a reformed smoker, a moment of acute discomfort.

"Is that a polite way of asking if I drove him to despair?" she replied with another tightly controlled smile. "I'd say we were at least as happy as most couples that I know. If you ask me 'was I in love with Vic?', the honest answer is 'no' but then I can't imagine anyone still being in love – in the giddy, head-over-heels sense – with their partner after 10 years. That's not to say I didn't love him because I did. I take it the distinction's not lost on you Sergeant?"

She looked at Worsp curiously. He has no idea what I'm talking about, she thought.

"If you ask me did Vic and I still make love," she continued coolly, "then the answer would be 'occasionally', certainly not as often as I would've liked. But then 14-hour days don't do much for the libido. If you ask me whether I made up the shortfall elsewhere, then the answer's 'no' but, in the spirit of candour you've so skilfully encouraged, Sergeant, I'll admit that it crossed my mind from time to time. I doubt that makes me much different from most wives – and certainly not from most husbands."

What a bitch, thought Worsp. He cleared his throat and said, "One or two people at the office had the idea you didn't go much for his job and the company scene generally."

Mrs Appleyard traced her right eyebrow with a bright red fingernail. Constable Greendale got the impression that she'd already decided that talking to Worsp was a pointless exercise.

"You've obviously been talking to Janet – my number one fan," she said off-handedly. "The company's okay as companies go but it forces people into a very narrow existence.

42

Some of them probably don't have to be forced – as far as they're concerned, the world outside Berkeley and their areas of business may as well not exist – but there was a lot more to Vic than that. I thought they were using Vic, just dumping more and more on him. I suppose he could've said 'no' but that wasn't Vic's way; he'd just take a deep breath, square his shoulders, and carry on. Lately though, I think he'd started to question whether he wanted to spend the rest of his working life in such an environment."

"So you think this questioning process led to him . . ." Worsp left the question hanging in the air.

Louise Appleyard looked at Worsp with almost clinical interest. Constable Greendale caught the look. Here it comes, she said to herself.

"Oh that?" said Louise. "For a while I thought we were going to sit here and talk about my sex life all morning." Worsp squirmed on his substantial buttocks thinking, no wonder the poor cunt jumped.

Louise Appleyard re-crossed her legs and leaned forward. "Let me spell it out for you Sergeant, as plainly as possible," she said. "Vic did not kill himself. Let's say for the sake of argument that it all got too much for him – the pressure, the disillusionment, wondering what it's all about, the fact that I wouldn't give up smoking, that I didn't want babies, all my other failings that Janet would've filled you in on. The point is that if Vic was anything, he was considerate and he was also insured for well over half a million dollars. So if he was going to commit suicide, he wouldn't have done it like this – he would've made it look like an accident."

Worsp and Greendale made a no more than cursory inspection of Victor Appleyard's study on the basis that if he was going to leave a suicide note, he wouldn't leave it in the bottom drawer under the manuals explaining how to programme auto-dial into his telephone. Worsp lapsed into sullen silence on the drive

43

back to town. The fact that Louise Appleyard had treated him with such transparent disdain was bad enough; what was much worse was that it had been witnessed by a 22-year-old female constable.

"What about the insurance thing then?" asked Constable Greendale as she piloted the police car past Westhaven at 20 kph above the speed limit.

Worsp perked up: "Love, the hardest thing for a suicide's family to accept is that they were the last thing on his mind. You see, suicide is the ultimate act of selfishness," he said, grateful that the phrase he'd heard or read somewhere had popped back into his mind when it was needed. "If Appleyard had really cared about her, he wouldn't have jumped off the Bridge would he, so why the hell should he worry about stuffing up her insurance? Believe me love, I've heard that line before today. The way I see it, the pressure and that got too much for him. Now ask yourself: is he really going to spend his last hours on earth trying to come up with some tricky way of doing it so his missus – who he probably couldn't stand anyway and who'd blame him? – gets her hands on the insurance? Do me a favour. And of course it might've been done on the spur of the moment – you know, he's been thinking about it for a while, then one night coming home across the Bridge, he decides tonight's the night.

"See, the other thing you've got to remember when you're talking about making it look like an accident as if it's the easiest thing in the world, is that it's not that easy. There aren't an unlimited number of ways you can kill yourself, you know. It's a question of what means are available. Plus, of course, for most suicides, there's only one or maybe two ways that they can actually bring themselves to do it. Just because a bloke might be quite prepared to poke a gun in his mouth and pull the trigger doesn't mean he could face slashing his wrists; a lot of people are just too bloody scared of heights to jump off a bridge. You know what I mean? It's illogical, sure, but that's the way it is. So it's not like they've got 101 ways to choose from and can pick the one most likely to fool us and the insurance company."

"I'm not sure that's quite what she meant," said Constable Greendale but she didn't pursue the discussion. She'd heard enough of the wit and wisdom of Ted Worsp for one day.

The contents of Victor Appleyard's Saab were spread out on a desk. Worsp poked disinterestedly through the contents of the black airline pilot's briefcase; others had already done so without finding anything of interest. There was a fat hardback book about Japanese management techniques. As Worsp idly flipped through it, a folded card, slightly smaller than the normal-sized Christmas card, fell out. Worsp examined it. It was white with decal edging; on the front was a rather florid crest and the words "Prince Albert College Ball, 1970".

Something stirred deep in Worsp's memory. He opened the card. Printed on the top of the inside left-hand page were the words "Dance Card"; written on the dotted line below in a loopy, girlish hand was "Bronwen Ticehurst". Worsp, feeling slightly dizzy, put the card down and sat back in his chair.

After a few seconds he picked up the card again. Below her own name and on the facing page, the long-dead Bronwen Ticehurst had written the names of her partners for the various dances at the 1970 Prince Albert College Ball. One of them was that of the just-dead Victor Appleyard.

Worsp put the card down again and stood up. "The suicide note," he said to no one in particular. "He left one after all."

# CHAPTER 4

*D*espite his almost cherubic appearance, Jackson Pike competed with the Prime Minister, the Minister of Finance, and one or two of the more nauseating television personalities for the unofficial title of the most hated person in New Zealand.

Pike was rarely troubled by this. Whenever he felt particularly put-upon, he consoled himself with the knowledge that, as the editor and joint proprietor of the monthly magazine *New Nation*, his unpopularity was more than matched by his influence.

As a young and dedicated journalist, Pike had often worried about the future of print journalism. One Sunday morning, in the course of a two-hour run along the waterfront, he realised that the remorseless decline in the quality, quantity and readership of the nation's newspapers presented a golden opportunity. Within six months he had secured backing for his venture; a further six months later the first issue of *New Nation* appeared. The print run of 15,000 copies sold out within 72 hours.

*New Nation* set out to be all things to all people. It combined news and lifestyle, weightiness and frivolity, hard-hitting investigative journalism and racy and irreverent celebrity profiles. Determined to avoid the fence-sitting blandness of most newspapers, Pike had launched his organ vowing that, whether the subject was restaurants, rugby or race relations, *New Nation* would leave its readers in no doubt where it stood. He further vowed that the magazine's stance would be determined by the merits of the case rather than prevailing orthodoxy or current fashion: one month a sacred tenet of political correctness would be ridiculed, the next the outcome of yet another experiment in economic rationalism would be subjected to equally scathing scrutiny.

While this broadened the magazine's appeal, it also meant that, over time, it had offended virtually every shade of political opinion and special interest group. Very early on, Pike had decided that if he was going to give offence, he might as well be hung for a sheep as a lamb. Therefore when *New Nation* took aim at someone, it did so not with a popgun but with an artillery piece.

Even though Pike was widely loathed, his magazine's popularity meant that he could not be ignored by those who wished to influence public opinion, whatever their particular brand of snake oil. After more than a decade of being paid grudging tribute, Pike had become as selective as a diva about whom he hob-nobbed with. Cabinet ministers could bombard his secretary in vain with luncheon invitations; tycoons could spend months trying to entice him to a weekend at their rural retreats. The exception was a man who was so old, he was widely assumed to be dead; in 13 years Pike had never missed his monthly lunch with Garth Grimes.

Pike and Grimes had instituted their monthly lunch when Grimes retired. There had been a period, after *New Nation* had really taken off and when Grimes still ventured out, during which the lunches would take place at one of the few and invariably very expensive restaurants in Auckland which found favour with both of them. But since reaching the age of 90, Grimes' excursions had been limited to his twice-daily shuffles along Takapuna beach.

From then on Pike would arrive at the old man's seafront bungalow with a hamper of food, a month's supply of overseas magazines, and a very good bottle of wine. He would make Grimes his first gin and tonic of the day and himself a Campari and soda. They would discuss current events, both domestic and international, and Grimes would give a brisk analysis of them which Pike usually found more illuminating than anything he'd come across in the seven daily newspapers and 15 periodicals which he made it his business to read. Grimes would then deliver a detailed critique of the last issue of *New Nation* while Pike took notes. They would then have lunch, either at the table by the full-length window or on the deck overlooking the beach, depending on the weather. Over lunch Pike would pass on all the unprintable gossip which he and his team of writers had picked in the preceding four weeks.

When Pike ran out of gossip, they would reminisce about the defunct *Auckland Evening Standard* where they'd both worked in the 1970s, Pike as a feature writer and Grimes, as he had been since returning to New Zealand in 1952 after 32 years overseas, as the star columnist. Occasionally, when Grimes was feeling particularly frisky, his reminiscences would include the unusual, even bizarre, sexual fantasies he had entertained about some of the *Standard's* female reporters. As he listened to Grimes' mellifluous purr, Pike would reflect that he was in the presence of almost certainly the dirtiest-minded nonagenarian in New Zealand and possibly in the world.

After lunch, Pike would make coffee and take notes as Grimes proferred story ideas and any leads or tidbits he'd picked up from the surviving members of what had been a legendary network of contacts. Thus it was that on one of the few rainless days of that spring, Pike and Grimes sat on the deck and discussed the strange death of Victor Appleyard which had occurred four weeks previously.

Garth Grimes regarded himself as fortunate to have been born in 1900. It meant that he was too young for the First World War and too old for the Second. He'd enjoyed what he referred to as "the last fluttering heartbeat of civilisation" – the 1920s – and the post-1945 boom during which he'd managed to position himself for a comfortable retirement. Now and again, when he was advancing this view, someone would ask "What about the Depression?" Grimes would reply that he'd spent most of the 1930s in Shanghai smoking opium and hadn't noticed. This was something of an embellishment of the truth which was that, during his time in Shanghai, he'd never been so short of funds that he couldn't afford both "a fine meal and an evening with the innkeeper's daughter".

Grimes had left New Zealand in 1920 and spent the next three decades roaming the world as a foreign correspondent, mostly for Reuters. Being inclined to pessimism, he'd concluded in the late 1930s that only the United States was likely to be spared the chaos that he foresaw engulfing the world and accordingly had taken steps to secure himself a posting in Washington. When the threat of nuclear war between the USA and the USSR emerged in the early 1950s, Grimes decided that, in the event of hostilities, his apartment building less than a mile as the crow flew from the White House would be vaporised by the first Soviet missile. It was time, he felt, to go home. In 1965 Grimes' American wife died suddenly. Virtually overnight he ceased to care a great deal either way about his and the human race's continued existence; ever since he had maintained a sunny, untroubled disposition which was the envy of all who knew him.

Grimes had always assumed that the rather self-indulgent, at times debauched, life he'd led and the fact that the only exercise he'd ever done was ascending stairs two at a time would ensure he was spared the indignities of extreme old age. It came as something of a surprise therefore when, on reaching 70 and on the brink of retirement, he underwent a thorough medical examination and was pronounced to be in rude health and good for a couple more decades.

Taking the doctor at his word, Grimes, to the

consternation of those journalists at *The Standard* who'd been jockeying to take over his thrice-weekly column, announced that he wouldn't be retiring after all. For another decade he continued to produce his urbane columns, melanges of opinion, gossip and arcane knowledge, and to supplement his income with what he called his "letters to friends".

To the rest of the trade, this was known as "ratting" – writing, usually on the sly, for other publications. The fundamental principle of ratting was maximum income for minimum output; the ideal rat was done during work time and involved only the most superficial changes to a story which had already been written for the newspaper which paid one's wages.

Grimes was King Rat. Each afternoon he methodically went through the tray on the news editor's desk containing copies of all stories filed that day, tut-tutting gently over grammatical imperfections, stylistic gaucheries and inept intros. Selecting any stories that might be of interest to his paymasters on four continents, Grimes would re-nose and re-angle them where necessary then stroll down to the main post office to arrange for their transmission to various overseas newspapers and magazines. Their voraciousness for New Zealand news never ceased to amaze him.

Under normal circumstances, the fact that the highest-paid journalist on the paper was at least doubling his income through the labours of others could have caused resentment in the newsroom. However Grimes, as well as being regarded with something approaching awe because of his age, reputation, and exemplary professionalism, played the role of mentor to many *Standard* journalists. Any reporter, no matter how lowly, could go to him for general guidance or help on a story in the knowledge that it would be provided with the utmost affability. The young Jackson Pike, despite his burgeoning reputation as a feature writer, never filed anything until it had been given Grimes' seal of approval.

Grimes finally retired on his 80th birthday. After long and careful calculations based on the assumption that he would live to the age of 95, he established that he'd accumulated sufficient wealth to afford his daily intake of a quarter of a bottle of gin, a bottle of decent wine, a glass of cognac and 10 cigarettes for the rest of his life without having to sell his house for which in 1979 he'd been offered just over $1 million. He had absolutely no desire to live anywhere else.

In retirement he'd settled into a routine from which he seldom deviated. He rose at 8am and made himself a cup of tea and a boiled egg, read the paper, and smoked two cigarettes. Regardless of the weather he would then go for a walk on the beach. Several of the organisations for which he'd ratted had neglected to take him off their mailing lists when he'd retired so each day's post brought newspapers airmailed from Hong Kong, London and New York. On his return from the beach, he would sit at the table by the big window which looked out to where sea met sky and read them with care. At midday he'd mix himself a gin and tonic; at 12.30 he'd have lunch, usually cold meat and salad, and a glass of wine from the bottle he'd finish with his evening meal.

After lunch he'd walk on the beach again, then take a nap from which he'd be roused by his middle-aged daughter who did his shopping and some cooking and often daydreamed of the house she and her husband would build on the site when Grimes died. She was sometimes troubled by her inability to suppress a twinge of resentment whenever anyone remarked on her father's durability.

Before dinner, which was always unfashionably rich when his daughter cooked, Grimes would drink two gin and tonics while reading a book or one of the magazines supplied by Pike. Sometimes he would watch the news on television although doing so usually caused a deterioration in his mood. After a leisurely dinner he would retire to bed with a book, perhaps something by P.G. Wodehouse – he re-read all the Blandings Castle and Jeeves novels each year – and a digestive. After reading for an hour or so, he would turn off the bedside light and lay his head on the pillow. As he lay in the darkness, he'd wonder if this would be the sleep from which he'd never wake up. Just in case, he'd select one incident from his extensive and varied sexual experience and recollect it in every detail. Garth Grimes did not believe in an afterlife.

"This might make something for you," said Grimes stirring his coffee. "Remember that Appleyard business?"

"The Berkeley guy?" said Pike. "Goodbye cruel world off the Harbour Bridge?"

Grimes, who remembered Pike when he'd been less callous about such matters, nodded. "That's the fellow. I seem to remember the coroner hedged his bets somewhat."

"Had to; Appleyard didn't leave a note. What about him?"

"Had a ring the other day from my man Worsp," said Grimes. "The sergeant at Central. The man's as vain as an archbishop; I mentioned him in a few columns 20 years ago and he's been ringing me ever since, mostly to tell me how clever he is. For once he had a rather interesting tale to tell. I don't suppose the Prince Albert College hanging means anything to you?"

Pike shook his head.

"It happened in 1970. I made a few bob out of it as it happens – The Daily Mail couldn't get enough of it although they kept asking me to get some sex into it. What happened was that a girl named Bronwen Ticehurst, who'd been at the college's annual ball, was found dead in the bell tower. She'd hung herself using a school tie."

Pike nodded. "Yeah, it rings a bell."

Grimes smiled thinly at Pike's unintentional joke. He tended to think that all that held Pike back from being a great editor was that he took everything, himself included, a shade too seriously. He continued: "Well as you can imagine there was a tremendous palaver. By all accounts she was a radiant little creature from a nice home; in those days, parents who allowed their daughters to go to private school balls rather expected them to come back alive. It was all too much for the headmaster, a very queer fish called Hogbin; he took to barking like a half-witted sheepdog in the middle of communion and had to be confined to a padded cell."

Pike pushed aside his notebook. "This is absolutely riveting Grimy but what's it got to do with Appleyard?"

Grimes regarded Pike placidly over his half-moon glasses. Perhaps, he thought, he could do with a little more patience as well. "Is my narrative too discursive? I hope not; one associates long-windedness with senility. The connection is that the police found Bronwen Ticchurst's dance card from the ball in Appleyard's briefcase; his name was on it."

Pike had a quick mind and Grimes enjoyed watching him use it. Pike put his elbows on the table, pressed his folded hands to his mouth, and looked intently at Grimes for half a minute. "He was with the girl that night, kept the card ever since, then bales out," he said slowly. "So what's the theory – he killed her and then went through 20-odd years of torment till he couldn't bear it any more?"

"That seems to be the sergeant's theory which in itself is cause for scepticism. The coroner made no mention of it; couldn't really I suppose – it does involve a couple of hefty assumptions and I don't suppose there's much inclination to re-visit the girl's death." Grimes took a piece of notepaper from his cardigan pocket and spread it on the table in front of him. "I persuaded the sergeant to give me all the names on the card; you might find a couple of them interesting."

Pike's eyes narrowed and he reached for his notebook.

Grimes read the names slowly: "Appleyard of course; Dermot Looms – he must've been her partner because he was down for several dances; Maurice Trousdale; Basil Batrouney; Caspar Quedley and Trevor Lydiate."

Fuck me gently with a chainsaw, thought Pike. Baz Batrouney had been a big name on the local rock music scene in the 1970s; at the height of his fame and amidst suggestions that he was severely drug-addled, he'd abruptly retired to Waiheke Island and become a recluse. Quedley was a high-powered public relations man, while Lydiate was a debarred lawyer who'd been imprisoned for embezzling a couple of million dollars from a client.

He reached across and picked up the list. "What about these two characters, Looms and Trousdale – they mean anything to you?"

"Looms no," said Grimes. "I suspect Trousdale's one of the carpet Trousdales."

"Perfect," said Pike. If Grimes was right, that made him a member of one of Auckland's wealthiest families. "This could be a beauty. It'll take a bit of work though – we're bloody stretched at the moment. I might have to put a freelancer on it. Any suggestions?"

"As a matter of fact I have," said Grimes. Pike noticed a glint of amusement in Grimes' watery eyes; look out, he thought, the old trickster's up to something. "Guess who I heard on the radio the other day talking about being run out of France? Our old chum Reggie Sparks."

Pike's smile vanished. He pushed his chair back hard, stood up and began pacing around the deck. "Grimy, this is a brilliant story idea and I'm extremely grateful and all that, but Sparks? You've got to be joking. He's a fucking psycho – remember the time he stabbed Col Dumpley?"

Grimes chuckled. "How could anyone forget? A great day for journalism. Surely you're not going to hold that against him? The boy was on drugs at the time. Good Lord, I remember when I ate magic mushrooms in Mexico – the very last thing you'd want in that state is to be confronted with a sight as horrible as the Dump. I'd have gone for him with whatever I could lay my hands on too."

Pike continued to pace. "Grimy, you know I normally follow your advice without question but not this time; I'm not having that maniac running round town representing my magazine."

"Well it was just a thought," said Grimes imperturbably. "It simply occurred to me that since Reggie would've gone to Prince Albert with these fellows" – he waved the list – "he might have a bit of a head start so to speak."

Pike stopped pacing and stared at Grimes. He came back to the table and sat down heavily.

"If you change your mind," said Grimes selecting a cigarette, "you should be able to get in touch with him through his mother; she lives somewhere in St Heliers. I think you're being harsh on Reggie, Jackson – I always found him a pleasant young man. By no means the worst reporter either. Not a lot of flair, I grant you, but quite a toughie behind that dishevelled exterior. I knew his father Stanley you know – the original likeable rogue. He bought property over here around the same time as I did; we probably got advice from the same source."

# CHAPTER 5

*C*ontrary to his and Detective Sergeant Ihaka's expectations, Detective Inspector Finbar McGrail was not enjoying the Wallace Guttle investigation.

The post-mortem had established that the private investigator's death had been caused, not by Margo Dugdale's well-worn Goodyear, but by the three .32 calibre bullets which had penetrated his forehead in close formation. The fact that the killer, using a handgun in poor light, had been able to place three rounds into such a small target – Wallace Guttle's forehead had been more simian than professorial – strongly suggested that he, or conceivably she, was a professional.

Getting to grips with Guttle's shambolic files had been a major undertaking in itself. McGrail's preliminary review of their contents had been conducted with the grim fastidiousness of a man who doesn't own a dog removing dogshit from his front lawn. His distaste for the whole exercise was in sharp contrast to Ihaka's lip-smacking enthusiasm which extended to marking the subjects of Guttle's photos out of 10 for appearance and technique. After three painstaking weeks, they'd compiled a list of people who might have held a grudge against Guttle. It was a long one. They and their team then embarked on the slow, often embarrassing and ultimately fruitless process of checking out everyone on the list. After more than a month of interviewing, there was only one name left.

McGrail paused outside the half-open door of the small meeting room at Central Police Station from which the Guttle investigation was being coordinated. He listened to the guffaws from within with disbelief tinged with irritation. Wouldn't he ever get bored with those damned photos?

He went in. Ihaka was flourishing a photograph of a man performing cunnilingus and telling a pair of constables: "I didn't recognise this bloke when I went to see him – I was expecting someone with a moustache."

The constables tittered nervously. McGrail said, "May I interrupt the gynaecology lecture?" The constables slipped out of the room, closing the door behind them. Ihaka sipped his tea.

McGrail looked at the photo. Extraordinary, he thought; Guttle must've been close enough to smell them.

"Well Sergeant, what can you report?"

"I'm seeing Mrs Broome, the one who's been overseas, at 11 this morning. She's the last."

"We haven't got a lot to show for six weeks' work, have we?"

Ihaka shrugged. "We got fuck all."

McGrail sat down opposite Ihaka. The desk between them was piled high with files, photographs and transcripts of interviews.

"We had to go through this process of course but if it was a hit – and I'm sure of that – the answer isn't in there," he said, pushing a pile of folders a centimetre or two.

Ihaka nodded. He and the inspector had had this conversation before.

"All anyone in here," said McGrail giving the stack another nudge, "would've got from killing Guttle is satisfaction. For them the damage had been done – getting rid of him wouldn't repair their relationships. You've got to feel pretty strongly to kill someone just for revenge – it's got to be churning your guts day and night. And when you hate that much, you're more likely to do it yourself than hire someone."

Ihaka knew McGrail didn't expect an answer so he didn't give him one.

McGrail opened a manila folder and began sifting through it. "You've talked to them, sergeant, you've read the transcripts. Most of these people are well off, professional types. How many of them would know where to find an assassin?"

Assassin, said Ihaka to himself. He thinks he's back on the Bogside. "Very few sir," he said. "I don't suppose there's a lot of call for assassins in Remuera."

From the start of the investigation, McGrail had urged Ihaka and his team to look beyond Guttle's files and photos. "Nine out of 10 times," he told them, "hiring a killer is a business decision rather than an emotional act."

McGrail's theory was that Guttle hadn't been killed because of something he'd done; he'd been killed to stop him going any further with something he was working on or to stop him acting on something he'd found out. Ihaka thought the theory made sense the first time he'd heard it; he still tended to think so even after hearing it repeated twice a week for six weeks. The problem was that Guttle enjoyed his secrets too much to share them with anyone. No one knew what he'd been working on when he was killed; he hadn't kept a diary or notes of work in progress. Plus, he was a one-man band; he'd had a woman who came in for a couple of afternoons a week but only to do administrative chores.

They'd wasted a week tracking down Tony Rispoli, Margo Dugdale's mystery companion. Rispoli had been subjected to one of McGrail's legendary interrogations – dispassionate, detailed and demoralising – at his home in front of his wife. Ihaka had gained the impression that Rispoli would have the distinction of being Guttle's last victim. Even in death it seemed, Wallace Guttle was able to put asunder those whom God had joined together.

McGrail stood up. "Okay, see this woman then give me a

progress report. When I've seen that, I'll review this whole investigation. Doesn't look like either of us are going to make our names on this one sergeant."

Ihaka met McGrail's expressionless gaze then reached for his favourite file. "A pain in the bum sir," he said, "in every respect."

If the cigarettes and whisky had caught up with Stanley Sparks a month earlier, he would have died a very rich man. Not that the October 1987 crash reduced him to penury; it simply restored the status quo by wiping out the gains he'd made riding the stockmarket in the mid-1980s. As it was, Stanley had left his widow with more-than-adequate capital and a large and comfortable freehold house in one of St Heliers' nicer streets. It was there that Reggie Sparks had taken up residence on his return from France.

Reggie's major achievement since his homecoming had been to persuade his mother to subscribe to Sky Television. As time passed, he strayed less and less from the sofa in front of the television set in the downstairs den. He'd seen a lot of movies and gained what he felt was a reasonable grasp of the situation in the Balkans. Mostly though he watched sport. South African rugby featured prominently on the sports channel and Sparks had watched enough of it to recognise the players' names, most of which, at first hearing, sounded like someone clearing their throat prior to spitting.

Although Sparks didn't realise it, the phone call from Jackson Pike was ideally timed. His mother Mareena was a patient and tolerant woman but didn't possess inexhaustible supplies of either quality. She'd accepted that Reggie would need a period of readjustment and if that meant lying on a sofa watching television for up to 15 hours a day, so be it. Reggie had made some contribution to the household, revealing a hitherto unsuspected interest in cookery. His specialities were the traditional French casserole dishes like *boeuf bourgignon*, *navarin de mouton* and *coq au vin*. But the sense of well-being induced by *etuvee de veau au vin rouge* and a few glasses of South Australian shiraz only lasts for so long; in Mareena's case, it tended to evaporate almost completely by midday the following day, particularly if the cook was still in bed.

It was nine weeks to the day since Reggie's return. That was as much readjustment as Mareena was prepared to countenance; it was time, she felt, for Reggie to get off his backside, find a job, and either move out or start paying rent. So Mareena stood in the doorway to the den, arms folded, regarding her unkempt son without affection and steeling herself for confrontation when the phone rang. She answered it; it was Mr Jackson Pike of *New Nation* magazine calling for Reggie Sparks.

The previous night, Reggie had stayed up till four in the morning watching caribou racing live from Lapland and drinking malt whisky. Three aspirins and two glasses of Berocca had had no discernible anaesthetising effect on the starbursts of pain behind his eyes. Neither Jackson Pike nor *New Nation* meant a thing to him but even with his perceptive faculties dimmed to a level barely above sleepwalking, he'd sensed that his mother was on a mission. That could only mean one thing and it was a thing he would take every opportunity to postpone. He hauled himself off the couch and picked up the phone.

"Hello."

"Sparks? It's Jackson Pike here. We worked together on *The Standard* a long time ago."

Sparks closed his eyes and made a superhuman mental effort — Pike: short, dark, wrote features, up himself.

"Yeah. How are you?"

The half-hearted note of familiarity disappeared from Pike's voice altogether. He was all business.

"Listen, what are you up to these days? You still a hack?" He didn't wait for Sparks to respond. "I run a magazine called

*New Nation* and I need someone to chase down a story. Could be a good yarn. You interested?"

Sparks listened to Pike with mounting unease. The feature story the editor outlined sounded like an extremely tricky and demanding assignment and it was a long time since Sparks had attempted serious journalism. Given the state of his morale and assuming his firestorm of a hangover ever abated, he reckoned he could just about process a press release into a 10-paragraph news story. Pike was talking about something else altogether. Christ, listen to him.

". . . okay, the basic story is these six guys who were involved with this girl who died 20-odd years ago, how it affected them, and what's become of them since. But I see it as, like, an extended metaphor for the way the country's changed in that time: you know Lydiate, the lawyer who's inside, could symbolise the collapse of ethics in business, the way greed and corruption have taken over; Batrouney, the musician, he stands for the dark side of sex, drugs and rock 'n' roll, the end of seventies innocence; Quedley, the PR man, symbolises the rise of the image maker, the manipulator, that whole image industry – advertising and PR – and the way it's been able to suck money out of the taxpayer by advising government departments and all that shit. Appleyard's obviously the starting point and you're going to have to get a handle on what the hell was going on inside his head – could he have killed the girl? Was he haunted by her death all this time? I don't know about the other guys but I'll bet they're good stories too. I mean, Trousdale's apparently the heir to a massive fortune. What d'you say? If it comes off, it'll be a cover story and a bloody good way for you to get back into it and get some profile."

What's this fucking maniac talking about? Sparks wondered. He desperately wanted to hang up and lie down in a dark room. He couldn't do that, not with Mareena standing right next to him looking expectant. He muttered his acceptance and half-listened as Pike jabbered about money, deadlines, photographs and posting him out the newspaper clippings on Appleyard.

"Okay, all set," said Pike. "Keep me posted on how you get on."

"Hang on," said Sparks. "Where do I find these guys?"

"You ever heard of the phone book?" said Pike testily after a meaningful pause. "You went to school with these wankers, Sparks; if you can't even find them by yourself, what sort of crap are you going to come up with?"

Sparks said "Yeah, okay" and put the phone down. He smiled weakly at his mother.

"Well Mum, back to work."

He told her about the assignment. She was doubly pleased because it meant the moment of reckoning could be postponed, perhaps indefinitely. Who knew where this might lead? As she headed upstairs to make lunch, she called over her shoulder: "I'm sure Gavin can help you get in touch with those people; he's got a couple of friends in the Prince Albert Old Boys' Association."

Sparks slumped on the sofa. There were three thoughts running through his head and he wasn't sure which was the most depressing.

There was the fact that his mother's mind had moved much faster than his when it came to tracking down the dead girl's dancing partners; there was the prospect of having to spend time with his brother and, worse, ask him for help; and there was Pike, the hotshot magazine editor – another contemporary who'd outstripped him.

In the first few weeks after his return, Sparks had made an effort to get in touch with old friends but the reunions had proved dispiriting experiences. Even those who'd been just as directionless and irresponsible as him now seemed to have something for themselves. They had homes, families, jobs that they actually seemed interested in, reputations, even a little fame in one or two cases; they had something to show for being

40-odd. What did he have? Big fat zero. Sure, some of them had changed for the worse; some of them had become conventional and boring and smug. But they had a focus and, for better or worse, seemed happy about it.

He'd come to dread the questions that invariably followed the greetings and nostalgia: So what've you been up to, Reg? What are your plans? You going to buy a place? Better move fast, the market's heating up. Don't tell me you didn't bring a little mademoiselle back with you? When do you hit the big four-O Reg – or is that a rude question? Reggie, one word of advice – superannuation; we've got to look after ourselves now, mate, because the government sure as hell won't.

All of them growing up, settling down, making it, going places, carving out their little niches, finding a meaning in their existences to sustain them through the home stretch, the hard stretch, the real thing.

Starting to feel like the train's left the station boy and you ain't on it.


Tito Ihaka parked in front of Priscilla Broome's smart Mairangi Bay townhouse with a view. He wondered where the ex-husband was living now and decided it would be somewhere just as good if not better. Despite everything you heard about blokes being taken to the cleaners in divorce settlements, it was Ihaka's experience that the legal system was piss-poor when it came to separating rich men from their money.

You sound just like your old man he thought, smiling at the idea. Ihaka doubted that his late father, despite the firebrand rhetoric, had ever laid a finger on a genuine class enemy. By all accounts though, he'd thrown his considerable weight about very effectively in the murky and often violent factional disputes in which he and his fellow communists often engaged. In fact, continually engaged; they just never seemed to find the time to overthrow the system.

His father had been something of a maverick: a fervent

admirer of the politically unsound – in Moscow-aligned circles – Josef Broz Tito, hence Ihaka's christian name. Had he lived to see it, the gory dismantling of Tito's legacy would have been the second great disappointment of Jimmy Ihaka's life; the first had been his only son's decision to become a policeman. Although a heretic on some issues, Ihaka senior held straight-down-the-line Marxist views on the police's role in the class struggle.

Priscilla Broome had overdone the sun-bathing during her six weeks in Noosa. In Ihaka's opinion, one of the few direct benefits of being born brown was that one felt little compulsion to waste summer lying in the sun cultivating skin cancers, as Mrs Broome, whose complexion bore a resemblance to the skin of a passionfruit, obviously did.

Mrs Broome was unable to contribute much to the investigation. Her attitude to violent death was essentially that she'd like to rule it out of her life altogether but if it had to happen to someone she knew, who better than Wallace Guttle? It was a sentiment Ihaka found difficult to fault.

Ushering Ihaka to the door, Mrs Broome decided to give him the benefit of her thoughts on the subject of death.

"I'd never known anyone who's died mysteriously or violently and then all of a sudden, it happens to two people I know within a few weeks. When I say that, I didn't really know Guttle and quite frankly wouldn't have wanted to, but I knew poor Victor Appleyard quite well. And even more of a coincidence, not long before he died, Victor rang me to ask about Guttle and get his phone number."

Like most policemen, Ihaka was not a great believer in coincidence.

"Appleyard – he was the bloke who went off the Harbour Bridge? Bit of a high flier? Hang on, let me re-phrase that – a big-time businessman?" She nodded. "What did he want Guttle for?"

"He didn't say." Mrs Broome looked slightly embarrassed.

"I'm more a friend of Louise, Victor's wife – widow I should say. I suppose she must've told him that I'd used a private detective to . . . when my marriage got into trouble. Victor must've told me three or four times that it was nothing to do with him and Louise; he said it was a business matter that he wanted Guttle for. Between you and me sergeant, I wasn't sure I believed him. I wondered if I should tell Louise – I thought my loyalty was really to her but you've got to be so careful when you get involved in other people's relationships; you can do more harm than good. Then of course when Victor . . . well, it's the last subject you're going to bring up, isn't it?"

"I guess so," said Tito Ihaka thinking, is this a clue? Did Rose Kennedy own a black dress?

# CHAPTER 6

$G$avin Sparks, the accountant, checked the time on his assertive sports watch again. It was a nervous reflex – so Reggie was late, so what else was new? The second pre-dinner Scotch was also a sign of nerves; Gavin drank, as he did most things, in moderation – two snorts before dinner on a week night was loose behaviour by his standards.

It was all of 30 years since Gavin had felt entirely comfortable in his brother's company so it was par for the course that he wasn't looking forward to the evening. To make matters worse, their mother had got it into her head that this story for *New Nation* was make or break for Reggie and was expecting – no, demanding – Gavin's cooperation and encouragement.

Gavin was profoundly unenthusiastic about the whole project. The thought of his erratic and disaster-prone brother and that scandal rag *New Nation* combining forces to rattle the skeletons in Prince Albert College's cupboard was gravely disturbing. It could have professional ramifications; the old boy network was good for business. Besides, his son James was due to start there the following year.

Despite his reservations, Gavin would do what he could for his brother because Mareena had asked him to and Gavin was as good and dutiful a son as he was a father, a husband, and an accountant. Gavin Sparks took his obligations seriously and took pride in performing well in his various roles. He saw himself as a contributor, a good citizen. Of course he earned a good living, but that didn't mean he thought money was the be-all and end-all; he just wanted to do the best he could for his family. If everyone had Reggie's attitude, where the hell would we be?

The prickly defensiveness of this train of thought was prompted by Gavin's certainty that, in the course of the evening, he and everything he stood for would be subjected to mockery: mocked for being an accountant, a suit, for making money, for taking life seriously – mocked for not having failed! Of all the things about his brother which irritated Gavin Sparks, the most grating by far was Reggie's assumption of superiority. What in God's name did he have to feel superior about? He took a deep breath. Tonight was another night; whatever the provocation, cordiality must be maintained. Reggie, according to their mother, was taking a tentative step in the right direction and nothing could be done to derail his comeback from semi-retirement.

The doorbell chimed. Gavin let in his brother. As they shook hands, he registered that Reggie hadn't shaved, needed a haircut, and was wearing their late father's favourite sports jacket. That jacket's at least 15 years old, thought Gavin, and it's in a hell of a sight better condition than anything else he's got on.

"G'day Gav," said Reggie handing over a brown paper bag containing a $12 bottle of red wine. "Nice jeans. Iron them yourself?"

Heather Sparks stood, unnoticed, in the doorway to the lounge and observed her husband and brother-in-law. Gavin stood straight-backed to the left of the fireplace; Reggie was half-sitting, half-lying in the armchair, his legs splayed out in front of him.

The odd couple, she thought; nothing in common except their name and their noses. Start at the top: Gav's hair's still black; looks a lot better since he started going to that new place too. Maybe a lighter touch with the blowdrier my darling – it's just a tad too neat. Reggie boy, do my eyes deceive me or do I see a few grey hairs? God, you'd think he didn't own a comb, the way it sticks out all over the place. I bet Gav walks into one before the night's out; he'll recommend the guy who does his hair and Reg'll have that crooked grin on his face and say something like "Why the fuck would I want hair like yours?" So sweet to each other. Gavin, why are you wearing those designer jeans I got you? You don't like the damn things, you're always saying you're not built for jeans. He's trying to avoid – what was it Reggie used to say? – looking like he's cracking walnuts in his arse. Same reason he's put on that Country Road shirt. The sweater with the diamond pattern's not quite right though; you can never avoid the golf club look entirely, can you my dear? Reg, Jesus, where'd you get that disgusting jacket? Otherwise the old uniform, old being the operative word: old jeans, old sneakers, old shirt. More to the point, what's underneath? Gav keeps fit but he was skinny to start with; all the jogging gives him that stringy look. Reggie's got more meat on him, but the sort of life he leads, maybe it's gone soft and flabby? Oh I don't know – there's nothing hanging over his belt and that backside still looks nice and firm. Get that shirt off Reggie; let's have a good look at you. That'd really make Gav's night.

Instead she said, "Which one of you boys is going to carve?"

Although Reg Sparks liked to think he didn't envy his brother one iota, it wasn't true. He envied him Heather. Watching them during dinner, he thought, as he always did, how did a quince like him get a woman like her?

Afterwards, back in the lounge with a glass of port, Gavin gave voice to his concerns.

"Do you really think this is such a good idea? I mean, dragging up all this stuff is going to upset a few people."

"Christ, the story's going to get done whether I do it or

68

not. You should've heard Pike on the phone – the guy was raving."

"But do you have to do it? I can tell you, it's not going to make my life any easier."

It wasn't the smartest thing Gavin could've come out with. Reggie had never seen his role in life as making his brother's life easier and wasn't about to start.

"Well, it's up to you," he said. "I mean, this wasn't my idea. Mum just thought you could give me a hand getting hold of these guys but if you're not happy about it . . ."

That had Gavin protesting that he'd never said he wouldn't help and all right, let's have a look at the list, most of them would be his year so he'd probably know himself. Reggie thinking, Jesus Gav, you're such a pushover.

Darkness rolled across Gavin's face as he read the list. His brother sat in silence thinking, what's the bet one of them's his biggest client?

When Gavin finally spoke, his voice was flat and lifeless.

"Looms, he was off a farm up north. He's probably still there; the Old Boys' Association's bound to have an address. Batrouney was the pop star, wasn't he? Wouldn't have a clue where he got to. Trousdale's family used to own Fabrice Carpets; they sold it for a fortune. Maurice hasn't done a stroke of work in his life – as far as I know, he sits around in his apartment in Herne Bay waiting for his mother to die. Trevor Lydiate stole a couple of million off a client and blew the lot; he's in some minimum security prison. The client was actually Barry Plugge, the strip club king, so they say Lydiate's better off inside where Plugge can't get at him. And Quedley – well, just look in the phone book."

Gavin handed back the list, gulped the rest of his port, and leaned back in his chair staring at the ceiling.

"What's up with you?" said Reggie.

"Quedley hasn't changed. He's still the golden boy, too much charm for his own good. We bumped into him a couple of years ago. It was one of those nights when Heather overdid it . . ."

Over the years Reggie had heard the odd story about what his mother referred to as "Heather's problem". As far as he could tell, it boiled down to the fact that when she'd had a few, she became a bit of a flirt – pinched a bum or two, turned the New Year's Eve kiss into a tongue wrestle; the same sort of stuff most men do given half a chance. If Gavin's stricken look was anything to go by, she'd given Quedley a lot more than a cheap thrill.

"We went to a party on the Shore somewhere. A client of mine was there and baled me up in a corner; I just couldn't get away from him. When I finally managed to escape, I couldn't find Heather anywhere so I went looking for her."

Reggie knew what was coming; it was just a matter of how bad. He felt slightly queasy. He was also very curious.

"I found them – Heather and Quedley – in the spare bedroom, down to their underwear. Heather had played up a few times before – you know, embarrassing stuff but nothing to get too worked up over. She never took any of it seriously, you know? This time though, she was . . . gone – way gone."

Gavin was still staring at the ceiling, replaying the scene in his mind as he'd done a thousand times. Reggie wasn't sure what he felt for him; eventually he decided it was respect. You're a tougher man than me pal, he thought.

There was one question he had to ask: "What did Quedley do when you walked in?"

Gavin shook his head slowly. "Didn't turn a hair. He just said '*C'est la vie*', picked up his clothes, walked out and left us to it. He was just the same at school – had a nerve you wouldn't believe."

On his way out, Reggie stopped by the living room where Heather was playing scrabble with James. Saying his goodbyes, he was unusually attentive to his nephew. That's nice, thought Heather. Normally he acts like Jamie doesn't exist.

70

Tito Ihaka had expected more of a reaction when he broke the news to Louise Appleyard that her late husband had hired a private investigator specialising in confidential enquiries. What he got was "Really?" accompanied by expectantly arched eyebrows. The tone and expression implied that Ihaka would have to come up with something better to justify his visit.

"You don't believe it?"

"If you say it's so Sergeant, I believe you."

"But?"

"Look, I think we're at cross-purposes. I'm prepared to believe Vic hired this character but it wasn't to check on me."

"How do you know?"

"Because there was nothing to check," she said with the diminishing patience of a teacher explaining something glaringly obvious to a backward child. "Vic knew that so why would he waste money confirming what he already knew?"

"So why did he hire the bloke?"

"Obviously to find out something that he didn't know," she said in an even sharper tone.

Ihaka had checked the Appleyard file beforehand. "Could it have had something to do with the girl's dance card that was in his briefcase?" he asked.

Louise Appleyard knew all about the dance card too. Its discovery had led to another trying session with Senior Sergeant Ted Worsp.

"Possibly," she said reflectively. "The thing had stayed with him, no doubt about that. It seemed a little morbid to me although it was never the sort of fixation that that buffoon Worsp made it out to be – all that drivel about Vic brooding on it for 20 years. If you want my opinion, Vic hadn't had the card for long; if he had, he would've shown it to me at some stage. I suggest it would be a more productive use of your time, Sergeant, trying to find out where the card came from than worrying about whether I was a naughty girl."

71

If you had been a naughty girl, thought Ihaka as he drove away, I sure às hell wouldn't have minded seeing the pictures.

About the time Tito Ihaka was trying to visualise Louise Appleyard in the throes of passion, Reggie Sparks was speaking to her on the phone seeking an interview. An hour earlier, the approach would have been unceremoniously rebuffed. However Ihaka's visit had given Louise pause for thought. This had been her first exposure to the police mentality and it had left her unimpressed: their matter-of-course assumption of sexual shenanigans on her part; their apparently unshakeable determination to view Victor as a suicide; their breathtaking leap of logic to link her husband with the Ticehurst girl's death. There was something to this Guttle connection but the police would just sit on their fat collective arse . . . unless she could find some way of pressuring them to pursue it. Like a story in *New Nation*.

So at 11.05 the following morning Reg Sparks, wearing a new pair of Levis, an ironed shirt and his late father's jacket, knocked on Louise Appleyard's front door. A minute went by then the door was jerked open. There was a gust of perfume, a swirl of black hair and a female voice saying very quickly, "Come in Mr Sparks, make yourself comfortable. I'm just on the phone but I'll be with you in two ticks."

She led Sparks through to the large kitchen, which opened out onto the deck, then disappeared. Sparks looked out through the condensation on the sliding glass doors at the rain which was coming down in a silver sheet. Spring wasn't like this when we were kids, he thought. It was dry and crisp and at morning break there was a race to get the best positions to bask in the sun for a quarter of an hour. Now it's always grey and gloomy and pissing down with rain. Must be the greenhouse effect – all that spray-on shit.

There was music coming from a ghetto blaster on the kitchen bench. It sounded like Lloyd Cole. He listened to the words: "Now when you're puttin' on your face/Guess that you feel kinda low/Knowin' that you're past your best/And you got nothin' to show." Sounds familiar, he thought. Then the chorus: "Only this time round you might have to . . . pay for it."

It was not a good moment to be reminded of his short and ignominious career as a gigolo but the memory flash was so vivid that Sparks felt his cheeks burning. It was all that fucking German's fault, what was his name? Klaus something. Standing there in that bar in Toulouse, about seven foot tall, checking his biceps and his profile in the mirror, looking like the prototype for the master race, bullshitting about the money he'd made as a gigolo on the Cote d'Azur, finally coming out with why didn't Sparks go down there and try it? Sparks, ordering two more beers, saying "All very well for you mate, but I don't look like some genetic engineer's wet dream."

"Not at all, not at all," said Klaus vehemently. "The most important things are that you can be very charming and you can get hard at the right time, even if the ladies are a little old and not so beautiful. Okay? It is not necessary that you are handsome, just that you are not ugly. Also you must not be short, you must not be fat, you must have all the hair. So you are fine. Of course" – he looked Sparks up and down – "you must dress in the correct way."

If Sparks had dispassionately assessed himself in terms of Klaus' specifications, he would have had to acknowledge that he was not renowned for his devilish charm. Furthermore, his ability to stand and deliver on demand was untested. However, it was late at night and he was drunk, a combination conducive to the formulation of hare-brained schemes. Two days later he was in the bar of the Hotel Negresco on Nice's Promenade des Anglais, dressed in a pale green linen suit he'd bought in Bangkok and casting meaningful glances at any woman of mature years who entered.

His first assignation was with a 50-year-old spinster from

Somerset. When he discovered that she was staying not at the Negresco but at a much more modest establishment several blocks back from the beach, Sparks began to wonder whether they were thinking in similar ballparks with regard to his fee. As it turned out, she had no figure in mind; indeed she was quite oblivious to the fact that she was party to a commercial transaction. He discovered how it was done on his second attempt when the lady, an Austrian, demanded payment from him before she'd removed a single garment. Sparks fled with guttural oaths ringing in his ears, caught the next train back to Toulouse, and avoided the company of women for several weeks.

The traumatic recollections left him ill-prepared for his interview with Louise Appleyard. After she'd spent 15 minutes explaining why she was sure her husband hadn't committed suicide and urging him to follow up the Guttle connection, she felt compelled to ask Sparks if he possessed the memory of a chess grandmaster since he was neither using a tape-recorder nor taking notes. Half an hour later she watched Sparks trudge through the rain towards his mother's car. If that's an ace newshound, she thought, I'm Opo the dolphin.

# CHAPTER 7

While the meeting with Reggie Sparks did little for Louise Appleyard's spirits, it had quite the opposite effect on him. He sensed that she hadn't been overly impressed with him and was determined to give her cause to revise her opinion. It had been some time since he'd had a goal in life.

Gavin had supplied phone numbers and addresses for Looms, Trousdale and Quedley. Directory service provided the phone number of the prison one hour's drive south of Auckland where Lydiate was incarcerated and Jackson Pike's secretary had rung with Batrouney's address on Waiheke Island. If Batrouney was on the phone, he had an unlisted number.

Dermot Looms was indeed still on the farm. He responded with the no-nonsense gruffness one associates with the rural sector: "If you want to come all the way up here, that's up to you. Sounds like a waste of time to me." *New Nation* seemed to carry more weight in Quedley's office; his secretary arranged an appointment for the following Monday morning on the spot. Trousdale had his answering machine on so Sparks left a message.

When Trevor Lydiate, the disgraced lawyer, got the message left by Sparks, he swore under his breath and requested permission to make an immediate phone call. He rang a South Auckland car dealer, one of the few people in what had been his social circle who would still take his calls, and told him to drop what he was doing and get down to the prison that afternoon.

When the car dealer got back to Auckland after visiting Lydiate, he followed to the letter the procedure the lawyer had laid down before entering prison. He stopped at the first public phone he saw and dialled the number he'd memorised. The man who answered the phone said: "Service department."

"Is Danny there?"

"Yeah, speaking."

The car dealer said, "A journalist from *New Nation* magazine, called Reggie Sparks, wants to talk to Mr Brown," then hung up.

The car dealer got back into his car, his mind abuzz. He wondered who Danny was; he wondered what Lydiate was up to; he wondered if he'd been wise to agree to help Lydiate on a no-questions-asked basis. He also wondered how long Reggie Sparks had left to live. Some two months before, the car dealer had relayed another message from Lydiate to the taciturn Danny, that "a private investigator called Wallace Guttle is sniffing around Mr Brown". A week later he read in his morning paper that Guttle had been shot dead in a Newmarket carpark.

Most of all the car dealer wondered if being Lydiate's go-between made him an accessory to murder.

After the call from the car dealer, the man named Danny, who repaired electrical appliances, left his workshop and walked across the road to a phonebox. He dialled a number that he'd known off by heart since long before Lydiate had become a guest of the Crown. After two rings the receiver at the other end of the line was picked up. There was no greeting or acknowledgement. Danny repeated the message that the car dealer had given him and hung up. Unlike the car dealer, he neither reflected on the consequences of his action nor was he curious as to the identity of the silent party at the other end of the line. As long as his unknown benefactors continued to pay $50 into his TAB account each week, Danny was quite happy to go on being a link in the mysterious chain.

His call had gone to a red telephone, one of three on a large and tidy mahogany desk in an office above The Blue Angel strip club in Auckland's Karangahape Road. The man behind the desk groaned when the red phone emitted its distinctive ring; lately that sound had heralded nothing but bad news. After he'd heard Danny's message, the man planted his elbows on the desk, put his head in his hands, and said in a loud and troubled voice: "Just one motherfucking thing after another."

The man was Barry Plugge. Gavin Sparks had described him as "the strip club king"; a Sunday tabloid had once dubbed him "Auckland's Sultan of Sleaze"; Plugge saw himself simply as a businessman, someone who identified a need and catered to it.

At the peak of his fortunes in the late 1970s, Plugge had earned close to $1 million a year from a dozen flourishing strip joints and massage parlours around Auckland. However the 1980s had been a difficult decade: first came the relaxation of the censorship laws which resulted in pornographic videos becoming freely available; then came AIDS; then came some serious competition.

Plugge took a dim view of all three. He considered sex should stay in the strip clubs and massage parlours where it belonged, not on the shelves of neighbourhood video rental shops. Porn videos, he felt, simply encouraged masturbation, a practice of which he disapproved as unyieldingly as did the Vatican. Plugge, who'd been happily married for 27 years, could think of nothing more demeaning for a grown man than masturbating in front of a television set. However, there was also a commercial dimension to his disapproval: masturbation was bad for business. "Wank, wank, money in the bank," he would say. "A bloke's not going to go to a massage parlour if he's just jerked off."

AIDS, he insisted, was something which happened to male homosexuals and drug addicts and his girls were neither; a few of them were undoubtedly lesbians but, to quote another of his aphorisms, "no one ever caught AIDS off a dildo".

Plugge, an ardent nationalist, was proud to be a New Zealander who employed New Zealanders and who provided entertainment for New Zealanders while performing a useful social service in the process. It infuriated him the way offshore operators had tried to muscle in on his patch in recent times – the Italians from Sydney and, even worse, the Asians who flew in "students" from Thailand and Hong Kong, girls who'd work for next to nothing and were often prepared to dispense with a condom for a few extra dollars. And when Plugge, having seen his revenues decline precipitously, swallowed his pride and his principles and brought in his own Asian girls, what did those little yellow animals do? They put a fucking contract out on him!

These negative trends had forced Plugge both to look around for opportunities to diversify and to consider resorting to the sort of strong-arm methods he had always shied away from. And it was the combination of the two which had reduced him to sitting at his fine desk with his head in his hands, feeling sorry for himself.

Throughout his career, Plugge had followed three basic rules: never a borrower or a lender be; never take commercial advice from a lawyer; and never make decisions when in the grip of emotion, whether the extreme of mood was up or down. Brooding on his problems, Plugge reflected bitterly that he was now paying the price for having broken two of these rules. At the time though, it had seemed too good to be true; ever since he'd been in business, he'd been ripped off by lawyers. Then, right when his cash flow was being squeezed, he'd been presented with a scheme for getting it back with interest.

It all began with an invitation to lunch. It came from Trevor Lydiate, a partner at Trubshaw Trimble & Partners, a law firm whose exorbitant fees matched the plushness of its downtown offices and the self-esteem of its principals. Plugge had had little to do with Lydiate, indeed regarded him as just another of the supercilious nancy boys with limp handshakes of whom there were plenty at Trubshaw Trimble. But Plugge, who wouldn't shout his best friend a meat pie if he could possibly avoid it, would put up with a lot for a free lunch anywhere, let alone at Antoine's. Obviously Lydiate would want something but he was too well-bred to raise it until after the food and drink had been ordered. And then . . . well, thought Plugge, I've told much more intimidating characters than Mr Trevor Lydiate to get fucked before today.

They lunched well. Lydiate proved to be an excellent host, avoiding any mention of business until the dessert plates had been removed and the neighbouring tables vacated.

Then Lydiate made his pitch: "Barry, I'm leaving Trubshaw Trimble to set up my own practice and I have a proposition for you."

The liqueur trolley arrived. Plugge chose the oldest and most expensive cognac on offer and was impressed when Lydiate nodded his approval and followed suit.

"You've got $200,000 in our trust account," continued Lydiate. "Off the top of your head, how much would you have invested in the share market, sitting in bank accounts, that sort of thing – I'm talking about money which could be redirected at short notice?"

Plugge didn't need to think about it. "Nine hundred grand give or take a few bucks."

Lydiate whistled softly. "Now I gather the business is currently making around $300,000 a year after tax. You don't have to answer this but I shouldn't imagine you declare every single dollar that comes in the door?"

79

Plugge swilled his brandy and felt the heat rise to his face. The lawyer interpreted his smug expression as agreement.

"For the purposes of this discussion, we'll assume that's the case. Okay, here's my proposal: you clean out your bank accounts, cash in your shares, and get your money out of Trubshaw Trimble. Then you hide it offshore – I don't know, stick it away in the Cayman Islands or something; we can work that out later. To all intents and purposes though – and there'll be all the paperwork to verify it – you will've given me that money to use through my trust accounts. All right? Then for a couple of years, you take as much as possible out of the business and do the same thing – hide it offshore and pretend I've got it. When we've built the amount up to, say, two million, I own up that I've stolen it and blown the lot. You get reimbursed the full amount from the lawyers' fidelity fund and I go to jail. While I'm doing time, you put my share into an offshore account so that it's waiting for me when I come out. That's basically it."

Lydiate leant back in his chair and sipped his drink. Plugge, his large ears by now bright pink, stared at him with newfound respect.

"That easy huh?"

"Yep, that easy. Believe me, I didn't dream this up last week; I've been thinking about it for years."

"Say we get two mill – how'd we divide it?"

"Well I'm the one who's taking the fall – I get disbarred and sent to the slammer – so I reckon that entitles me to a round million."

"A mill for you, a mill for me – that seems reasonable."

"Not quite. We'll need a partner, an accountant. The books are going to have to be absolutely shipshape."

"You got someone in mind I suppose?"

Lydiate smiled cheerfully. "He gets $200,000. Of course on top of that, I'll need play money."

Plugge's eyes narrowed. "What the fuck do you mean, play money?"

"I'm meant to've blown two million right? That means gambling, high living, conspicuous consumption. If it's going to stack up, I'll need to've established a pattern of behaviour – you know, overseas trips, first-class travel, five-star hotels, spending sprees, and so forth."

"How much are we talking about?"

"I'd say another $200,000 should do it."

"Jesus wept. What does that bring my cut down to?"

"Six hundred thousand – but remember that's pure cream. And you don't have to do a bloody thing for it."

The lunch had taken place almost four years previously and since then events had unfolded very much as Lydiate had outlined as they worked their way through most of a bottle of 1951 cognac. It all went without a hitch; at least, it had done until the day his red phone rang and Danny relayed the message that a private investigator was asking questions about Lydiate.

Plugge was not by nature or inclination a violent man. The types of characters his industry attracted meant that now and again one had to deal with people who responded more readily to a fist in the face or a boot in the groin than to reason. When such measures had been required in the past, they'd been satisfactorily performed by the large and stupid men whom Plugge employed as bouncers. But earlier that year, when Plugge found himself under siege from the Italians on one side and the Asians on the other, both groups having abandoned any inclination to peaceful co-existence and now clearly hell-bent on driving him out of business, he'd had to rethink his attitude.

In the space of three weeks, one of Plugge's clubs was firebombed, the word went out that there was $25,000 to be earned by putting him on a slab, and the head of his "security" team was dragged into an alley where his left achilles tendon and right thumb were severed. The other bouncers decided that Plugge's wages and the occasional free blowjob were not worth the risk of being subjected to this sort of fiendish oriental cruelty and took to their heels. In fact the knifework had been performed by a 49-year-old Henderson grandfather of Croatian descent who'd just returned from doing a spot of ethnic cleansing in Bosnia. It was done on behalf of the Italians from Sydney for $2,000 and the promise of tickets to see his favourite soccer team, AC Milan, next time he was in Europe.

Desperate times require desperate measures and Herman Pickrang, whom Plugge recruited on the advice of one of his heavier underworld connections, certainly qualified under that heading. Pickrang took the fight to the enemy; on his first day on the job, he walked into an Italian restaurant, seized one of the trouble-makers from across the Tasman, pushed him head first into a pizza oven, and held him there until his eyeballs crackled and popped like frying eggs.

Then he accosted the wife of the Hong Kong gentleman who'd put the bounty on Plugge's head, surprising her while she was walking her prize Pekinese. Pickrang snatched up the dog by its hind legs and flailed it against a concrete telephone pole, reducing the beast to hairy jelly. As the horrified woman tried to flee, he seized a large handful of her hair and yanked it out by the roots leaving her with a monk-like bald patch. The contract was cancelled the following day.

Plugge was not comfortable with such methods but told himself he had to fight fire with fire. The Guttle business, however, was another story; that was overkill. It was partly his fault: that was the second time he'd broken one of his rules. He'd just heard that his two best strippers had found God and were retiring to devote themselves to His service when the call came through on the red phone. Plugge didn't lose his composure very often but when he did, a search party had to be sent out to get it back. He'd rampaged round his office, throwing things, bellowing that no snotbag snoop was going to poke his nose into his affairs and get away with it, and demanding of Pickrang was he going to stand around scratching his arse or do something about it, the long streak of piss? Pickrang did something about it all right; the fucking madman went out and blew Guttle away. Hadn't he ever heard of breaking a guy's legs, for crying out loud?

# CHAPTER 8

*R*ummaging through the accumulated flotsam and jetsam in his mother's basement, Reggie Sparks found his old record collection which included Basil Batrouney's farewell album, *Going Mad in Public*.

The cover photo showed Batrouney standing in the middle of a downtown intersection wearing only a Napoleonic hat, gumboots and a pair of underpants the waistband of which had been hitched up well above his navel, accentuating his genital bulge. Beneath the flamboyant headgear and framed by lank black hair was a pale, oval face dominated by a pair of bulging, frog-like eyes. All in all, Batrouney looked thoroughly deranged.

Mad as a snake, thought Sparks.

The only track off the album which Sparks could remember was the notorious *Smack gets in your Eyes*, a paean to drug use which had goaded several parliamentarians into demanding Batrouney's imprisonment. These calls were resisted although the song was banned from the state-controlled airwaves. The album's ability to offend the establishment more than compensated for its total lack of musical or lyrical merit and ensured its commercial success.

Sparks caught the Quickcat to Waiheke Island and took a taxi from the wharf to the township of Onetangi. The address he'd been given turned out to be a nondescript weatherboard house a block back from the waterfront. Sparks mounted the steps to the veranda and knocked on the front door. It was opened by a stout man of early middle age. His receding wiry grey-black hair was pulled back into what Sparks assumed was a bun or a ponytail and bushy white muttonchop sidewhiskers emphasised the pumpkin-like shape of his face. He peered benevolently through large round spectacles with lenses like the reinforced windows on a despot's limousine.

"Does Basil Batrouney live here?"

"That's me."

It hadn't for a moment occurred to Sparks that this portly Dickensian figure was the former wild child of New Zealand rock music. He was so thrown by the admission that all he could think of to say was, "We went to the same school."

Batrouney stared at him blankly for 20 seconds.

"School," he said eventually. It was neither a statement nor a question. It reminded Sparks of the way little children utter words because they like the sound.

Off to a promising start, thought Sparks. "Yeah, Prince Albert College."

There was another long silence. "Groovy. But as my old amigo Bobby Zimmerman said, 'that was in another lifetime'."

Jesus, what a fruitcake, thought Sparks. "Look, I'm a journalist," he said doggedly, "and I'm doing this story for *New Nation* about a group of guys – including you – who were at Prince Albert College together . . ."

"A journalist, eh? Thought I'd finished with them."

Batrouney shrugged, turned and walked down the hallway. "If you want to rap, come in," he called over his shoulder. Sparks followed. Batrouney had a bald crown and a pony tail which hung like a dead animal between his shoulder blades.

He led Sparks into a room set up as a study. There was a large desk with a computer, a printer and a fax machine, an old kitchen table covered in files, magazines and drawings, and a draughtsman's board. Batrouney sat on the swivel chair at the desk and pointed Sparks to an old sofa against the wall.

"You still in the music game at all?" asked Sparks trying to get the conversation going.

"Man, I don't even have a transistor." Batrouney got heavily out of the chair and went to the table. "These days, I draw comic strips; just call me the Walt Disney of Waiheke." He picked a comic from a pile on the table and tossed it to Sparks. It was called *Grub* and subtitled *The Kiwi Lavatory Humour Comic*. On the cover was a cartoon of a hugely fat man sitting on the toilet. Underneath it said: "In this issue – how to leave giant skidmarks every time. Plus! Ron's Runs, Wendy's Wide-On, Perry and his Poo-Ring and much, much more!"

Sparks glanced up at Batrouney who was swinging to and fro in the swivel chair, humming tunelessly. "It's not everybody's bag," he said. Sparks put the comic down on the arm of the sofa.

"You do it all yourself?"

"No, no, a bunch of us put it together." Batrouney giggled. "I've just invented a new character – 'Jack Stack and his Magic Crack'."

I don't believe this, thought Sparks. He tried to look interested. "Yeah? What's that about?"

"Jack's a super-hero, kind of like Batman, except what he does is suck bad guys up his arse. Like a black hole out in space." He giggled again.

"Can't see it ever being made into a movie," said Sparks, "but I've been wrong before. So how many copies do you sell?"

"You'd be surprised," said Batrouney primly. "We did our homework. Scatological humour – that's like to do with arseholes and farting and stuff – is the big growth area in comics. So," he beamed at Sparks, "can I put you down for a subscription?"

"No thanks. I'm more your *Doonesbury*, that sort of thing."

Batrouney looked a little miffed. "Suit yourself."

He lapsed into silence. Christ, thought Sparks, now I've upset him. However after a minute or two, Batrouney came abruptly back to life: "Now this school thing: fact is, there's nothing I can tell you. All I remember from those days is this stuff." He waved the comic. "You know, schoolboy humour. See, I divide my life into BD and AD – before drugs and after drugs. What I remember from the BD period doesn't amount to shit."

Sparks was curious. "What about the bit in between, when you were actually on drugs?"

"It was a big bit. They really are missing years, man – just a blur."

"So all the fun, the groupies . . ."

Batrouney shook his head slowly. "You tell me. I might as well have been a clerk."

"That's tough," said Sparks sincerely. "But getting back to BD, to your Prince Albert days – surely you remember Bronwen Ticehurst, the girl who hanged herself? You danced with her at the ball."

Batrouney blinked rapidly behind his thick glasses. "Man, all I remember is it was a heavy scene. What did we used to say – bad karma? Yeah, that was it – it was bad karma."

Sparks sighed and closed his notebook. He suspected that what Jackson Pike had in mind went a little deeper than bad karma.

The class of '70 isn't holding up too well in the hair department, thought Sparks as he watched Dermot Looms, the farmer from up north, coming down the steps towards him. That was where any likeness to Batrouney began and ended: whereas the creator of *Grub* had the flab and pallor of a sedentary recluse, Looms was every inch the outdoorsman – tall and rawboned, his face and exposed scalp weathered the colour of varnished wood.

"Sparks is it?"

"Yes."

"You Gavin's brother?"

"Yes."

"You got kicked out, right?"

"Well, technically speaking I wasn't expelled . . ."

"Doesn't matter a bugger now. Let's go round the back."

Looms lived in an old colonial-style farmhouse, white-painted timber with a grey slate roof, at Tapora on the Okahukura Peninsula which juts out into Kaipara Harbour. To the right of the house was a double garage; behind it was a rose garden and a lawn which sloped away to some farm buildings. Beyond them, the paddocks rolled down to the sea. They sat in the sun on white wrought-iron garden furniture. Sparks explained his assignment.

Looms rubbed his forehead. "Christ, what a terrible thing that was. I hardly knew Bronwen, you know. Mum was friendly with her mother and they jacked it up between them, for me to take Bronwen to the ball. I was so bloody socially backward I wouldn't have had a partner otherwise but it was hard lines for Bronwen; she wasn't short of admirers. Trouble was, she wanted the one bloke who could take her or leave her. I suppose that's what it boiled down to in the end, the whole sorry business."

"Who was that?"

"The Ghost – Cas Quedley. You'd remember him?"

Sparks nodded.

"We called him the Ghost after the cartoon – Caspar the friendly ghost? Good name for him too."

"What was the story between him and Bronwen then?"

"They went out a couple of times. She was pretty rapt in him; so were half the girls in town for that matter. Anyway Cas gave her the flick – I mean, she wasn't the only one that happened to; he was a terrible bugger with the birds. At the ball I had a couple of dances with Bronwen, then she says she's got to talk to Cas, she'll be back in a minute. Off she went and that was the last I saw of her. Apparently she fronted Cas and he told her look, it's all over, don't be a pain in the arse, so she shot through. At least that's what I thought – that she'd just buggered off home. Her folks' place wasn't that far from the college. Of course, what she did was go up to the belltower and – well, you know the rest."

"What about Victor Appleyard? How did he fit in?"

"Oh Christ, poor old Vic. Well he was one of the bunch panting after Bronwen – in fact he was pretty stuck on her. He took it real hard."

"So he had the hots for her but she wasn't interested?"

Looms shook his head stiffly. "She wasn't interested in him or me or anyone but Quedley. It was Cas or no one."

"I've heard the cops think Appleyard might've jumped off the Bridge because he had a guilty conscience. Is it possible he could've killed Bronwen in a jealous rage, you know, just couldn't handle being rejected?"

Looms let out his breath explosively. "Whew, that's a bit of a shocker. Let's put it this way, Vic was just about the last bloke you could imagine doing something like that . . ."

"That's what the friends and neighbours always say, isn't it? 'He was such a nice, polite man, I'd never have picked him as an axe murderer'."

"Yeah, I guess so."

"How about Quedley? How did he take it?"

Looms sat back and folded his arms. "Well as I said, the Ghost was a good name for Cas. You never knew what was going on there. I mean, he wasn't what you'd call sentimental. His mother died when we were at school and no one knew till weeks later. But sure, it must've upset him. I wouldn't have liked to've been in his shoes."

"Why, did people blame him?"

Looms waved a hand at an invisible fly. "Oh you know, there was whispering behind his back. I think a few doors were shut on him, he wasn't welcome in some quarters anymore. But you couldn't really blame him. For a start, the birds knew where they stood with him – shit, he went through them like it was a race. And you know what it's like at that age – kids put each other through the emotional hoops all the bloody time."

They walked back to Mrs Sparks' Peugeot. Looms looked in the driver's window: "You know, after you rang the other day, I got to thinking about that year. When you think about it, two suicides within a few weeks – it's a bloody wonder parents weren't pulling their kids out of the place."

"I left at the beginning of that year and I sort of lost touch," said Sparks. "Who was the other one?"

"The chaplain, Padre Swindell. He drove his Morrie 1100 straight into a wall – couldn't have been more than a few weeks before the other business. They tried to make out it was an accident but apparently there was nothing wrong with the car, the weather was okay, and the old bloke never touched the piss. It looked like he just pointed the car at the bloody wall and put his foot down."

Sparks sat in the reception area of Quedley Communications (Counsel, Strategy, Crisis Management) trying to differentiate between the various attractive young women flitting to and fro. It was no easy task; there seemed to be a distinct Quedley Communications look – long hair, short skirts, high heels. After a 10-minute wait, a statuesque brunette swayed into his line of sight, breathed, "Mr Sparks? CQ will see you now," and escorted him down a corridor to Quedley's office.

It was a huge office, big enough to house a large desk in front of which were positioned three high-backed chairs, an eight-seat meeting table, a couple of long sofas arranged around a low coffee table, a small bar and assorted foliage. There's still enough room to land a helicopter, thought Sparks.

Caspar Quedley, wearing a beautifully cut dark double-breasted suit and displaying a very deep tan and very white teeth, rose from behind the desk and advanced on Sparks, hand outstretched. The handshake he administered was impressively muscular and of precisely calculated duration: sufficiently protracted to convey an enthusiastic welcome without suggesting freemasonry or arousal. The tan, the firm grip, the erect posture, the wide shoulders and the flat stomach all proclaimed that here was a man who sprang from his bed at 6am and ran 10 kilometres before breakfast, a man who pumped iron, a man who played a rip-roaring game of squash, skied like a daredevil and liked the sting of salt spray in his face. What an arsewipe, thought Sparks. He sourly noted that, unlike his contemporaries, not a square centimetre of scalp peeped through the glossy black curls which tumbled onto Quedley's forehead and lent a touch of boyishness to his slightly unreal good looks.

"Thanks for seeing me Mr Quedley," said Sparks. "Or should I call you CQ?"

Quedley grinned disarmingly. "You can call me Caspar or you can call me Shitface – it's entirely up to you. Take a seat."

As he poured the coffee, Quedley made small talk about *New Nation* and Jackson Pike – "We've all got to strive to stay on side with young Master Pike."

Sparks interrupted him. "Mr Quedley, I couldn't help but notice, you seem to've surrounded yourself with bimbos. Any particular reason for that?"

Quedley put down his cup and leant forward, half-smiling. "Well Reggie, bimbo is a somewhat judgemental term implying that these young women perform no function save the decorative. That isn't entirely the case. To answer your question: yes, there is a reason for it. The fact is that, despite everything one hears and reads about women in the workplace, 90 per cent of the time in corporate public relations we're dealing with men. And the simple truth of the matter is that on the day-to-day stuff, most men, whether they admit it or

91

not, would rather deal with an attractive woman than a man. The reality is that a lot of executives look upon dealing with PR issues as almost light relief, a bit of a break from the real work. So I've always had the view that it's important to ensure that there's an enjoyment factor – if you like, it's a case of giving 'em what they want, not what they necessarily need."

Sparks raised his eyebrows. "It makes it all sound pretty . . . superficial."

Quedley leaned further forward, looking thoroughly earnest. "Abso-fucking-lutely. If I can go off the record for a moment: this is a superficial industry for superficial people. If public relations ceased to exist tomorrow, it wouldn't detract in the slightest from the sum of human happiness; in fact, you could argue that mankind would be better off. Imagine a world in which companies and governments and institutions were judged purely and simply on their merits rather than all the outrageous bullshit they spread around – on what they do rather than what they say they do. But I put it to you, it requires a certain wit and cunning to make a good living out of something so fundamentally artificial and to do so, what's more, by gouging money out of the supposedly canniest, most hard-nosed, most financially literate sector of society – big business. Which brings us back to my bimbos, God bless each and every one of 'em."

Quedley paused from his dissertation and looked at Sparks appraisingly. "So you're Gavin's brother?"

"Yes."

"I believe I've met your sister-in-law. A delightful creature – what's her name?"

"Heather."

"By God Heather, that's right," said Quedley slapping his thigh. "How could I forget? Been quite some time since I've seen either of them."

Sparks glowered at him. "You married Mr Quedley?"

"No sir. Haven't got the temperament for it."

"I suppose it's difficult for a man about town like yourself to settle down?"

If Quedley sensed the hostility radiating from Sparks, he gave no sign of it. He regarded Sparks amiably. "Man about town – haven't heard that term for a while. If you mean that I like to do a bit of rootin' from time to time, well I'll own up to that. Don't you?"

Sparks ignored him. "I guess that was the problem with Bronwen Ticehurst – she just didn't understand your temperament?"

Quedley held Sparks' stare. "I don't know why Bronwen killed herself. That night at the ball she asked me if we could have a relationship and I said no. I heard afterwards from a couple of her friends that it hurt her – apparently she believed she was in love with me – so maybe you could argue I drove her to it. If so, it was by being honest. Obviously, if I'd thought for one second she was going to do what she did, I would've handled it differently although if you follow that line to its absolute logical conclusion, I couldn't ever have broken up with her – I'd have had to have married her to keep her alive. But who the hell knows? Maybe there were other things in Bronwen's life that made her unhappy, things that none of us knew about, and me giving her the elbow was simply the straw that broke the camel's back. Now personally, you or anybody else can write whatever the fuck you want about me – I've got a fairly thick skin and I'm pretty much beyond caring what people think about me – but don't you reckon Bronwen's family could do without *New Nation* raking over it after all these years?"

"Well I suppose that's the difference between journalism and PR; as they say, news is what someone, somewhere wants to suppress."

Quedley sniggered derisively. "Pomposity doesn't become you Reg. Besides, you know who said that? Some Fleet Street press baron, no doubt trying to justify running a 'what the butler saw'-type story. That's the sort of self-serving sound bite I'd be proud to come up with."

Sparks shrugged. "So who did you take to the ball? She must've been special – sounds like most of the other guys would've crawled over broken glass for Bronwen."

Quedley pursed his lips. "I wouldn't want this to be taken the wrong way but I don't remember. She was new, that was all."

"She was a challenge, was she? Yeah, I hear you like challenges." Quedley started to say something but Sparks pressed on. "What you were saying about *New Nation* raking over Bronwen's death, as if we're doing it just for the hell of it; that's crap. We've got something to hang it on – the Victor Appleyard connection."

Quedley sat up. "You know about that?"

"About what?"

Quedley's genial poise had slipped. "Well I'm not sure I want to . . ."

"If you mean, have we heard that Appleyard might've had some sort of fixation about Bronwen Ticehurst, the answer is 'yes'."

Quedley slumped back on the sofa. "Well I'm sorry to hear that but at least it didn't come from me."

"Well was it true?"

Quedley stood up and walked round in a little circle. "Look, Victor was a nice guy and I really don't want to go on the record about this but I guess you'd have to say that he seemed to have a bee in his bonnet about it. He came round and talked to me about it a couple of times."

"Where was he coming from?"

"Well that's it, I couldn't really work it out. He just seemed to want to go over and over the same old ground. You know, no one's ever accused me of being the most sensitive soul on the block and I make no apology for not accepting responsibility for Bronwen's death, but going through it all chapter and verse wasn't exactly my idea of a good time."

"Would you say he was obsessed with it?"

Quedley grimaced. "Obsessed is an ugly word. I don't know I'd say that. But he certainly had an itch he couldn't scratch."

On his way out, Sparks asked Quedley about the chaplain.

"Old Pard Swindell? Yeah well, there you go. Who knows what that was all about? Far be it from me to speak ill of the dead but I suspect he was well and truly screwed up. I mean, a clergyman, a bachelor, a boys' boarding school – nod, nod, wink, wink, know what I mean? He was probably a bit of a tortured soul and was punishing himself for some trivial lapse that you or I wouldn't lose a moment's sleep over."

They shook hands. Quedley's smile was full of sly humour. "Terrible things, consciences. We're much better off without them, eh Reggie?"

I can't help it, thought Sparks going down in the lift. I really ought to detest that man – but I don't.

# CHAPTER 9

When Maurice Trousdale, the heir to the carpet fortune, returned to his multi-million dollar Herne Bay apartment after his four-day, eight-restaurant trip to Sydney, he stood in front of the big window in his upstairs living room and looked out across Westhaven marina to Waitemata Harbour, the North Shore and the Harbour Bridge. After contemplating this scene for several minutes, he turned away sighing. Even the view no longer worked. There'd been a time when, on his return from overseas, he'd stand at the window thinking it was good to be back, good to be home. Now even that sense of belonging failed to uplift him. He could feel a blue period coming on.

Trousdale's occasional spells of gloomy introspection resulted from his dwelling on the fact that his only role in life – that of heir – essentially involved outlasting his mother. Given that his mother was almost twice his age, it was not a lot to ask and Trousdale felt that he'd pretty much got the hang of it. He felt ready for something a little more demanding, something that would stretch him.

Trousdale spent a quarter of an hour musing on his dilemma. Having failed to come up with any stimulating projects which didn't require high intelligence or physical courage or drive and energy – none of which he possessed – he played back the messages on his answering machine. Among the invitations to weekends at Pauanui, cocktail parties and gallery openings was a message which at first gave him a nasty jolt, then triggered some furious thinking. The conclusion he eventually reached transformed his mood like a blaze of sunshine after a summer shower.

The message was from Reggie Sparks and was a request for an interview in connection with an article he was preparing for *New Nation* magazine. The message concluded with a volley of names, some familiar – Victor Appleyard, Caspar Quedley – some all but forgotten – Bronwen Ticehurst, Basil Batrouney. The common thread seemed to be Prince Albert College.

Trousdale's initial alarm was caused by the mention of *New Nation*. The magazine had a gossip column, *Aucklander's Diary*, in which Trousdale featured from time to time. There'd been a reference several years previously which he could still recite from memory. It had read thus:

"A pall of gloom descends on the festive season! It is one's melancholy duty to report that yet another year has passed in which Maurice Trousdale, globetrotter, patron of the arts, *bon vivant* and heir to the Fabrice Carpet fortune, made no discernible progress towards finding a consort.

"It defies belief that, in this savagely materialistic age, a man who stands to inherit around $200 million when Mater, the doughty Lydia, turns up her toes, can be entering his 40th summer still a bachelor. It's hardly as if Auckland is devoid of women intent on marrying money; in the salons of Parnell and Remuera, the smart restaurants, the yacht clubs, the member's stand at Ellerslie, in fact everywhere the voluptuaries, phonies and *nouveau riche* white trash who make up what passes for Auckland society gather, one is in constant danger of being trampled underfoot by hordes of debs, 'models' and assorted bimbos flashing thigh and breast at anything they suspect is male, single and rich. So frenzied has the hunt become that even being of dusky hue is no longer unacceptable providing the tinted gentleman's net wealth is in the right ballpark.

"So how come, I hear you cry, Maurice is still fancy-free? Your diarist's theory is that for even the most single-minded gold-diggers, the thought of having to submit to the pudding-like albino's clammy caresses on a nightly basis is too horrific to contemplate. *Plus ça change, plus la meme chose* . . . as a lad at Prince Albert poor Maurice was dubbed 'The Troll' because of his general unsightliness and shunned by the smart set."

Trousdale and his lawyers had debated whether or not to sue. The hawks among his legal advisers had argued that the item was so malicious, so gratuitously offensive, that no court in the land would have an ounce of sympathy for *New Nation*. The doves cautioned that defamation cases could be brutal and demeaning affairs; the defendant could be expected to leave no stone unturned in exposing every unsavoury aspect of the plaintiff's character and the resultant humiliation could far exceed that caused by the original libel. In the end Trousdale decided to turn the other cheek, swayed by the unthinkable prospect that *New Nation* might produce as witnesses the women who'd participated in his rare and uniformly gruesome sexual experiences.

Forbearance had its price. From then on, the editor of *Aucklander's Diary* felt sufficiently emboldened to preface any reference to Trousdale with the label "pudding-like albino".

What galled Trousdale most of all though was the realisation that the diary item was another sally in the campaign of denigration and humiliation which had been mounted against him, intermittently, for almost 30 years. He'd suspected it straight away – "Pudding Bum", "Slimefingers", "the Albino" and "the Troll" were all lampoons invented at Prince Albert College by his once and future persecutor, the diabolical Caspar Quedley. Trousdale's suspicions had been confirmed by Quedley himself when they'd met shortly after the item appeared. Not that Quedley had owned up to planting it in *Aucklander's Diary*; he hadn't needed to. The malicious gleam in his eyes, the predatory grin, the greeting – "Bugger me blue

Trousers, you get paler every time I see you; you must live under a fucking bridge" – were all intended to let Trousdale know that the Ghost had struck again.

So while the very name *New Nation* had caused Trousdale to flush to the roots of his thinning hair, the remainder of Sparks' message prompted some careful thought. He'd often yearned to revenge himself on his tormentor but Quedley had seemed unassailable. If I handle this right, thought the carpet heir, I can get back at that swine through the very vehicle he used to ridicule me. Trousdale sat down at his antique writing desk, took a clean sheet of paper, unscrewed his red lacquer fountain pen and started making notes of what he would tell the man from *New Nation* about Caspar Quedley.

Sparks had two messages when he checked in at *New Nation*: the first was an invitation to join Maurice Trousdale for lunch at Le Brie restaurant the following day. The second was an instruction to call the supplied telephone number at exactly 2 o'clock that afternoon if he wanted to know the real story about Trevor Lydiate. He did so.

The call was answered on the fourth ring.

"Who's that?" said a deep male voice.

"Reggie Sparks. Who am I talking to?"

"Never mind that, pal. You want to know about Lydiate or not?"

"Sure."

"Okay, you know Potter's Park on the corner of Dominion and Balmoral? There's a kids' playground, right? Behind it, just up the rise, there's one of those round things that bands play in."

"A rotunda."

"What?"

"That's what it's called, the round thing – a rotunda."

There was a short silence. "Sparks?"

"Yep."

"Shut your hole. You want to know about Lydiate or not?"

"Yeah, I want to hear about Lydiate."

"Okay, be at that whatever the fuck it's called in Potter's Park in one hour. How old are you?"

"Thirty-nine."

"What are you wearing?"

"Jeans, blue shirt, brown jacket. How will I recognise you?"

"I'll be the one in the hotpants."

The anonymous caller hung up.

Sparks sat in the rotunda in Potter's Park for half an hour. He would have waited a little longer, even though by then he was pretty sure that he was wasting his time, but it started to rain and the temperature dropped appreciably. He ran back to his mother's car.

Herman Pickrang, who'd been observing Sparks through a pair of binoculars from his car parked in the car park of the Kentucky Fried Chicken outlet on the other side of Dominion Road and wondering how long it would take the dumb shit to figure out he'd been jerked, said "About fucking time" and started his car. Pickrang had set himself two objectives for the afternoon – to find out what Sparks looked like and where he lived. Neither proved difficult. Having paraded himself for identification purposes, Sparks continued to oblige, driving straight to a house in St Heliers where he put his car in the garage and went inside. After following him there, Pickrang, who felt rather pleased with himself, decided he'd go home and play with his electric train set.

Sparks rang Jackson Pike and gave him a brief and uninformative account of his progress. Pike was unconcerned by the lack of detail: the mere fact that Sparks had found and interviewed some of the dead girl's dancing partners meant that he'd already surpassed Pike's expectations. Sparks asked Pike if he had a means of putting a name and address to the phone number he'd been given by the no-show. He hung on while Pike called a contact in Telecom who reported that the number was that of a public phone box in New North Road. Sparks had expected something of the sort. He found it interesting, in a detached sort of a way, that expecting such an answer did absolutely nothing to allay the unease it caused.

When Sparks was ushered to the table, Trousdale took a hurried slurp of his dry martini, brushed some flakes of crust from the corners of his mouth, hauled himself to his feet and extended a pudgy hand.

Like the man who doesn't know much about art but knows what he likes, Reggie Sparks had no particular notion of what the heir to a fortune should look like but his luncheon companion certainly wasn't it. Trousdale was short – no more than five feet five – and plump. In the exact centre of his fat, pink face was an incongruously babyish button nose. Occasionally women, feeling obliged to find a redeeming feature in the swollen expanse of Trousdale's face, professed to find his nose cute. Trousdale himself considered it a damn nuisance since it failed to provide satisfactory support for his spectacles. Trousdale's hair was bone-white and very fine and, beneath it, countless tiny beads of perspiration glistened on his pink scalp. Trousdale sweated a great deal. Some of his acquaintances, who considered him close to being a glutton, assumed it was excitement which made him sweat so much in restaurants.

They ordered. Sparks, recently health-conscious, chose soup and grilled snapper with a green salad; Trousdale, for whom meals were an important filler of the all-too-many hours which make up an empty life, nominated garlic snails followed by venison casserole and vegetables du jour. Suspecting that his guest might decline the offer of wine, he called for a bottle of pinot noir without consulting him.

As they waited for the food, Sparks outlined his brief from *New Nation*.

Trousdale swallowed the last mouthful of his martini. "So what did you make of the exquisite Caspar?" he asked.

"Quedley? He struck me as a pretty smooth operator."

"A smooth operator?" Trousdale arched his almost invisible eyebrows and turned down the corners of his prim mouth. "I must say that if describing Caspar as a smooth operator is any indication of the level of insight and originality we can expect in this article, I don't think I'll bother to read it."

Only the brief flaring of his nostrils betrayed Sparks' urge to reach across the table and prong Trousdale's jaunty little nose with his fork.

"Well to be absolutely candid, my dear old sausage," he said calmly, "I don't give a rat's arse whether you read it or not."

Trousdale dabbed his forehead with a napkin, his other hand fluttering in appeasement.

"I do beg your pardon – that sounded rather impertinent. No, what I really meant to say was that describing Caspar as a smooth operator seems rather an understatement."

Sparks' gaze remained indifferent. "Well I get the impression that you're just itching to tell me about him so why don't you?"

Trousdale, hot and flustered, wriggled on his seat; his armpits were positively frothing. This was not how it had been meant to go at all: he'd planned to manipulate Sparks like a puppeteer, have him dancing his tune without even knowing it. Still, there was the opening. He took a deep breath.

"Well, I think one must always remember that Caspar's family was of comparatively modest means and at school he was very, very conscious of the fact. You know, see him swanning around town today as to the manner born and it's easy to forget his rather humble origins. His father was a vicar, you see, and the only reason Caspar went to Prince Albert was

102

because of the clergy's discount on school fees – they only paid 50 per cent from memory. As I say, he was very aware, was Caspar, that he was something of a have-not compared to most of his schoolmates. I remember going to the movies with him and a few others during the school holidays, in our fifth form year I think, and someone commented on the fact that wherever we saw Caspar out of school – at a party, at the football, in town, whatever – he seemed to be wearing exactly the same clothes. I'm sure it was said in all innocence – just one of those thoughtless, flippant things teenagers say – but Caspar was quite hurt by it."

Trousdale felt a fresh outbreak of sweat on his forehead and applied the napkin. The fact of the matter was that he himself had drawn attention to the pathetic paucity of Quedley's wardrobe. It had been a put-down worthy of Quedley himself in its calculated nastiness, a moment to savour. Quedley had blushed absolutely crimson and the others, sensing his vulnerability like sharks scenting blood, had gleefully twisted the knife in the wound.

"Anyway, Caspar became terribly money-conscious. He always had some sort of little money-making scheme on the go. Believe it or not – and this is strictly off-the-record by the way – in our last year he somehow got hold of an advance copy of an exam paper, university entrance history I think it was, and sold sneak previews."

"What, to a public exam? How the hell could he do that?"

"No, no, no. It was the internal school exam but he sold it to all the fellows who failed UE the year before and were trying to get it accredited on internal assessment."

"Even so, how'd he get hold of it?"

"God only knows. Maybe he sneaked into the masters' common room one night and made a copy of it. As I said, he always had something on the go, he was always hatching a plot."

Trousdale attacked his food, noting with approval that

103

Sparks was scribbling furiously in his notebook. I just hope he's up to the task, thought Trousdale. God, Quedley will hate this stuff coming out.

Sparks put his pen down and took a hurried mouthful of fish.

"What about Appleyard? Anything you can tell me about him?"

"Nothing much really – we weren't close either at school or subsequently. Although funnily enough, I did see Appleyard not that long ago – no more than a few weeks before he died, I guess – over in Sydney. I bumped into him in the lobby of the Regent Hotel and he insisted on having a drink. Now you're interested in that Ticehurst girl aren't you? Well, I swear, that was the only subject he could talk about. He was awfully het-up about it, asking me all these questions about her and the ball. What could I say? Without wishing to appear callous, I had one rather off-hand waltz with the poor thing; it was hardly worth committing the details to memory."

"What did he say about it?"

Trousdale arranged his knife and fork on a spotless plate. He was more interested in dessert than the subject of Victor Appleyard.

"Oh, I don't know. To be frank, it was going in one ear and out the other. All I can remember was him rabbiting on that he'd come across someone in Sydney who'd shed some light on it all."

Sparks had a moment of genuine excitement. "Who? Did he say who it was?"

"Oh no. I actually asked, out of politeness rather than curiosity, but he said he'd been sworn to confidentiality or some such. I must say, I found his behaviour rather extraordinary; it did occur to me that he might've been slightly off his head and what do you know? Next thing, he's jumped off the Bridge."

CHAPTER *10*

$R$eggie Sparks had virtually no interest in clothes. As far as he was concerned, one wore clothes to avoid pneumonia and arrest. In France he'd had two comparatively expensive items in his wardrobe: a linen suit and a Burberry raincoat. After the ignominious gigolo episode, he'd given the linen suit to the tramp who sometimes slept in the doorway of his apartment building, on the condition that, in future, he would urinate somewhere else. He'd kept the raincoat, wisely as it turned out, since in Auckland that spring fine weather, like the ideal guests, came rarely and didn't stay for long. Sparks was wearing the raincoat when he called on the widow Appleyard for the second time. She opened her front door, looked him up and down, and checked her watch.

"Is school out already?"

"What?"

"The coat, Mr Sparks. You look like every parent's nightmare."

Since their first meeting, Louise Appleyard had seldom been far from Sparks' thoughts. He'd been keenly anticipating her instant, unguarded reaction to his unannounced visit, thinking that it would be a pointer, at least, to whether her attitude towards him was essentially positive or negative. He'd envisaged a range of responses, some of them wildly optimistic, some, on the basis of being prepared for a let-down, less so; being likened to a child molester had not been among them.

He forced a stiff grin. "Thanks for reminding me; I'm almost out of boiled lollies." She acknowledged his re-bound with a slight incline of the head and half-smile. He moved rapidly to the matter at hand.

"I just thought I'd drop round and let you know where I've got to. I've talked to all but one of the guys on the dance card. A couple of interesting things have come up."

He was admitted. They went into the kitchen where he sat on a bar stool at the bench while she made coffee.

Sparks began his report: "The first guy I saw, Batrouney, the ex-rock singer who lives on Waiheke, he was basically a waste of time. Guy's as crazy as a shithouse rat."

Louise raised an eyebrow.

Sparks misread her reaction. "Sorry, pardon the French. Thing is, the guy admits he gave himself one hell of a hammering with the drugs. He's only half here. You know what he does with himself these days? Draws dirty comic strips."

"What sort of dirty?"

"Stuff for grubby-minded kids."

She looked at him expectantly. "Give me an example."

"You know, it's full of . . . bodily functions," he said, stirring his coffee. "The stories are like 'Ron's Runs' and 'Wendy's Wide On'."

Louise giggled. "'Wendy's Wide On'? You're kidding."

"Absolutely not. You wouldn't believe some of this stuff. Jesus, I thought I had a pretty basic sense of humour." He shook his head. "Anyway, as I say, old Basil's out there on his own private planet. More to the point, his memory's completely shot – he'd have trouble remembering how to get to the bathroom let alone what happened at that ball in 1970."

"Oh well, strike one. Who was next?"

"Dermot Looms. He's a farmer up near Wellsford, one of your good, keen men. He was Bronwen's partner at the ball but reckons that didn't mean much because their mothers jacked it up for him to take her. He did point out something

106

interesting though: a few weeks before the ball, the college chaplain also killed himself."

"What's interesting about that?"

He shrugged. "I suppose interesting's the wrong word – strange maybe. Don't you think two suicides at the same school within a few weeks is a bit of a coincidence?"

She took a thoughtful drag on her cigarette. "Hmm. What else did he say, the farmer?"

"Nothing much. He said your husband and a few others were pretty keen on Bronwen."

"Oh I knew that," she said smiling. "Under that earnest exterior, there was a genuine romantic. Vic used to say he was hopeless when he was young, falling in love at the drop of a hat. But that one was strictly one-way traffic, wasn't it?"

"Yeah, well she had the same problem with Caspar Quedley. He was my third call."

"Oh yes, I've met him. He's rather gorgeous-looking, works in advertising or something like that? I'm thinking of the right one, aren't I?"

"I don't know," lied Sparks. "Quedley's a public relations man."

"It's not exactly a common name. What does he look like?"

Sparks shrugged, frowning. "I guess . . . smooth."

Louise Appleyard smiled enigmatically. "Okay, so what did Mr Smoothiechops have to say for himself?"

"Well, Quedley said your husband went round to see him about Bronwen Ticehurst. He said he wouldn't say he was exactly obsessed about her but he wasn't that far off. Then I talked to this strange little bloke Trousdale who said pretty much the same. Trousdale ran into Victor in Sydney just before he died and reckoned he really got into his ear about the girl and the ball and whatnot. Anyway, this is what I wanted to ask you about: Trousdale was saying your husband had met someone in Sydney who'd shed some light – those were his

107

words – on the Ticehurst business; said he was quite worked up about it. Any idea who it was?"

She shook her head. "No. He never said anything to me."

"Did he have a diary or something, maybe an address book, that he put phone numbers in?"

"He kept a desk diary at Berkeley. I doubt if that'd tell us much – he wouldn't have taken it away with him." Her hand holding the cigarette stopped in mid-arc, halfway to her mouth. "Christ, of course – the electronic organiser." She ground the just-lit cigarette in an ashtray and hurried from the kitchen, returning a minute later with the biggest briefcase Sparks had ever seen. She laid the briefcase on the kitchen table, clicked it open, rummaged inside for a moment and produced a flat black rectangular object, slightly smaller than a paperback book. To Sparks it looked like a calculator.

"The police went through his briefcase," she said. "They probably thought this was a calculator."

Sparks said nothing. She opened it out, revealing a keyboard and screen.

"Lucky I'd forgotten about this otherwise I might've wiped all Vic's stuff and used it myself, to keep track of my frenetic social life. Now let's see, when was Vic's last trip to Sydney?" She pulled a calendar off the wall and flipped through the pages, then began jabbing the small keyboard.

She peered at the instrument's small screen. "Okay, he went over on the 20th of July and had dinner that night with TR – that'd be Toby Redsell who runs Berkeley in Australia. Wouldn't you know it, it's all bloody initials." She punched another button. "Hang on, here we go – on the 25th he had an appointment with Lloyd Chennell and on the 27th with Julian Gage. I can't remember Vic talking about either of them. They mean anything to you?"

Sparks nodded, trying hard not to look pleased with himself. "I'm pretty sure there was a teacher at Prince Albert called Chennell. Gage rings a bell too. Can I use your phone? I know someone who'll know for sure."

Herman Pickrang sat in his car parked 50 metres down the road from Louise Appleyard's house and watched the rivulets of rain run down the windscreen. He'd followed Sparks there and now he was going to have to wait for him to emerge. Although he didn't particularly enjoy sitting in a car watching the rain, he would do it for as long as he had to. Among the many things Pickrang had learned during his 25 years in the army was the art of waiting for something to happen.

Pickrang was 49 years old. On his tax return and for similar official purposes, he described himself as a security consultant. In fact he earned his living by scaring, hurting, and occasionally even killing people. Pickrang sometimes wondered if he was what the newspapers called a psychopath. He'd tell himself that he couldn't be a psycho because he did what he did for money rather than for pleasure. Every now and again though, a voice from deep inside his head would point out that that really didn't prove much because he enjoyed doing it anyway. Pickrang would bring these interior debates to a close by deciding that it made very little difference to his victims whether he was a psychopath or not.

Pickrang was highly qualified for his work on several counts. In the first place, he had a frightening appearance. He was the son of Janey Wang, a Chinese/Samoan whore who'd worked the logging camps of the mid-North Island, and one of her customers. Watching Herman grow, Janey decided that his father must have been a tall pakeha which narrowed the possibilities down but not enough to point the finger with any real conviction. Not long after she became pregnant, Janey had set up home with a Maori logger named Joe Pickrang. Janey gave her son Joe's surname and the Christian name of her very first customer, the scion of a wealthy German family with large land-holdings in Samoa.

Pickrang had inherited his mother's tiny cat-like head

109

and slightly slanted eyes. These attributes gave Janey, who was barely five foot tall, an exotic look. However on Pickrang, who had also inherited his unknown father's long and sinewy frame and who at 19 was six feet five inches tall, the effect was quite unearthly and had earned him the nickname "Pimplehead" when he joined the army. The unusual pattern of his hair loss over the following 30 years had heightened his menacingly alien appearance: he was completely bald except for a swathe of black fuzz which swung across the back of his head from ear to ear like a hammock and a greying V-shaped clump, all that remained of what had once been a widow's peak, which sat in splendid isolation high on his forehead. People noticing Pick-rang walking towards them in the street would often wonder why he didn't wipe the bird shit off his head.

As a youth, Pickrang had been a keen and promising rugby player, his height, spring and athleticism making him an adept lineout forward. At first his brutal inclinations helped rather than hindered his career, selectors in country areas having traditionally valued "a bit of mongrel" in their forwards. One chilly afternoon in Tokoroa however, Herman Pickrang discovered the old adage that those who live by the sword sometimes perish by it. Before the game was quarter of an hour old, he'd delivered carefully targeted kicks to the heads of three members of the opposition and left livid sprig scrapes on the back and buttocks of several others. It was proving a most enjoyable afternoon until, returning to earth after a mistimed lineout jump, he was struck just below his right ear by a fist the approximate size and consistency of a cannonball which has been gathering barnacles on the seabed for several centuries. His head exploded in a flash of white light and the crackle of splintering bones. By the time he came off his liquid diet 10 weeks later, Pickrang had decided to quit rugby and join the army.

While Pickrang doubted, on balance, that he was a psychopath, most who crossed his path felt strongly to the contrary. In the army, an institution which has long valued psychopathic tendencies provided they are accompanied by a readiness to follow orders and a tolerance for uncomfortable uniforms and for being shouted at from close range, Pickrang found his natural home. He rose to become a sergeant-major in the SAS where his apparent relish for enduring extreme discomfort and eating disgusting things during survival exercises, coupled with his unflagging enthusiasm for making life hell for those under his command, made him a highly-regarded figure.

After 25 years in the army, Pickrang retired reluctantly into civilian life. It was a source of aggravation to him that, having spent two-and-a-half decades mastering numerous ways to kill people, he'd never actually had the opportunity to put this knowledge into practice. Just as disturbing was the dreary prospect of no more of the unarmed combat sessions at which he'd routinely exceeded the parameters of pain and punishment which instructors were permitted to inflict. What, he wondered, does a highly-trained fighting man with powerful if controllable sadistic urges do when he can no longer serve his country? After much thought, Pickrang reached the obvious conclusion: he became a thug-for-hire.

Pickrang's second career had gone swimmingly until the mix-up over the private investigator Wallace Guttle. The whole business still gnawed at him. Not only had Plugge refused to pay for what had been an outstandingly executed job but he'd had to stand there and take some of the ripest, crudest abuse he'd received since he'd been a raw private. For a man with 20 years' experience of screaming elaborately filthy insults at others, it had been an unsettling experience. Now he was having to traipse around after this clown of a journalist hamstrung by humiliatingly restrictive rules of engagement. It was an insult to his professionalism.

If Pickrang had been less engrossed in revisiting Plugge's irrational and unjust reaction to Guttle's flawless assassination, he might have noticed Detective Sergeant Tito Ihaka driving past in an unmarked car. Ihaka, on his way to call on Louise Appleyard, recognised Pickrang's distinctive features from one swift sideways glance. Ihaka drove on past the Appleyard house and pulled to the side of the road.

Pickrang had never actually been convicted of a criminal offence although he'd been interviewed by the police in relation to a number. Those of his victims who'd lived to tell the tale preferred not to. Ihaka wondered what a fully-fledged criminal monster like Herman Pickrang was doing in this pleasant and peaceful street on the shores of Lake Pupuke and whether it had anything to do with Louise Appleyard and her dead husband who had hired the also dead private investigator.

Reggie Sparks rang his brother Gavin.

"Got a couple of names for you; I think there's a Prince Albert connection."

"Fire away."

"Lloyd Chennell."

"Yep, he was a teacher there back in our time. He taught arts subjects, English, history, that sort of thing. He was quite good."

"Do you know where he is now?"

"He went to Australia. Last I heard, he'd done all right, got himself appointed headmaster of one of the top schools – I can't remember if it was Sydney or Melbourne. I could find out for you."

"Okay, second name – Julian Gage."

Gavin groaned. "Shit, I knew it. I won't be able to set foot in the place after this story comes out."

"Why, what'd he do?"

"Oh, even you'd remember Gage, surely? He was the character who everyone reckoned was gay. With good reason too from what I've heard of him since. I think he went to Aussie as well."

# CHAPTER *11*

*I*haka waited in his car across the road from the Appleyard residence. Eventually the front door opened and a man he didn't know came out. The man turned to Louise Appleyard, who was standing in the doorway, and went to shake hands. The gesture seemed to surprise and amuse her but she carried it off gracefully. The visitor then walked down the path, got into a Peugeot, and drove away. Ihaka watched in his rear view mirror as Pickrang did a U-turn and drove off after him.

Louise Appleyard thought the knock on her front door meant that Reggie Sparks had found an excuse to return and found herself smiling as she went to answer it. However it wasn't the journalist; it was the large Maori policeman whose name she couldn't remember and whom she suspected of being smarter than he pretended to be. Louise did what she always did when caught slightly off-guard, which seldom happened; she stood there saying nothing and looking good.

"Detective Sergeant Ihaka, Mrs Appleyard. How are you?"

"I'm well, thank you Sergeant. Do come in. Two visitors in one day – it's bordering on hectic."

Following her down the corridor to the kitchen, Ihaka said: "Yeah, I saw the bloke who just left. Who was he, if you don't mind me asking?"

"I'm sure you have a reason other than nosiness for

wanting to know so I'll tell you: his name's Sparks, Reggie Sparks. He's a journalist."

"A journalist eh? Now why would Herman Pickrang be tailing a journalist?"

"I'm sorry?"

"While you and Sparks were in here talking about whatever it was you were talking about, a fella called Herman Pickrang was sitting in his car just down the street. When Sparks left, Pickrang followed him. Who's Pickrang? He's probably the nastiest thing on two legs in this town. In fact, that's being unfair to rottweilers. He's a hood, a heavy, someone who earns a crust by bashing people up – or worse."

Ihaka had been looking forward to testing the thickness of Louise Appleyard's coolly ironic exterior. He was glad to find that it wasn't double-glazed. Her hand jumped to her mouth: "Good God. Is Reggie in some sort of danger?"

Ihaka nodded slowly. "If Pickrang was stalking me, I wouldn't be laughing about it."

"We've got to warn him," she said, pawing through the bits and pieces on the kitchen bench. "He left me his phone number – it's here somewhere."

"If you don't mind Mrs Appleyard, I'll do that – I'd like to talk to Mr Sparks. So he's working on a story, is he?"

Louise, disoriented, rubbed her forehead. "Yes he is, for *New Nation* magazine. I suppose in a way it's what we were talking about last time you were here – the Ticehurst girl's dance card. He's talking to the men on the card, I think to do a story on what's happened to them since. It was Vic's death that gave them the idea."

"Yeah, well that's the press for you. To be honest, I'm surprised you're helping them."

Louise brought her chin up. "They didn't get the names from me, Sergeant. Mr Sparks had them already. And as for helping him, why shouldn't I? At least he's going about it with an open mind; you people seem to have taken the view from

114

the very beginning that my husband committed suicide and probably murder to boot. I can't see that I've got much to lose."

It took Ihaka less than five seconds to work out how *New Nation* had obtained the names on the dance card. Ted Worsp, he thought; that sack of shit could talk under wet concrete.

He said, "Where do I find Sparks?"

When the *New Nation* editor Jackson Pike was told by his secretary that there was a Mr Sparks wanting to see him, he half-expected that Sparks had come in to admit defeat. However the Reggie Sparks who entered his office was not the twisted substance abuser who'd lunged at Col Dumpley with a copy spike all those years before, nor the clueless wimp to whom he'd given the assignment. While Sparks didn't look like a convert to temperance, clean living and early nights, he was by no means the burnt-out shell Pike had expected. What surprised Pike even more was that, far from weasling on the story, Sparks clearly had the bit between his teeth.

He went straight into his pitch: "Mate, I wouldn't try to tell you how to do your job but I reckon we might be coming at this thing from the wrong angle. The sort of story you were talking about, using these guys as symbols of what's happened to the place over the past 20 years – well, let's face it, you can do that state of the nation stuff any time. I mean, how interesting are these turkeys anyway? Batrouney's a rock 'n' roll casualty – what would that make him? Number 900 in an unlimited series? Quedley's a slick PR man; well aren't they all? At the end of the day, he's a bit of a show pony. Looms is just down on the farm minding his own business and Trousdale's a pathetic little blob who's only interested in his next feed."

Pike leaned back in his excessively large chair and gave Sparks what he thought of as his "first base" look. It was intended to be both encouraging and challenging, to say "Okay, you've got my attention, now let's see if you can convince me".

Sparks, who assumed the editor was holding in a fart, was mildly flattered. Realising that the look hadn't conveyed the message, Pike spread his hands and said, "I'm listening."

"I think Appleyard found out something about the death of Bronwen Ticehurst – maybe that it didn't happen the way they said it did or that there was a lot more to it. To me, that's the story – what did Appleyard find out? Because whatever it was, it was enough to make him jump off the Bridge – or enough to make someone throw him off."

Pike lurched forward and planted his elbows on his desk. "Hang on, I must've missed something. How did we get to that?"

"You know the cops' theory is that he had something to do with the girl's death and was driven to suicide by guilt. I don't think that stands up. Mrs Appleyard's absolutely convinced he didn't kill himself. I know that in itself doesn't prove a thing, but surely to Christ she and others would've noticed something if the guy had been dragging this terrible secret around with him all these years. That's the first thing. Second, if he'd known all along what really happened to her, why does he suddenly get a bee in his bonnet and go round quizzing people about it? As far as him being murdered: well, if he didn't jump, what did happen? Either he stopped his car on the Bridge to sniff the sea air and fell – and both parts of that proposition are hard to believe – or someone shoved him. There's one other thing: Appleyard had hired a private detective."

"What for?"

"Well we don't know, do we, because a couple of weeks later someone blew the guy's brains out."

Pike's eyes widened.

"It was a guy called Guttle. Mrs Appleyard says he definitely wasn't hired to check up on her. Okay, again you can take that with a grain of salt. All I can say is, I've talked to her and I'd be surprised if it turns out she's bullshitting."

116

Pike thought about it for a minute or two. No matter how much Sparks had cleaned up his act, it went against the editor's usual practice and instincts to let a freelancer, particularly such an unknown quantity, drive the story. On the other hand, sometimes the best stories, the real ball grabbers, came when a journalist got this sort of gut feeling. And Sparks did seem to have a reasonable grasp of it.

"All right Reggie, we'll do it your way for the time being. So what's the next step?"

Sparks grinned. "I'm glad you raised that."

After Ihaka had left with a promise that he, personally, would alert Sparks to the Pickrang menace, Louise Appleyard made herself her fifth cup of coffee and lit her tenth cigarette of the day and sat down to review recent events. Pickrang's sudden materialisation was genuinely alarming but at least the police were aware of it. On the subject of the police, Ihaka was certainly a vast improvement on Worsp. There definitely was, she'd decided, a shrewd mind behind the immobile brown face. Under the circumstances, his sheer bulk was quite reassuring as well. Her thoughts didn't dwell on Ihaka and Pickrang for long; there was another, more diverting, development to consider.

By and large Louise Appleyard didn't care what other people thought of her; she considered it one of her few strengths. Even so, there was one reputation she was reluctant to risk gaining – that of merry widow. Hence she'd resisted all attempts to draw her back into the social swing. These attempts had begun in earnest the previous week, exactly four weeks after her husband's funeral. Four weeks seemed to be regarded as the appropriate period of mourning and self-denial. She hadn't known whether to laugh or cry when she received that first dinner party invitation accompanied with a delicately worded rider to the effect that there'd be an unattached male of suitable age and

117

social status among the guests for her to cast an eye over.

All the same, her own instinctive responses were now telling her it was time to get on with life. She suspected that Reggie Sparks fancied her and far from being offended or unnerved, she'd quite enjoyed the faint buzz of the electricity of attraction which flowed between them, albeit predominantly in one direction. I'm not quite sure where I stand on that one, she thought. He's not exactly every maiden's dream but then again, he's not the tongue-tied scruff and all-round no-hoper I took him for at first.

Somewhat more tantalising than the rumpled and awkward Sparks was the prospect held out by Audrey Benn, the wife of one of Victor's colleagues at Berkeley Enterprises. While other would-be hostesses had been euphemistic, in some cases to the point of inscrutability, Audrey had been refreshingly direct when she'd called that morning.

"My dear," Audrey had said briskly, "it's time to throw off the widow's weeds. I know you've been knocking back invites right, left and centre but be warned – there'll be high dudgeon if you don't take your place at the dinner table here next Saturday night. I've moved heaven and earth to snare Auckland's most eligible bachelor for the occasion. I'm sure you know to whom I'm referring – Caspar Quedley."

Louise had said she'd think about it. It wouldn't do to appear too eager.

Ihaka had checked Sparks' phone number against his mother's listing in the phone directory and then driven to St Heliers. There was no sign of the Peugeot or of Pickrang. He rang the doorbell. After identifying himself and assuring Mareena that her son was not about to be led away in handcuffs, he was invited in for a cup of tea and a peanut brownie.

After two cups of tea and three peanut brownies and a discussion about race relations, a subject on which Mrs Sparks proved to be surprisingly well-informed and enlightened by what he assumed were the standards of St Heliers matrons, Ihaka, sitting by the window, observed Sparks pulling into the drive. He was closely followed by Herman Pickrang.

During the afternoon Pickrang's frustrations had finally boiled over. Fuck this, he thought. Any prick with a car and a pair of eyes could do this job. First chance I get, I'm going to scare the living shit out of Sparks and if Plugge doesn't like it, he can blow it out his arse.

Pickrang didn't decide to flout Plugge's express instructions solely because of his resentment at being treated as just another hired hand rather than as a highly qualified specialist. During the hours he'd spent dogging Sparks, it had occurred to Pickrang that he'd effectively rendered himself obsolete as far as Plugge was concerned. Since his retaliatory missions against Plugge's Asian and Australian rivals, peace had returned to Karangahape Road; Plugge was treating him in this demeaning fashion because he'd outlived his usefulness. If Plugge's going to give me the flick, thought Pickrang, why the hell should I worry about pissing him off?

Sparks hadn't noticed Pickrang's red Mitsubishi, which had been parked just down the road from his mother's house all morning and had followed him around town for most of the afternoon, so he was only mildly curious when it pulled up behind him. Curiosity turned to amazement when Pickrang got out of his car. Fucking hell, he thought, what sort of a mutant is that? Amazement turned to bowel-activating fear when the creature spoke.

"Hey cuntbag," it said. "I'm going to rip your fucking ears off."

Ihaka came out of the house and strolled down the drive to join them. For a couple of sickening seconds, Sparks thought he was pincered. However when the newcomer spoke, it was apparent that he and the ear removalist were not working as a team.

"G'day Herman," said Ihaka. "Eaten any babies lately?"

119

Pickrang checked his inclination to fling the insolent intruder to the ground and stomp his testicles into powder. The fact that this big buck knew his name and felt bold enough to insult him could only mean one thing.

"You're a cop."

"I'm a cop and you're a headcase – that's why we're here. Whose dirty work are you doing today, Herman? Who told you to lean on Mr Sparks?"

Pickrang took a couple of paces backwards and opened his car door. He gestured rudely, got into the car, reversed out of the drive, and sped off amidst the thump and whine of violent gear changes.

"He said he was going to rip my ears off," said Sparks. "Would he really do that?"

"Herman must like you," said Ihaka. "He usually goes straight for the nuts. So what did you do to upset him?"

Sparks noticed he was trembling slightly. He put his hands in his pockets. "I'm not sure. I guess it must be something to do with Trevor Lydiate."

"Who?"

"I'm doing this story for *New Nation* magazine . . ."

"I know about your story," said Ihaka. "I've been talking to Mrs Appleyard."

"You know about the dance card?"

Ihaka nodded.

"Lydiate's one of the names on it. He's a lawyer who's doing time for embezzlement. The other day I got this anonymous phone call from a guy saying to met him in Potter's Park if I wanted the oil on Lydiate. Well I went but no one turned up. The guy on the phone was your Herman whatsisname – the thing that time forgot. I recognised the voice as soon as he opened his mouth."

CHAPTER *12*

*C*aspar Quedley, the public relations wizard, lived in a smart new townhouse in Mission Bay. It had two bedrooms, a study, a living room with a fine view of Rangitoto Island, a heavily marbled bathroom with a large spa in which Quedley now and again stage-managed romps involving sufficient quantities of champagne, cocaine and partner swapping to constitute an orgy in these austere and unspontaneous times, a wine cellar, a dining room and state-of-the-art kitchen neither of which were often used, and a two-car garage which housed his Lexus and four-wheel drive. He also owned a hideaway, which he liked to think of as spartan, at one of Coromandel Peninsula's more spectacular and inaccessible beaches. Despite the various attractions of his two homes, Quedley was happiest in his office.

As he'd indicated to Reggie Sparks, Quedley was unreservedly cynical about the public relations industry. In fact, in his case public relations was just a conveniently vague term for a range of shadowy activities.

Quedley's office was the hub of a far-flung network of friends, acquaintances, contacts and informants who were constantly feeding in information, speculation, rumour and gossip. This Quedley filtered, processed and distributed in whichever direction best served the agenda he happened to be pushing at the time. His network extended across most sectors of business, through the media, and to the uppermost reaches of the major political parties. Quedley's clients paid handsomely for his information, analysis, advice, and, they mistakenly believed, loyalty. Most of those who dealt with him, whether as client or contact, underestimated the extensiveness of his network, his access to the highest offices and biggest boardrooms in the land and his capacity for manipulation: many would have scoffed at the notion that his influence matched their own; only the very well-connected, the real insiders, understood that Caspar Quedley was one of the two or three dozen most powerful people in the country.

Quedley also enjoyed the interaction of office life. Although he chose to live alone, he enjoyed having people around him, especially if they were young, bright, attractive and female, as most of his staff were. It was often whispered where PR people gathered that Quedley conducted staff recruitment interviews on the casting couch; he'd heard the stories and found them highly offensive. To Quedley, seduction was sport. In sport there was little or no satisfaction in gaining victory over a handicapped or disadvantaged opponent; likewise where was the challenge, where was the achievement, in getting a woman into bed through the use of pressure or inducements? It was one step up from paying for it.

He had, it was true, slept with a number of his employees, but always at their instigation and after exhorting them to look upon it as nothing more than a short-lived exercise in mutual physical gratification; it would not, he would warn, lead to a deeper relationship nor to advancement within the Quedley organisation. Sometimes these warnings went unheeded and the liaison's aftermath would be an embarrassing scene. When that happened, Quedley, who detested emotionalism, would vow never again. These vows were seldom observed for long; Quedley was no more capable of adhering to his own rules than to anyone else's.

However, this particular Thursday morning in late October, office affairs were far from Caspar Quedley's mind.

122

In his morning mail was a hand-addressed letter, postmarked Sydney and labelled "Private and Confidential". Quedley opened the envelope; it contained a single sheet of unfamiliar handwriting which read:

'Clifftops'
Ocean View Road
Palm Beach NSW 2108

Caspar,

I am at my beachhouse for what is almost certainly the last time. Although my doctor still can't bring himself to state the obvious, he no longer bothers with the customary encouraging platitudes. I can almost read my death certificate in his eyes. I can hardly do anything for myself now; even the simple act of writing is beyond me and I'm having to dictate this to my friend Dean Delamore, whose unstinting care and support has been all that has sustained me of late.

By contrast, your support has been conspicuous by its absence. I see from my diary that it is nine months to the day since I told you of my condition. When we spoke then, you promised to visit me at the first opportunity. Not only have you not come to see me but you haven't even bothered to pick up the phone and give me a single, solitary call. Surely you were well aware how much a visit from you would have meant to me and, conversely, how wounding your indifference has been. I'm deeply shocked that, after all we went through together, you could turn your back on me at this time.

No doubt a religious person – someone like poor Chaplain Swindell for example – would say that someone in my position should feel forgiveness rather than bitterness. Personally, I've always thought deathbed conversions or transformations were cowardly. So I'm going to behave bitterly but in a way which should appeal to your finely-developed sense of malice. A few weeks ago, before I became a real cot-case, I sat down and wrote a little memoir of those strange days at our dear old alma mater. It's a rather riveting read, if I say so myself. If you don't put in an appearance before I go, Dean will send it to an appropriate and interested party.

I'd better stop there and get this in the post. Time is short.

Julian

After he'd read the letter, Quedley said "Fuckfire" in a hoarse whisper. He checked the postmark; it had been posted four days earlier. Christ, he thought, I hope the little queer hasn't croaked already. He leant back in his chair and thought furiously for a couple of minutes. Then he flipped through his address book, found a number and dialled it. The phone rang three times then there was a click and a recorded message came on:

"Hello, this is Julian Gage. I can't come to the phone right now but if you leave a message after the beep, I'll get back to you as soon as I can."

The beep sounded. Quedley put the phone down. Would it be a good idea to leave a message, he wondered? What the fuck, the sooner you make contact, the better.

He rang the number again. When the beep sounded, he put every ounce of shame, regret and wheedling salesmanship he could muster into his voice and blurted, "Julian, it's Caspar. Please forgive me. I'm absolutely ashamed of myself. I've been unbelievably busy but there's no excuse for it. I'll come over as soon as I can – this weekend. In the meantime, don't . . . do anything hasty."

Quedley hung up. That's a holding action at best, he told

himself. The question is, how am I really going to deal with this? Of course, Bill Tench. If it wasn't for me, Tench and that trash he employs would be breaking rocks in Mt Eden jail rather than getting fat on some of the plummest security contracts in town.

Quedley went to his address book again, dialled the number and was put through.

"Bill, it's Caspar Quedley. I need you to do me a favour old chief, bit of a delicate one. I need someone to go to Sydney straight away, like this afternoon, and perform a little task for me. It could be quite tricky – not exactly by the book, shall we say? I'll pay top dollar."

"We talking about the sort of bloke who won't take 'no' for an answer here?"

"Exactly. That's precisely the sort of operator I'm after."

"There's one bloke who comes to mind," said Tench. "Leave it with me. I'll see if he's available and ring you back. If he's on, how do you want to play it?"

"I'd much prefer to stay at arm's length. How about if I brief you and you brief him?"

Quedley ordered coffee and waited for Tench to call back. Yes, he thought, that's the way to handle it. Get someone over there pronto to intercept Julian's poison arrow.

His private phone rang.

"All set," said Tench. "This bloke's a starter."

"Billy my boy, you've surpassed yourself. Let's meet for a sandwich in Cornwall Park in an hour's time and I'll tell you all about it."

Caspar Quedley wasn't the only prominent Auckland identity to be rattled that morning.

Unease descended on Barry Plugge, the striptease impresario, as soon as Detective Sergeant Ihaka entered his office. It was the grin, Plugge decided. When a cop wore that sort of big, friendly grin, it meant he was about to shove it up you in a major way.

Plugge's secretary brought in coffee and biscuits and set the tray down on the low table separating her employer and the policeman.

"Mallow puffs," exclaimed Ihaka. "That just about amounts to bribery."

He picked up a mallow puff between thumb and forefinger, studied it fondly, and popped it in his mouth. He thought about having another then dragged his eyes away from the tray and looked at Plugge.

"Barry, they tell me you've got Herman Pickrang on your payroll these days. He's a bit heavy-duty for you isn't he?"

"Give us a break, Sergeant," said Plugge indignantly. "You know the ructions we had around here. When it reached the stage I had a fucking contract put out on me, I decided well shit, I better get myself some protection. You can't blame me for that."

"I don't think the journalist that Pickrang's been heavying is trying to put you away Barry."

Plugge frowned. "A journalist you say? Don't know anything about that; it can't have been on my account. Don't forget, Herman's a free agent, he doesn't just work for me."

Ihaka was grinning again. "Yeah Barry but the word is, he's been pretty much your man full-time since you pooed your pants over that contract. What I can't figure out though is why you of all people should care if a journo wanted to talk to Trevor Lydiate?"

Plugge's expression froze and he made a low grunting sound. Ihaka gulped another biscuit.

"Isn't it unbelievable these lawyers ripping off their clients?" said Ihaka shaking his head. "So many of 'em, you can't keep track. Anyway, the point is, here's your boy Pickrang following this journo all round town and threatening to do Christ knows what to him – well shit, I don't mind admitting, it made no sense to me. I asked myself, 'Why should Plugge give a flying fuck if every man

126

and his dog want to talk to Lydiate?' So I had a chat to a mate of mine in the Fraud Squad; he thought it was pretty strange, too. He said it almost made him wonder if there wasn't more to Lydiate's little number than meets the eye. Anyway, he and his boys are going to talk to the Law Society and have a good long look at the whole thing. I just thought you'd like to know."

Ihaka wolfed a final mallow puff and stood up. Plugge sat in silence, looking as if he'd swallowed something vile and was waiting for his system to reject it.

Ihaka paused with his hand on the doorknob. "Speaking of Lydiate – you remember a private investigator called Guttle who got smoked a while back? He was working for a bloke – who's also dead now, by the way – who was poking around in something where Lydiate's name came up. I guess we're going to have to have another look at that too."

Louise Appleyard had found phone numbers for Lloyd Chennell and Julian Gage in the directory section of her late husband's electronic diary. Sparks rang them from Auckland to try to set things up in advance. Chennell was wary; to secure the interview Sparks had had to feed him a long and inventive spiel, claiming he was doing a story, using Prince Albert College as a case study, about whether private schools should be responsive to social change or maintain their traditions at all costs. The call to Gage got an answering machine. He didn't leave a message.

Sparks caught the mid-afternoon Air New Zealand flight to Sydney and took a cab from the airport to his Kings Cross hotel. There was a fax from Gavin waiting for him. It read: "LC was deputy head of history at PAC from 1968 to 1974. The head of department supervised the teaching of history at scholarship and bursary level while LC did so at UE and school certificate level. His responsibilities included setting internal exam papers."

Just after seven o'clock Sparks went out for a stroll and something to eat. He walked through the Cross, running the gauntlet of pimps, whores and hustlers, towards Potts Point. He crossed the street to avoid a melee involving a trio of skeletal hookers, their skimpy outfits revealing decaying blue-tinged flesh, and a ragged wino whose eyes rolled comically in his plum-coloured face. Sparks didn't see Herman Pickrang in the rear seat of the taxi which halted for him at the pedestrian crossing, and Herman Pickrang was having too much fun observing the dementia of the street people to notice Sparks.

CHAPTER *13*

Adversity, it is often said, brings out the best in people. It was a moot point whether there was any "best" in Barry Plugge to be brought out but once he'd recovered from the shock of Ihaka's bombshells, the Sultan of Sleaze surprised himself with his self-possession, decisiveness, and ruthless cunning.

Admittedly the lack of histrionics once the policeman had departed was mainly due to the fact that the gravity of the situation had stunned him into a state bordering on catalepsy. After sitting virtually motionless for 25 minutes, Plugge cleared his mind of nightmarish visions of penury, imprisonment, and being sodomised by large, brutal men with tattoos and dreadlocks, and forced himself to think.

Of the two related crises, the Guttle matter required the more urgent attention. Despite Ihaka's needling, it would take the Fraud Squad some time to get around to reviewing Lydiate's scam given the apparent epidemic of white collar crime and the fact that they already had a conviction. But murder was murder. What linked him to Guttle was Pickrang — Pickrang whose unbelievable incompetence, whose chronic inability to follow instructions, whose savage impulses had got him into this mess. Pickrang's job had been to discourage interest in Lydiate and thereby ensure that the Plugge-Lydiate connection remained hidden from view. He had achieved the exact opposite. And what, Plugge asked himself, would the useless turd do when the cops got their hands on him, which wouldn't take long? Save his own hairy arse, more than likely. There was no dodging the fact that Herman Pickrang had become a liability.

Pickrang hadn't been heard from for a couple of days which, in the light of Ihaka's visit, was in itself disturbing. First thing the next morning, Plugge dispatched his new chief bouncer to establish Pickrang's whereabouts. Just before midday the bouncer reported that Pickrang was not answering his home or mobile phone and hadn't been sighted in any of his usual haunts.

"Get out to his place and have a look," Plugge told him. "Break in if you have to."

"What if he's there?"

"If he's there, you won't have to break in will you?" said Plugge in an eerily calm voice. He put the phone down thinking, the bastard knows he's fucked up so he's gone to ground; maybe that'll take the heat off. Even as he permitted himself that glimmer of hope, it occurred to Plugge that if Pickrang wanted to melt into a crowd, he'd have to hide out in a leper colony.

Half an hour later the bouncer rang again.

"Boss, I'm out at Herman's place – I kicked the door in like you said – and I reckon he's gone to Sydney."

"Sydney?" yelped Plugge. "What the fuck would he be doing there?"

"Well I wouldn't know. It's just that I found this thing from a travel agent on his kitchen table. It's got Herman's name on it and it's a sort of schedule, all typed up, saying when he's got to be at the airport, what flight he's on, where he's staying and all that. According to this, he went over to Sydney yesterday afternoon."

"When's he meant to be coming back?"

"Doesn't say. It says 'open return'."

"Okay. Get back here and bring that schedule thing with you."

Plugge hung up and stared at the wall. A plan was taking shape in his mind. The more Plugge thought about it, the more he liked it. It was simple, easily executed and would solve the Pickrang problem at a stroke. It was one thing to identify Pickrang as a threat which had to be neutralised; it was quite another to actually do the neutralising. Plugge was well aware that his other employees would sooner rub themselves down with raw offal and jump into the shark tank at Kelly Tarlton's Underwater World than tangle with Pickrang; his plan overcame that problem. He went into his private bathroom and splashed some cold water on his face. As he looked at himself in the mirror above the handbasin, he said out loud, "Herman, you're about to find out the hard way that it doesn't pay to screw around with Barry Plugge."

Rocco Perfumo was just seeing out the last of the lunch customers at the inner-city pizzeria restaurant which doubled as the headquarters of his family's New Zealand business interests when a waiter told him he was wanted on the phone. He walked to the far end of the restaurant and picked up the receiver.

"Yeah?"

"Is that Rocco Perfumo?"

The caller sounded like he had a mouthful of industrial strength glue. Perfumo wondered why he was going to such lengths to disguise his voice; all New Zealanders sounded the same to him.

"Yeah. What do you want?"

"Remember Herman Pickrang?"

Remember Herman Pickrang? Was this arsehole some kind of comedian? What does he think – that every second day some fucking gorilla who looks like Doctor No on steroids comes in here and shoves my brother head-first into the pizza oven?

Rocco's brother Martino had suffered impaired eyesight and severe facial scorching as a result of his insertion in the wood-fired oven, the virtues of which were extolled in the restaurant's advertising. He was now convalescing back in Sydney. His sight was nearly back to normal but it would require costly plastic surgery to repair his complexion. Without it, he faced the prospect of going through life looking like a sand-blasted beetroot. The brothers had demanded revenge but their uncle, the head of the family, had ruled that an escalation of the dispute might draw unwanted attention to the family's presence in New Zealand. Rocco had chafed under the veto, convinced his uncle would have put family pride ahead of profits had it been his son whose head had been baked.

"Course I remember him, the cunt," snapped Rocco. "What about him?"

"I just thought you'd like to know – he's in Sydney right now, staying at the Grosvenor serviced apartments in Potts Point."

The caller hung up. Perfumo looked at his watch. He had time to get the late afternoon flight to Sydney. He rang his mother's apartment in Sydney's inner west. His brother answered.

"Marty, it's Rocco. I'm coming over for the weekend. We got some business to take care of."

Lloyd Chennell, the headmaster of St Bartholomew's College, a private boys' school in the posh Sydney suburb of Bellevue Hill, looked at the antique clock on his antique desk. It was 4.15 on a Friday afternoon; another week over. It had been a testing week: a cache of the drug Ecstasy had been found in a stationery cupboard; persons unknown had released a cage of laboratory mice in the head of maths' new car; and a Taiwanese multi-millionaire had removed his son from the school after the lad had been left traumatised by a bullying campaign culminating in a mock lynching, dealing a severe setback to

132

Chennell's strategy of cultivating the Asian community to make up for the fall-off in enrolments from hard-pressed country folk.

On the positive side of the ledger, the senior tennis team had won its rubber against traditional rivals, Marsden Grammar. In his eight years as headmaster of St Bartholomew's, Chennell had learned that the Friends of St Bart's, the all-powerful grouping of old boys and parents which dominated the board of governors, would turn a blind eye to pure heroin being sold from the tuck shop as long as victory was achieved in the various sporting tussles with Marsden.

Chennell was spending the weekend in the Blue Mountains and was anxious to be on his way. First though, he had to do this bloody interview. He cursed the conceit which had caused him to agree to the thing in the first place. He had done so for one reason only: being written up in New Zealand's leading magazine as the headmaster of one of the southern hemisphere's most prestigious schools would be an unwelcome reminder for his former colleagues at Prince Albert College – those patronising oafs now washing down the bitter taste of failure with cheap sherry in the staff reading room or languishing in their dim provincial colleges and second-rate prep schools – that he'd gone on to far greater things.

He vaguely remembered this journalist fellow Sparks droning on about the theme of his article, some idiotic guff about whether private schools should respond to social change. As if I bloody care, he thought. To Chennell, a private school was a meal ticket, a way to make a living without having to endure the nameless horrors of the state system. He would spend another cloistered decade at St Bart's and then take a comfortable retirement; after that, it was all the same to him whether they outlawed private schools, burnt them to the ground or turned them into loony bins. A career of dealing with the children of privilege had left Lloyd Chennell with an outlook which verged on nihilism.

At 4.30 Reggie Sparks, wearing a respectable pair of corduroy trousers, a new sports jacket and his late father's lawn bowls club tie, was shown into Chennell's office. The gloom created by the dark wood panelling and the heavy drapes, illuminated only by the single lamp on the large desk in the corner gave Sparks a nasty moment of *deja vu*. However the figure who rose to greet him bore no resemblance to the schizoid colossus Dr Foster Hogbin.

Sparks had only the haziest recollection of Chennell; he'd put it down to his indifferent memory but the fact of the matter was that Lloyd Chennell was rather forgettable. He was of medium height, slim and moved with a loose-limbed, boneless slither. He had sandy hair, spectacles, a high, brainy forehead, a loose, wet mouth and wore a tweedy brown suit and brown brogues which gave him the appearance of a boffin masquerading as a squire. Sparks was intrigued by his ears which were bright red, almost crimson, and unusually fleshy; they looked as if the slightest perforation would unleash spouts of blood of the sort one associated with decapitation. Chennell's pallor also made Sparks wonder if this build-up of blood at the extremities was depriving other organs.

For half an hour, they addressed the ostensible subject of the interview. If Chennell had been more experienced in dealing with the press, it might have occurred to him that Sparks, having opened proceedings with the broadest of catch-all questions, made no effort to shepherd the discussion in any particular direction with more specific follow-ups. Chennell accepted the opportunity to blow his own trumpet and was doing so tunefully, to his ears anyway, when Sparks brought the recital to an abrupt halt.

"When you think about it, some pretty strange things went on at Prince Albert back in 1970. I mean, first the chaplain steered his car into a brick wall; then the girl hanged herself at the ball; now I hear there was a black market in exam papers."

Chennell stared at Sparks, his ears glowing like horseshoes fresh from the furnace.

"You have the advantage on me there," he said finally.

"You'd remember a bloke called Caspar Quedley?" Chennell nodded. "Apparently, before the exams, he was flogging the UE history paper around the place. You were in charge of setting that paper; how do you think he got hold of it?"

Chennell rose. Something was terribly wrong here. How it had come about could be established in due course; the immediate priority was to terminate the interview.

"Mr Sparks, I have no idea what you're talking about so there's little point in pursuing this discussion. I'm going away for the weekend and I've delayed my departure on your account but I'm not prepared to do so a minute longer for this sort of scurrilous nonsense."

Sparks seemed quite unflustered by the headmaster's indignation. He flipped his notebook shut and put his pen in a jacket pocket. He looked up at Chennell who was now standing next to him.

"What about Victor Appleyard – had you come across him lately?"

Chennell decided not to wait for Sparks to get to his feet. He walked to the study door and held it open. "Appleyard? I heard he died, that's all."

Sparks stopped at the door and extended his hand to Chennell. As Chennell withdrew his hand after a fleeting touch, Sparks looked at him quizzically and said, "That's odd because I know for a fact that Appleyard had an appointment with you the last time he was over here. I suppose you're going to tell me you haven't clapped eyes on Julian Gage for 20 years either?"

The reference to Gage was a stab in the dark but the effect was spectacular: Chennell recoiled as if Sparks had requested one of his choirboys for use in a satanic rite.

"Get out of here this minute," he hissed. "And rest assured your editor will be hearing about this."

Sparks nodded. "You bet."

Herman Pickrang walked down the avenue in Potts Point checking the street numbers, enjoying the warm afternoon sun and congratulating himself on his good fortune. This Sydney job couldn't have been better timed. Even before Ihaka's appearance, Pickrang had been well aware that he was losing ground with Plugge; Plugge would've gone apeshit if he'd found out the cops had somehow got involved. All in all, it was better for everybody if he spent a bit of time out of Auckland. Maybe he should've let Plugge know about his run-in with the cop but he could talk his way out of that if he had to – I figured the best bet was to lay low for a while, keep my head down blah, blah. Not that he particularly gave a shit about Plugge except he could do without the guy going round town badmouthing him; it wouldn't do his reputation any good. In the meantime, he was going to make sure he did the business on this job; whoever he was working for was paying bloody well and there might be more down the track – providing he didn't fuck it up.

Pickrang stopped outside a handsome three-storey terrace and checked the number against the address Tench had given him. He opened the cast-iron gate, walked up three steps to the tiny porch and rang the bell. The door was opened by a young woman whose pale face contrasted with her uniformly black colour scheme: she had black hair cut page-boy style, a black dress, black stockings, black shoes and black rings under her eyes. Pickrang leered down at her thinking, I'd give you one love if you asked me nicely.

"I'm looking for Julian Gage," he announced. "Is he in?"

The woman half-closed the door and moved nervously behind it shaking her head. "No," she said huskily. "He's gone away – overseas."

Pickrang consulted his piece of paper.

136

"What about Dean Delamore?"

"He's gone too."

"Who are you?"

"Miranda. I'm house-sitting for Julian. He should be back in a week or so." She started to close the door. "Maybe you could come back then . . ."

Pickrang dropped his shoulder and rammed it hard against the door. It flew open, knocking the woman backwards. She began to protest.

"Shut your gob," snarled Pickrang. He entered the house shutting the door behind him. "Gage's got something that belongs to a friend of mine and he wants it back. I'm going to find it so if you want to stay in one piece, just keep quiet and stay out of my way."

Pickrang searched the terrace literally from top to bottom, beginning on the third floor and working his way down. It was not a difficult task – the house was immaculately tidy and there were few obvious hiding places – but his search proved fruitless. By the time he reached the last room, the kitchen, he was in a foul mood which wasn't improved when he found there was no beer in the fridge. He summoned the woman. She came hesitantly, hands clasped in front of her.

"I'm looking for something like a letter, you know, a few pages with writing on them. It might be in an envelope or some sort of package or maybe a folder or notebook. Have you seen it?"

The woman shook her head.

Pickrang said "Fucking shit" then brushed past her and stalked down the corridor. He stood in the doorway and said, "I'll be back," then left, slamming the door behind him.

Miranda, whose real name was Dean Delamore, stood in front of the large mirror in the hallway and removed the wig. He ruffled his hair which had been plastered to his scalp, then took a tissue from his handbag and wiped off his lipstick. He wondered what the frightening stranger would've done if he'd

137

told the truth: that Julian Gage had been dead for two days and that the previous day, he'd dropped a letter from Gage to Victor Appleyard into the airmail slot at the Potts Point post office.

Dean Delamore was pretty sure lying had been the sensible course of action. He decided he wouldn't tax his already fragile state of mind by contemplating what the frightening stranger would do when he found out he'd been lied to.

# CHAPTER 14

*C*aspar Quedley had woken up with a hangover too often to bother berating himself for having less sense than one of Pavlov's dogs. Similarly, he had given up making pointless and self-deceiving resolutions to stay off the booze for a week, a month or a year. Even the soreness at the back of his throat and the foul taste in his mouth, the residue of one of his occasional cigarette binges, didn't cause a twinge of self-disgust. Caspar Quedley had long ago accepted himself for what he was and looked upon the various facets of his nature – the admirable and the unattractive, the healthy and the perverse – with equanimity. The simple fact was that he was going to get shit-faced from time to time; it was as inevitable as death, taxes and flatulence. Yes, he felt dreadful but experience suggested it was nothing that a 10km run, a gargantuan break-fast, and a contemplative and productive 20 minutes on the toilet couldn't fix.

Quedley checked his watch – it was 9.30 – threw back the duvet, rolled out of bed, stretched, scratched, and pulled on a white towelling robe. On his way downstairs he checked the answer phone in the study; the flickering light showed he had two messages. He pressed the playback and was assailed by the strident and slightly hectoring tones of Audrey Benn.

"Caspar, Audrey Benn. It's 9.30 on Friday night and this is just a little reminder that you have a dinner engagement here tomorrow evening. I'm absolutely counting on you so don't let me down."

"Slutfire," said Quedley. "What in the world possessed me to agree to that?" Before he could grapple with that mystery, he found himself being harangued by a frantic Lloyd Chennell.

"Caspar, it's Lloyd Chennell. I've just had this journalist from *New Nation* magazine in to see me – an insolent shit called Sparks who was at Prince Albert. He made out he was doing a story on private schools but that was just a pretence to get in the door. Caspar, he brought up the exam paper; he brought up Julian. How much does he know, for God's sake? What sort of story are they going to do? Call me as soon as you can – I'll be in the Blue Mountains."

This is starting to give me a monumental slack, thought Quedley sourly as he erased the messages. *New Nation* must be taking this bloody thing seriously if they've sent Sparks over to Sydney. And how the Christ had he got onto Chennell and Gage? First things first. Quedley retrieved his address book from his briefcase, found the number for Chennell's cottage in the Blue Mountains, and dialled. Chennell answered, sounding peevish, after a dozen rings.

"Caspar here."

"Dammit Caspar, what time is it? I was sound asleep."

"Don't whine please Lloyd. The first sound I heard this morning was that of you wetting your panties, which is an extremely fucking disagreeable way to start the weekend, especially when one has a severe headache. I'm in no mood to be grizzled at."

"All right, okay. Anyway, what about this blasted journalist?"

"Exactly what did he say?"

"He said he'd heard that in 1970 you got an advance copy of the UE history exam paper and sold it to your pals; he wanted to know how you'd got hold of it. Then he threw Julian at me."

140

"In what context?"

"He asked if I'd seen him."

"What'd you say?"

"I refused to discuss it. I ejected him from my study."

Oh yes, thought Quedley, I can just imagine that. I bet Sparks is still shaking.

"Caspar, did you know Sparks was doing this story?"

"Yeah I did. He came to see me a couple of days ago."

Chennell, the quaver back in his voice, began demanding to know why he hadn't been alerted but Quedley cut him off.

"Stop bleating," he snapped in a voice without a trace of its customary banter. "I didn't take him seriously; obviously that was a mistake which now has to be rectified. Is Sparks still in Sydney?"

"I've no idea. He came to see me late yesterday afternoon."

"Assuming he's still there – any idea where I can get in touch with him? I mean, did he leave you a contact number or anything?"

"He did as a matter of fact. When we arranged the interview, he told me to leave a message for him at his hotel if I needed to change the time. It was the Plaza, I think. Yes, the Plaza. I believe it's in Kings Cross."

"Okay, leave it with me. I'll take care of it. If you hear from him again, find out where he is and let me know straight away."

"Thank you Caspar. I needed some reassurance. I really couldn't bear the thought of that business seeing the light of day."

Quedley put the phone down. What an old woman Chennell was. The generalised throbbing in his skull had centralised to a pinprick of intense pain high in his frontal lobe; he was in dire need of a fresh orange juice and a strong cup of coffee. As he made his way downstairs, he thought of something which perked him up enormously. He remembered

141

why he'd accepted Audrey Benn's dinner invitation: because the extremely fuckable – and now fancy-free – Louise Appleyard would be there.

Caspar Quedley was an expert and dispassionate analyst of the various forms of communication, spoken and unspoken, used in social conduct. He employed this expertise in various ways, one of which was to assess the attitudes of attractive women towards sex in general and sex with Caspar Quedley in particular. They were categorised under various headings ranging from "mattress crusher" to "convent fodder". In almost two decades of employing his system, he had only once been dangerously underprepared for an encounter. He'd made a point of avoiding politicians' wives ever since. He'd met Louise Appleyard a few times over the years and was sure he'd detected a spark of interest in her dark eyes. She was by no means a flirt: she'd simply held his look for that extra second or two; when he'd try to catch her eye again, she'd flick him a slightly mocking smile and look away. But back then, he told himself, her husband was always lurking around, boring someone shitless on the subject of interest rates or CBD rents or something equally fascinating. After allowing for the husband factor, Quedley had categorised Louise Appleyard as a "slow burner", one of those cool, self-contained types who like to be in control of themselves and the situation; they didn't let go often or easily but when they did, it paid to be in racing condition because one was in for a wild ride.

In the course of these musings, it occurred to Quedley that there was a second very good reason for devoting close attention to Mrs Appleyard. He hadn't really thought about it in all the excitement but the "appropriate and interested party" to whom Julian Gage was threatening to send his odious little memoir could well be the late Victor Appleyard. It makes sense, he thought: Appleyard could've seen Julian on one of his trips to Sydney and Julian's probably been too busy dying to have caught up with the fact that virtuous Victor is no longer with us.

Quedley squeezed three oranges, drank the juice, made himself a cup of coffee and returned to the study. Before I do anything else, he thought, I need to get a message to my man in Sydney on the subject of Reggie Sparks, who's becoming tiresome.

The army had eradicated any inclination in Herman Pickrang to lie abed; regardless of the day of the week or the state of his health, he liked to be up and doing by eight o'clock. So when the go-between Bill Tench tried to get hold of him to pass on Quedley's message, Pickrang was in downtown Sydney doing some shopping. He bought himself a baseball cap to protect his scalp and a diver's knife. He then followed the advice of his next-door neighbour and visited the Queen Victoria Building, Darling Harbour and the Opera House. Just before midday he picked up a hire car and drove out to Watson's Bay where, once again on his neighbour's advice, he ate fish and chips at Doyle's restaurant. When he received the bill, he made a mental note to do something moderately painful to his neighbour when he got home. After lunch, he went for a leisurely drive through the eastern suburbs. The more mansions he passed, the more resentful Pickrang became; he was so preoccupied with envy that he didn't notice the dark green Ford which had followed him since he'd picked up the hire car.

When Pickrang returned to his serviced apartment in the early afternoon, there was a message to ring Tench. He did so, reporting on his lack of progress and receiving his instructions with regard to Reggie Sparks. He had mixed feelings about this new assignment: while he was pleased that someone was prepared to pay him handsomely to have a second crack at the journalist, he was puzzled as to how it had come about. Was there any connection with Plugge and Lydiate? After a few minutes of unproductive mental effort, he reached his usual conclusion – who gives a fuck? What mattered was getting the job done.

143

Pickrang had planned to use the afternoon to check out Gage's place at Palm Beach but that could wait. Instead he walked over to Sparks' hotel and sat in the lobby. Watching the comings and goings, he observed that when guests left their keys at reception, they were put in cubby holes marked with their room numbers. Eventually he walked over to the desk and told the receptionist he wanted to leave a message for a guest, Mr Reggie Sparks. The young woman handed him a small notepad and a biro. Pickrang wrote "Meet me in the bar at 6pm, Bert", folded the piece of paper, and handed it to her. He watched her put the message in the cubby hole, noting the room number. There was a key in the cubby hole so Sparks had gone out. Pickrang selected a chair on the far side of the hotel lobby well away from the main entrance and sat down to await the journalist's return.

This time when the doorbell rang Dean Delamore looked through the peephole. He didn't know the man standing on the doorstep; he also looked too straight – with his sports jacket and his uncool hair, neither short enough nor long enough – to be a friend of Julian Gage's. On the other hand, he looked a lot less threatening than the gatecrasher of the previous day. Delamore opened the door as far as the security chain would allow.

"Yes?"

"Oh hi," said the stranger. "Does Julian Gage live here?"

"Julian's not here at the moment."

The stranger gnawed his lower lip. "My name's Reggie Sparks; I'm a journalist from New Zealand. I was really hoping to talk to Julian – are you expecting him back shortly?"

"No. He's gone away for quite a while."

"Bugger," said Sparks, grimacing. "Look, you're obviously a friend of his, you might be able to help. Did Julian ever mention a guy called Victor Appleyard?"

"I've heard Julian talk about him. What's your connection with Appleyard?"

"Before he died . . ."

"Appleyard's dead?" exclaimed Delamore. Sparks nodded. Delamore unhooked the security chain and opened the door.

"You'd better come in."

Sparks entered.

"We'll sit outside in the courtyard," said his host. "Down the corridor and through the kitchen."

Sparks walked through to the courtyard which was bathed in afternoon sun and sat down at the wooden table.

"I'm Dean Delamore by the way. Can I get you something – coffee or a juice?"

Sparks declined. Delamore was in his mid-20s with short dyed blond hair cut Roman style, troubled brown eyes, and a slim, wiry build. He wore an unbuttoned check shirt over a snug-fitting white singlet, black stovepipe jeans, Doc Martens and gold earrings. Sparks assumed he was gay.

Sparks told Delamore about Appleyard's interest in the events of 1970 and his meetings in Sydney with Gage and Chennell: "Whatever he found out, he went back to Auckland all fired up about it. Then he died and now I'm sort of trying to piece it together. Appleyard's wife's – widow's – helping," he added, as if it gave the enterprise legitimacy.

Delamore came and sat down opposite Sparks.

"Julian's dead. He died on Wednesday."

"Jesus Christ. How'd he die?"

Delamore lowered his eyes and fiddled with one of his earrings, then looked defiantly at Sparks. "He had AIDS."

Sparks, expressionless, held Delamore's gaze for a few seconds then looked away.

"I'm sorry."

Delamore nodded. "So am I."

He went into the kitchen and came back with an apple. As he ate it, he told Sparks about the threatening note Gage

145

had sent Caspar Quedley and how, two days previously and according to his instructions, he'd posted Gage's letter to Victor Appleyard.

Sparks whistled softly. "What did it say?"

"No idea. I just dropped it in the post."

"Had he ever talked to you about any of this stuff?"

Delamore shook his head.

"Well I guess we'll know soon enough. I'll ring Louise and let her know it's coming."

"There's another thing," said Delamore. "Quedley must've got a big shock when he got Julian's letter. He left this smarmy message on the answering machine – you know, please forgive me, I'll come over and see you as soon as I can. I think he sent someone over here to find what Julian wrote. This guy barged in here yesterday, really rude, and searched the place. You should've seen him – he was unreal, like maybe two metres tall and kind of Asian-looking. And he was bald except for this chunk of hair right here," he said pointing to the middle of his fringe.

Holy shit, it can't be, thought Sparks. "How big was his head?" he asked.

Delamore looked puzzled. "What do you mean?"

"Did he have a really small head?" asked Sparks, making a shape with his hands.

"Right, yes he did, a tiny little head, like really out of proportion with the rest of him. Do you know him?"

It must be, thought Sparks. The sort of biological quirk which results in a Herman Pickrang happens once a generation at the most. But if Pickrang works for Quedley, where does Lydiate come into it? Maybe it was Quedley all along who was trying to scare me off and the Lydiate stuff was just a smokescreen.

"I'm pretty sure I do and if it's who I think it is, just stay well out of his way. The guy's an animal."

Delamore shrugged. "Tell me about it. I'm not going to

hang around here. I've got to do a show tonight, then I'm spending a couple of days up at Julian's place at Palm Beach. It's my last chance; they're putting it on the market."

On the way out Sparks asked Delamore what sort of show he was in.

"A drag show," said Delamore brightening up. "It's a hoot. If you've got nothing on tonight, you should come and see it – Oscar's in Oxford Street. It'll broaden your horizons."

Sparks paused at the bottom of the steps down to the street. "What makes you think my horizons need broadening?"

Delamore looked down at him gravely. "You might be different but I find most people's do."

Herman Pickrang's failure to intercept Reggie Sparks that Saturday afternoon was due more to nature than dereliction of duty. After Pickrang had sat in the lobby for two hours monitoring every arrival, the several beers he'd had at lunch began to make their presence felt. Stoically, he remained at his post for a further 30 minutes until the pressure from his bladder became unbearable. The sight of Herman Pickrang mincing at high speed through the lobby with his thighs clamped together and his bottom protruding in the manner of a female baboon in mating season attracted the attention of most people in the area. No one eyed him more intently than Sparks, who was about to enter the hotel through the large glass doors. Instead he spun on his heel and walked quickly away.

So what do I do now, he wondered. I'm being pursued by a violent maniac who appears to have taken up residence in my hotel; my credit card is in a safety deposit box in the hotel and I have exactly $70 on me; I don't know a single person in this entire city. Except Dean Delamore.

Sparks walked back to Gage's terrace and rang the bell. There was no answer. His mind was racing. That club, what the hell was it called? Oscar's. Sparks looked at his watch: 5.15pm. He found a public phone box, inserted a handful of coins and dialled Louise Appleyard's number. It was, he reflected, the only phone number he knew off by heart. She answered on the seventh ring.

"It's Reggie Sparks."

"Reggie, sorry to do this but I was literally on my way out the door; I've got a taxi waiting."

"Not to worry. I just wanted to let you know you'll get something in the post in a day or two addressed to your husband. It might explain quite a lot. It's from Julian Gage, one of those guys Victor saw over here. Gage died a few days ago – it's a long story. I'll let you go – have a nice night. I'll tell you all about it when I get back."

Sparks replaced the handset wishing he'd never made the call. Now he was going to feel low all weekend; it sounded like she had a big evening lined up. Later Sparks would wonder about that call and whether things would have turned out much differently if Louise Appleyard had either let the telephone ring or been in less of a rush to get to her dinner party.

# CHAPTER 15

*I*n the large mirror above the fireplace, Louise Appleyard watched the two men eyeing her, or to be precise, eyeing her legs which were displayed to advantage in the black lycra bodysuit she was wearing under a boldly embroidered jacket. They'd been eyeing her on and off from the moment she'd arrived; she wondered how long it would be before their wives noticed. She also wondered when the fat man, whose name she'd forgotten and to whom she was pretending to listen, would finish eulogising her late husband and release her hand from his moist grip. Not till we're called to the table, she guessed.

The drawing room in which Audrey Benn's guests were having pre-dinner drinks was at the front of the house, close to the front door, so the words with which Caspar Quedley greeted his hostess carried clearly: "Audrey, you appalling old gargoyle, what's for dinner?"

The eyes of all the guests, even of the pair who'd been admiring what was visible of the curve of Louise Appleyard's buttocks below the hem of her jacket, swivelled to the doorway. Quedley sauntered into the room with a simpering Audrey Benn on his arm. He wore a rumpled, navy blue suit with loose-fitting jacket and baggy trousers and a black polo-neck sweater. He surveyed the gathering, inclined his head grandly, and said, "Greetings earthlings."

Audrey steered him straight over to Louise. He shot a

suspicious glance at her companion, who had at last let go of her hand, and asked: "Is this man bothering you?"

"Not at all," she said, faintly embarrassed by the lack of conviction in her voice.

Quedley looked dubious. "I'm not sure I believe you. You do realise Harvey here's a well-known snowdropper?"

"A what?"

"A snowdropper. You know, a person, usually of the male persuasion, who steals ladies' undergarments off clotheslines. Lord knows what he does with them – chews the crotches out of 'em more than likely."

Louise, struggling to keep a straight face, turned to Harvey, who'd gone crimson and started to pant. "Harvey, can this be true?"

Before he could reply, Audrey cut in to ask Quedley what he'd like to drink. Harvey used the diversion to beat a retreat.

"I thought you'd never ask," replied Quedley. "I'll have bourbon, thanks Aud, providing you serve an acceptable brand. Wild Turkey or Maker's Mark would be the shot; if I must, I'll settle for Jack Daniel's. Three fingers with plenty of ice if you'd be so kind."

Audrey raised her eyebrows at Louise. "I'll see what I can do."

As Audrey Benn departed on her mission, Quedley smiled benignly down at Louise. "Alone at last. Long time, no ogle. So how the hell are you, old girl?"

She shrugged. "Oh pretty good."

"I'm sorry as hell about Vic. He was a good lad."

"He was that."

He nodded. "Managing okay?"

"Yes, I'm fine."

"Not sitting around moping I hope. You get out much?"

"As a matter of fact, this is my social comeback."

He whistled. "Strewth, you picked a beaut. Why this show? You'd have more fun at the dentist."

150

"Well if I read Audrey right, she's rather relying on you to provide the sparkle."

"She's a devious critter, isn't she? She used the fact that you were coming to get me along; wild horses couldn't get me here otherwise."

Louise, wide-eyed: "And to think little old me did the trick – flattered I'm sure."

"Now Louise," said Quedley, mock-serious, "you know bloody well I've been slobbering over you from a discreet distance for years. If it wasn't for the fact that the very thought of adultery is deeply abhorrent to me, I'd . . ."

Louise, looking over his shoulder, saw Audrey Benn coming and interrupted him. "Ah here we are – here's your drink."

Audrey belligerently thrust a heavy crystal tumbler at Quedley. "All I can say Caspar is you damn well better enjoy this. I had to send my son next door for it and he wasn't impressed."

Quedley sipped and smacked his lips. "Dashed decent of him. Sorry to be a pest Aud but, as I was saying to Louise, this is no mere whim – this is a deep and enduring yearning."

They were placed next to one another at the table. As they sat down Quedley said quietly, "By the way, have you heard about the story *New Nation* are doing?"

"Yes I have," said Louise. "In fact, I've talked to the journalist a couple of times."

"That doyen of journalism, Reggie Sparks? I shudder to think what sort of dog's breakfast he'll come up with."

"Oh I don't know, I suspect Reggie's a bit more capable than he sometimes appears. He rang me tonight actually – from Sydney. He went over to see a couple of people that Vic had talked to about . . . well you know what it was about; he came to see you, didn't he? Anyway, Reggie said one of them – Julian someone . . ."

"That'd be Julian Gage," cut in Quedley. "I heard he was at death's door?"

"I'm afraid he's knocked, entered and shut the door behind him – just this week. But Reggie was saying that, before he died, Gage wrote to Vic all about that business at Prince Albert. Apparently his letter's in the mail."

Quedley shook his head. "I could probably tell you right now what it'll say." He lowered his voice. "Listen, why don't we leave the living dead to it as soon as we decently can and have a drink somewhere? I'll tell you all about little Julian. You should know the whole background before you read it – and definitely before you even consider passing it on to *New Nation*." His concerned expression lifted, replaced by a lop-sided grin. "It won't take long. Then we can talk about you and me."

At 8pm Sydney time, an hour after Audrey Benn's guests had taken their first sip of toheroa soup, Herman Pickrang left Sparks' hotel. His quarry had not appeared and the long and fruitless stake-out had left Pickrang ravenous and in a volcanically bad mood. He found a McDonalds where he ate three hamburgers, three helpings of chips and an apple pie. He then bought two six-packs of beer and returned to his serviced apartment.

At 9.30pm Pickrang came out of the apartment building with a six-pack under his arm and got into his hire car. He switched on the interior light and spread out a map of greater Sydney. When he eventually located Palm Beach, he swore foully; it looked a good distance away. However, as the hours had crawled past in the lobby of the Plaza Hotel, Pickrang had become increasingly convinced that Julian Gage and the item he'd been sent over to secure were out at Palm Beach, at the address Tench had given him. Besides, he thought, what else is there to do: sit in that shoebox watching TV or go back up the Cross and buy himself a root. Fuck that. Pickrang had decided that the prostitutes in Kings Cross were the most repulsive representatives of the oldest profession he'd ever come across. And you've blocked some shockers in your time, he said to himself, smiling grimly at the memories.

By 10.30pm Pickrang was in the northern suburb of French's Forest, pulled over on the side of the road studying the map for the third time since leaving Potts Point. Fifty metres back down the road Rocco Perfumo cursed, flicked off his headlights and swerved in behind a parked car.

"I'm telling you, the cunt's lost," repeated his brother Martino.

Rocco looked across at his brother. Martino's face was starting to flake again.

"Course he's fucking lost. Question is, where the fuck's he trying to get to?"

Martino opened the glovebox and brought out a .38 calibre revolver.

"Why don't we do the fucker here and now, just pull up beside him and blow him away?" He extended his arm and sighted down the gun barrel just as a man out walking his dog strolled past their car.

"That's why, for fuck's sake," said Rocco heatedly. "Put that fucking thing away." He cuffed his brother affectionately on the shoulder. "This is great, man – the longer he fucks around out here, the better for us. We'll just wait a bit longer, till no one's around, then do it. He's dead meat, mate – no worries."

It was between the rack of lamb with rosemary and the caramelised pear tart that Louise Appleyard decided in principle that she would go to bed with Caspar Quedley. It briefly occurred to her that perhaps she should send him a signal that she was thus disposed; if he carries on knocking back the red wine at this rate, she thought, sleeping with him might turn out to be exactly that. However as she shrank from unambiguous gestures such as casually dropping a hand on his

153

inner thigh, she was forced to pin her faith on Quedley's constitution and to hope that he could see some benefit in stopping short of intoxication.

It had been more than a decade since Louise Appleyard had seriously contemplated having sex with anyone other than her late husband so she was understandably nervous. Apart from anything else, she was not entirely sure of Quedley's aspirations. He was not the easiest person to read: he paid attention to her in short bursts, radiating charm like heat off a bonfire; in between times he had fierce discussions on sport with the other men, once even threatening, when chided by Audrey Benn for antisocial behaviour, to lead a breakaway male group into the kitchen.

The other diners hung on his every word, solicited his opinions and sought his approval of theirs, cackled at his witticisms, and cooed like pigeons at his revelations of political and commercial intrigue. They were, by and large, a staid and conventional crew, middle-aged-going-on-old in attitude if not in fact. In their company, Quedley stood out like a black panther in a pet shop. Every now and again, he bared his teeth as if to remind them that suburban dinner parties were not his natural habitat.

Harvey's wife Eleanor, a permed and powdered supporter of worthy causes, was defending the Aotea Centre, Auckland's star-crossed performing arts centre, against well-rehearsed charges of being a white elephant when Quedley intervened.

"Personally I don't give a toss whether it makes money or not. I mean, it's there so surely to God it's only common sense to use it? Whether or not the events they stage make a profit says a lot more about the management and the Auckland public than about the building. If we're going to debate the merits of the building itself, we should be concentrating on the aesthetics of it: is it pleasing to behold? Is it beautiful? Eleanor?"

"Well yes, I happen to think it is rather . . ."

"Fine. Eleanor, I take it you subscribe to the view that

architecture is an artistic medium and therefore that a building can be a work of art?"

"Of course."

"Okay. I submit that the defining quality of art is poetry. Poetry has two meanings: in the specific sense, it's a composition usually involving rhyme and metre, the stuff we were taught at school. In the wider sense, poetry is that quality in a work of art – be it a piece of music, or drama, or a novel or a building – which engages our emotions, uplifts our spirits, puts us in touch with our higher selves. It's what separates art from entertainment. Now I've got a place down at Coromandel. It's pretty rough and ready: instead of a proper toilet, I've got an outhouse, a long-drop – your basic little wooden sentry box built over a bloody great hole in the ground. In summer, believe me, she gets ripe in there. You get these bluebottles – they're as big as hummingbirds but their radar's not as good so they keep flying into your mouth. Anyway, the point I wanted to make Eleanor, with all due respect, is that there's a thousand times more poetry in my nasty, smelly, flyblown little outside shithouse than in the Aotea Centre."

Throats were cleared around the table; there were a few nervous chuckles. Louise looked at Quedley expecting to see his usual ivory grin. He was looking at Eleanor with an almost quizzical expression, head slightly tilted and smiling pleasantly but without showing his teeth; the smile hadn't reached his eyes which gleamed coldly. It reminded Louise of the way her brother would look at her when they were children playing Monopoly, when he'd put a hotel on Park Lane and she'd landed on it.

By the time coffee and liqueurs arrived, most of the men were the worse for drink. Quedley though, who'd had as much as anyone, seemed quite unaffected. Someone proposed that everyone should tell a joke and the motion was carried by acclaim. Once again Louise was reminded of her childhood; the jokes were the sort of dismal, sanitised little yarns her parents and their friends used to tell when they'd had a sherry or two and shed some of their excessive decorum. The men hooted and the ladies made indulgent, boys-will-be-boys faces at one another when Harvey told the story of an engineer who came up with a new method for getting rid of the stench from the local abattoir: he suggested running pipes from the killing chain into a gigantic tank so that the odours would dissipate in water. The mayor derided his theory saying, "Come off it mate; haven't you ever farted in the bath?"

When it was Quedley's turn, Audrey Benn instructed him, "Now Caspar, no filth thank you very much."

Quedley shrugged. "I'll have to pass then. I don't know any clean jokes."

The other men, none of whom had had the nerve to tell a proper dirty joke, set up a chorus at this, demanding that Quedley should have his turn.

Quedley held up his hands in a gesture of surrender. "If you insist but don't say I didn't warn you. It's actually a salutary little tale this: a woman gets a part-time job as a barmaid at the local pub. So on her first day, a Saturday, she kisses her husband on the cheek and heads off full of enthusiasm. Everything's going well until a couple of hard cases wander in. They swagger up to the bar and she goes over to serve them, putting on her brightest smile. 'And what would you like, sir?' she says to the first hard case. He looks her up and down and says, 'I'd like to smear raspberry jam all over your tits – and then lick it off'."

There were a few snorts of suppressed laughter. Audrey Benn peered closely at something in her coffee cup.

"Well as you can imagine, the woman's a bit thrown but the boss had warned her she'd have to put up with a certain amount of crude and uncouth behaviour. So she keeps her smile in place and turns to the second guy. 'And how about you sir: what would you like?' 'I would like'", said Quedley speaking very deliberately, "'to fill your vagina' – he didn't use that word but in deference to Audrey's sensibilities I shall – 'I would like to fill your vagina with ice cream and then eat it all out'."

Eleanor, her cheeks flushed, got to her feet. "If you'll excuse me, I'm just going to powder my nose."

"If I was you, old thing, I'd have a widdle while you're there," said Quedley. "Save having to make another trip. Where was I? Yes, so this is all too much for the poor woman. She bursts into tears, dashes out of the pub, jumps in her car, and hightails it. She's still distressed when she gets home where her husband's got his feet up watching television. He leaps up when he sees her: 'Darling, what's happened?' So she tells him about the two hard cases and how the first one wanted to smear raspberry jam all over her breasts et cetera. The husband's outraged. 'No one talks to my wife like that,' he declares. 'I'm going down there to have a piece of these bastards.' He puts on his jacket and as he's going out the door he says, 'By the way, what'd the other one say?' 'He said he wanted to fill my vagina with ice cream, slurp, slurp, yum, yum.' The husband stops in his tracks, turns around, takes off his jacket, goes back to his chair, sits down and turns on the TV. 'What are you doing?' asks his wife. 'I thought you were going to sort those horrible men out.' The husband looks at her and says, 'Anyone who can eat that much ice cream is too big for me'."

Louise Appleyard had felt the tension build in the room as Quedley told his joke. She knew that, whatever the outcome, she wouldn't be able to stop herself laughing. The gross and unexpected punchline came as a release; she threw her head back and roared with laughter. Some of the men joined in while the other women exchanged dazed shakes of the head. When the laughter died down, Audrey refilled Louise's coffee cup and said: "You two obviously have something in common."

"Grubby minds," said Eleanor, pinch-faced, from the doorway.

Louise, still laughing, looked at Quedley thinking, well that's not a bad start.

# CHAPTER *16*

*T*he ambiance at Oscar's Night Club turned out to be less confrontational than Sparks had anticipated. Earlier in the evening, over several espressos in a Darlinghurst coffee bar and when not brooding about Louise Appleyard, he'd given some idle thought to what he might encounter there. His speculations were largely populated by the stereotypes of gay subculture: musclemen with shaven heads, self-mutilators with metallic items embedded in every appendage, deviants using colour coding to advertise their readiness to indulge in various unthinkable sexual practises. However, at first sight the clientele resembled a gathering of ardent young Christians although Sparks couldn't remember whether the Mormon missionaries who'd doorknocked around Auckland during his childhood had been permitted to cultivate hair on their upper lips. Most of the moustaches sported by Oscar's patrons were under-stated if not apologetic affairs even when accompanied by Vandyke beards; there were no cowpuncher handlebars or walrusy tea-strainers. Nor were there peaked caps, chains, or leather trousers customised to expose the buttocks. Oscar's, it seemed, was not the favoured haunt of the flamboyant and exhibitionist among Sydney's gay community but more of a rendezvous for those who only fully emerged from the closet at weekends and even then preferred not to make a fuss about it.

The club itself was long and narrow, on three levels. At

one end was a raised stage, at the other a long bar with stools and an open kitchen. In front of the stage was a small dance floor with most of the remaining floor space given over to tables and chairs and more seating along the walls. Sparks watched the show – a series of impersonations of Hollywood's *grandes dames* – from the bar. He thought he spotted Delamore as Carmen Miranda but it was hard to tell under the fruit. In between the acts a disc jockey played dance music. Sparks, mooching at the bar, received only one invitation to dance. Taken by surprise, he declined the invitation more emphatically than was called for. The rejected party, a well-built young man, shrugged his impressive shoulders and muttered something to his two companions which caused them to shoot oblique accusatory glances in Sparks' direction.

Shortly before 11pm the MC announced the last live act of the evening. The Rexettes performed in the style of the all-girl groups of the 1960s, their repertoire including *He's a Rebel* and *Big Girls Don't Cry* which was particularly well-received. Delamore, in a black wig and abbreviated body-hugging white dress, wiggled becomingly and emitted a piercing falsetto. After six energetic numbers, the Rexettes waved and blew kisses to the audience and tripped girlishly off the stage to the accompaniment of whoops, whistles and wild applause.

Sparks decided he needed another beer before he was ready to venture backstage. He was sipping it morosely when Dean Delamore, still in full Rexette costume, tapped him on the shoulder.

"I thought it was you – it's hard to tell with the lights," he said. "I didn't expect to see you here. So – what'd you think?"

"It's good," said Sparks nodding. "Especially the Rexettes."

"Yeah, everyone likes them. I tell you, it's hard work doing that Frankie Valli falsetto though; I start running out of breath towards the end." He patted his cheeks. "Are my cheeks red? I feel like I've got a real glow on."

159

Sparks shook his head. "No, they're fine. Would you like a drink?"

"Yes please, a Coke."

Sparks turned round to attract the barman's attention asking himself, what are you doing? That's a bloke, remember? You're carrying on as if he's Sharon Stone. He ordered the drink then turned back to Delamore.

"To be honest, I didn't really come to see the show," said Sparks. "I'm in a bit of strife. You know the gorilla who turned up at your place? I didn't tell you this but I had a run-in with him in Auckland a few days ago – he was all set to give me a hiding to make me drop the story. Anyway, right now he's camped out in the lobby of my hotel. My credit card and cash are in the safety deposit box and I don't know another soul in Sydney. I was wondering if I could crash at your place tonight?"

"Well sure, except remember I said I'm going out to Palm Beach tonight?"

"How far's that?"

"About an hour or so."

"Well, if it's not a hassle. I can get a bus back tomorrow."

"It's no problem at all. I'll just get my stuff and we'll get going. It'll be nice to have someone to talk to on the way."

Delamore was back in a couple of minutes, wearing a faded denim jacket over the white dress.

"I can't be bothered getting changed. You right? My car's just outside."

Sparks finished his beer as Delamore started for the exit. As he passed the group at the other end of the bar, Sparks noticed him exchanging words with his would-be dancing partner. Outside the club he caught up with Delamore and asked what the conversation had been about.

Delamore looked at him curiously. "Nothing."

"No come on, what'd that guy say? I'm only interested because he asked me to dance before."

Delamore put the key in the car door and looked at Sparks over the roof of the car.

"If you really want to know, what he said was, 'Do you get off going with straights?'"

They got into the car.

"What'd you say?"

Delamore started the car and steered it out into the traffic. Without looking at Sparks he said, "I said it depends on the straight."

In the end it had all been resolved with a minimum of fuss: as the dinner party began to break up, Louise Appleyard had murmured that she'd better order a taxi; Caspar Quedley had offered her a lift home; she'd replied, expressionless, "Whose?"

When they got to Quedley's place, they decided, without actually discussing the matter, to postpone both the drink and the discussion about Julian Gage and his letter. Instead, after some imperfectly coordinated kissing and urgent thrustings against one another and without shedding any more clothing than was absolutely necessary, they fornicated on the long leather couch in the living room which looked out to Rangitoto Island. The spontaneity suited Louise Appleyard who'd been looking forward, albeit nervously, to the sex but slightly dreading the preliminaries. Afterwards, as they sprawled on the couch breathing heavily, she reflected that, all in all, the exercise had gone better than could have been expected apart from a slight hiccup when the image of her late husband had flashed into her mind.

Quedley, noticing her pensive expression, reached over to brush the hair off her face.

"Post coitum omne animal triste est," he said.

"What?"

"It's Latin. Roughly translated it means that all creatures feel a bit down in the dumps after a legover."

161

"A legover?" she said. "How romantic."

He kissed her on the nose and stood up. "My dear, there was nothing romantic about what just took place. Not to put too fine a point on it, we coupled like beasts. Now if you'd care to hop into the spa, I'll fetch the champagne."

Quedley also fetched some cocaine which he deployed in rows on a silver tray. Louise thought about declining but decided it was a little early in her new career as a born-again party girl to start applying the brakes. After trying a couple of lines she concluded that cocaine was over-rated. Caspar Quedley, on the other hand, wasn't.

When the champagne and the cocaine were finished and their skins began to wrinkle, they got out of the spa and into Quedley's large bed where they made love again, this time in a more excursive manner, deriving as much enjoyment from the journey as the arrival. Insufficient clothing had been discarded during their first engagement to permit a thorough review of the other's physique; in the course of the leisurely repeat, neither suffered the disappointment which often attends the sexual experiences of the no-longer young: the discovery that artful outfitting and tailoring have concealed slackening muscles, subsiding flesh and coarsened skin.

They talked about Julian Gage on the way out to Palm Beach. According to Delamore, he'd owned a couple of wildly expensive light fitting shops which had done very well during the mid-1980s when money was no object for those who overnight conjured fortunes from their computer screens. Then, as the end of the decade approached, he'd been diagnosed HIV positive.

"He used to say he was lucky," said Delamore. "As soon as he knew, he sold his shops for a good price. Six months later the party was well and truly over – after the economy had gone south, there weren't many people still willing or able to shell out 10 grand for a lamp. He reckoned if he'd sold a year later, he would've been lucky to cover his loans. He sold the terrace in Potts Point too and rented it back so he had enough money to make the most of the time he had left. He bought his place at Palm Beach and did a lot of travelling. I was lucky too – I came on the scene just at the right time and he took me with him. It was wonderful – we always flew first class and stayed in the best hotels. You name it, we went there – Paris, Venice, New York, New Orleans, Rio. We went on the Orient Express and the QE2 and cruising in the Caribbean; we even went on safari in Africa although a person less keen on roughing it than Julian would be hard to find." Delamore stared ahead dreamily. "It was like a fairy story. I said that once and he said, 'Yes and we're the fairies'." Delamore smiled for a few seconds, then the smile faded and he continued in a voice which resonated with loss and bewilderment: "About a year ago, the symptoms started to appear. In a few months he went from being a normal, healthy person – as far as the outside world knew – to an invalid. A few more months and he looked like something out of a concentration camp, a skeleton with skin. At the end he was just a shell. It was like he'd been eaten by termites – you thought one tap and he'd crumble into dust and blow away."

They drove across the Spit Bridge in silence and headed out through Manly to the northern beaches.

Sparks eventually broke the silence: "So he never said a word about what happened at school?"

"Nothing specific. But seeing Appleyard definitely unsettled him. He said afterwards that he had a big decision to make because he had something on his conscience which he wanted to resolve before he died. I asked him what the decision was and he said it wasn't just him who'd be affected."

"He didn't say who else?"

"No."

"But that letter to Quedley sort of speaks for itself, doesn't it?"

"I guess so."

163

"Did he ever talk about Quedley?"

"Oh God yes, all the time. Once he even called him 'the love of my life'."

Sparks stared at Delamore for a moment then he noticed how far the hem of his dress had ridden up his slim thighs and hurriedly looked away. "You telling me Quedley's gay?"

Delamore looked at him coldly. "You make it sound like being a necrophiliac or something."

Sparks waved a hand apologetically. "No, no, I didn't mean that. It's just that the guy's got a reputation for being a big-time womaniser."

Delamore shrugged. "I never said he was gay; what I said was Julian adored him."

"What, you think it was all one way – what's that word . . . ?"

"Unrequited."

"Yeah, unrequited. You think it was like that?"

Delamore's mouth twisted. "It's hard to say. I suppose that was my basic impression but Julian could be coy and drop these little hints . . . I'd say it was probably one-sided, kind of a hopeless infatuation rather than a relationship, certainly as adults. But who knows what happened at that school? It was a boarding school after all. Didn't you say you went there too?"

"I was a day boy."

After that Delamore put on a tape and they listened to Edith Piaf for the rest of the way.

As forecast, a cold front had rolled through Sydney early that evening bringing steady rain and driving the temperature down. Even allowing for the hour, Palm Beach seemed abandoned; few lights showed as they drove along the sea front. Clifftops was perched right on the edge of the hill overlooking the far end of the beach. It was down a drive at the end of a no-exit road; the nearest house was about 50 metres away.

Delamore stopped in front of the white-washed wooden house and slumped back in his seat.

"I've just thought of something," he said. "We're assuming that Quedley sent that guy – what's his name, Pickrang? – over here, right?"

"It looks that way, doesn't it?"

"Julian was a bit of a show-off; he couldn't help himself. When he bought this place, he had some personalised stationery done with the address on it, you know? That letter he sent to Quedley, the one he dictated to me, was on that letterhead. What I'm saying is, Pickrang could know about this place."

"Yeah, that's a point but I wouldn't worry about it tonight," said Sparks after a few moments. "For a start, we know where Pickrang is – he's parked in the lobby of my hotel waiting for me. And even if he got sick of that, he's hardly going to drive all the way out here at this time of night and in this weather, is he?"

CHAPTER *17*

*D*espite having set out for Palm Beach more than two hours before Delamore and Sparks, Herman Pickrang got there five minutes after they did. Peering through the half-moons of visibility created by his windscreen wipers, Pickrang was frequently tempted to abandon his circuitous expedition to try again in daylight and, hopefully, more favourable weather the following day. Each time he'd remind himself that both the hour and the foul weather were ideal for his purpose. When he finally found his way to Palm Beach, he then faced the problem of locating 5 Ocean View Road. He briefly toyed with the idea of knocking on the door of one of the few houses from which lights glowed behind curtains before deciding that it would be unwise to ask directions to an address at which one intended to commit one and possibly several crimes. There was nothing else for it but to start at one end of the small community and work methodically across it, checking the street signs. Fortunately for Pickrang, he chose to start at the right end.

To ensure that Pickrang didn't notice he was being followed, Rocco Perfumo had taken to switching off his headlights for minutes at a time. There was hardly any other traffic on the roads so it was easy enough to follow Pickrang by his tail lights.

Pickrang found Ocean View Road at exactly one o'clock that Sunday morning. He drove slowly to its dead end and pulled over to the side of the road. When Perfumo saw Pickrang's lights go off, he cut the engine and drifted to a halt at the top of the street. Pickrang got out of the car. He could see lights through the trees and made his way carefully down the drive towards them. A car was parked outside the compact wooden bungalow. Staying in the shadows, Pickrang approached the house and went silently up the stairs to the veranda. The rain was easing and he could hear music over the dwindling hiss. He flattened himself against the side of the house, inched up to a window and peered in.

Pickrang was not greatly prone to self-pity. Even so, his recent string of reversals had left him in a put-upon and resentful frame of mind; he'd been feeling that it was about time he got a break. One peep through the window convinced him that, at long last, his luck had changed. In the foreground was the woman from Gage's house. She was wearing a sexy little white dress and wriggling around the room in time to the music with a glass in her hand. Over in the corner, slumped in an armchair and watching the woman with an odd sort of half-smile on his face, was the journalist Reggie Sparks. Pickrang leaned against the wall and breathed deeply. His nostrils flared. He grinned horribly, the rapacious, age-old grin of the predator in the night. He took three long strides along the veranda, threw open the door, and stepped inside.

"Howdy," he said.

Pickrang closed the door behind him and looked from Delamore to Sparks. Both of them stared at him in dumbstruck horror. He unzipped his light windcheater, reached inside and, with a slow flourish, produced the diver's knife with the thick eight-inch blade. He dropped into a half-crouch holding the knife extended in his right hand and crabbed towards Sparks, who sprang to his feet and looked wildly around for something with which to defend himself. When he'd closed to about a metre, Pickrang switched the knife to his left hand and feinted a thrust to Sparks' belly. Sparks bleated like a dying sheep and dropped his hands, his eyes bulging in agonised anticipation of the knife's cold plunge. With a snap of his hips, Pickrang came out of his crouch and slung a whiplash right hook to the side of Sparks' jaw. Sparks jitterbugged backwards, his legs splaying like a new-born foal, and spilled over the armchair he'd recently occupied onto the floor where he lay face down and utterly motionless.

Pickrang slowly straightened up and turned to Delamore who was clutching the wine glass in front of him in both hands.

"Wouldn't mind a drink myself," he said. "What've you got there?"

"White wine," said Delamore in a near-whisper.

"Cat's piss," said Pickrang. "Where's Gage?"

"He's dead. You're too late – that thing you're looking for is gone too. I posted it myself."

Pickrang's brow furrowed. "Posted it – where to?"

"Auckland. I didn't notice who it was addressed to; I just stuck it in the mail like Julian told me."

"You didn't notice who it was addressed to eh? Course you didn't." Pickrang grinned playfully. "We can talk about that later – after I've shagged the arse off you." He put the knife down on the arm of the sofa, unzipped his jacket and laid it on top.

Delamore wished to God he hadn't spent so much time cultivating a girlie voice. He tried to speak in a timbre redolent of pendulous testicles and jutting Adam's apples but all that emerged was a reedy squeak.

"Look there's something you should know . . ."

Pickrang chuckled, shaking his head. "Let me guess, it's that time of the month? I think you've got me mixed up with someone who gives a fuck."

Delamore pulled off the black wig revealing his short, slicked-down blond hair. "I'm not a woman."

Pickrang's amiable expression disappeared. He regarded Delamore through slitted eyes. "What the fuck is this?"

"I told you, I'm not a woman. I'm in a drag show – this is one of my costumes."

"What are you talking about?" snarled Pickrang. "You got tits."

"That's part of the costume too. Look." Delamore reached behind him, undid a couple of buttons on his dress and slipped it off his shoulders. He shrugged out of the padded brassiere and dangled it in one hand; with the other he pulled down the front of his dress to expose a flat, lightly tanned chest dotted with a few clumps of downy golden hair.

"You're a fucking transvestite," said Pickrang hoarsely.

Delamore shook his head. "No I'm not, I'm a performer, a singer. I only wear women's clothes in the show."

"Bullfuck. You had 'em on the other day."

"It was a new outfit," said Delamore wearily. "I was just trying it on."

"Don't shit me." A foxy glint came into Pickrang's eyes. "I got a blowjob from a trannie once – up in Singapore. I bet you've blown the old meat trombone plenty of times."

"I'm not touching you, you animal," said Delamore, eyes blazing.

"Oh we're choosy are we? Don't tell me you haven't gobbled matey here," he said with a jerk of his head towards the recumbent Sparks. Pickrang advanced on Delamore and was unzipping his fly when the door opened and the Perfumo Brothers walked in. Rocco shut the door and leaned against it with his arms folded; Martino pointed the revolver at Pickrang's chest.

Rocco, his lip curling with disgust, took in the scene. "Well wouldn't you know it?" he said. "Big, bad Herman turned out to be a screaming fag."

There was a long silence. Pickrang stood with his hands on his hips looking from brother to brother. Finally he said, "Who the fuck are you?"

"So you don't remember us, huh?" said Rocco as Sparks

169

groaned and sat up. "Take a geek at him. That's what happens to your face when it gets shoved in a pizza oven."

Pickrang nodded his understanding. He'd taken it for granted that this pair intended to kill him; now he knew why. There was one other thing he needed to know.

"How'd you know I was here?"

Rocco smiled maliciously. "I'm glad you asked that. You're on someone's shit list, mate. A little bird told us you were coming to Sydney, where you'd be staying, the works. We've had you in our sights since you got here, just waiting for the right moment. Now here we are – I mean, this is perfect."

Pickrang's curiosity was satisfied. He'd work out who'd tipped them off in due course. First things first. These guys are a couple of fucking clowns, he thought. One gun between the two of them; following me around waiting for the right time to do it. Jesus, talk about amateurs. You want to shoot someone, you walk up, no warning, no big speeches, no nothing; you point the fucking gun at them and pull the trigger. End of story.

Rocco Perfumo was talking to Delamore and Sparks, asking them if they were in some sort of three-way homo thing with Pickrang. Delamore was embarking on a laboured explanation when Rocco interrupted.

"Forget it, I don't want to know. It's got nothing to do with what we're here for so why don't you just fuck off back to New Zealand? Sounds like you got no reason to care what happens to this cunt and if you want to stay in one piece, you'll forget you ever saw us."

Delamore picked up his overnight bag and helped Sparks to his feet. "Of course," he said. "Thank you. Thank you very much. We're out of here right now."

Neither spoke till they were out of Palm Beach and back on the main road.

"You all right?" asked Delamore.

"Yeah," said Sparks thickly. He flexed his jaw. "Nothing broken anyway."

Delamore began shaking violently, causing the car to wobble. "Oh God," he said, "I was absolutely terrified. Pickrang thought I was a she and wanted to have his wicked way with me. They turned up just in time, those two."

Sparks stared at Delamore for a few moments then leaned back with his head on the headrest. "Jesus, no wonder you're still shaking."

"What do you think they'll do to him?"

"I don't know and I don't care – the worse the better far as I'm concerned. I just wonder if they know what they're up against." Sparks rubbed his stomach gently. "Jesus, I really thought it was all over when Pickrang went for me with that knife. I could almost feel it going in."

"I wonder what happened to the knife," said Delamore. "He didn't have it when they came in." He smiled wanly. "Maybe he thought it spoiled the romantic atmosphere."

Pickrang was propped against the back of the sofa, quite relaxed. "So what now?" he asked.

"What happens now," said Rocco, "is that we shoot you and you die. Then we'll go back into town, go to a nightclub, and have a bottle of champagne to celebrate. How does that sound?"

Pickrang looked thoughtful. "I don't know about the champagne; that shit gives me a hangover."

Rocco looked at Pickrang incredulously.

"Shall I shoot him now, Rock?" said Martino.

"Hang on, why don't we just see if there's an oven in this place?" said Rocco.

Martino nodded, giggling happily. His brother's path to the kitchen brought him within two metres of Pickrang. As Rocco walked past, Pickrang, in one swift, fluid motion, pushed off the sofa, effortlessly dragged him in with his left arm and wrapped him to his chest. He clamped Rocco to him with one arm, reached under his windcheater which was draped over the arm of the sofa and brought out the diver's knife which he held across Rocco's throat.

"Drop the gun," he said to Martino, who held the .38 at arm's length, unsure of where to point it, "or I'll cut his head off."

"Shoot him Marty," screamed Rocco. Pickrang clamped his left hand over Rocco's jaw to silence him and jabbed the index finger into his right eye for emphasis. He threaded his right arm under Rocco's armpit. With the knifepoint pricking Rocco under the chin, Pickrang hoisted him a few inches off the ground, effectively denying Martino a clear target.

"Put it on the sofa now," snapped Pickrang.

Martino lowered his arm. "I have to Rock," he wailed. "I have to."

He put the pistol on the arm of the sofa.

"Now back off. Stand over by the doorway."

Martino did so. Pickrang lowered Rocco to the floor. He retracted his right arm and positioned the knife point just below Rocco's right ear. He grinned and raised his eyebrows at Martino then, with a grunt of effort, forced the knife inwards and upwards. Two-thirds of the blade disappeared. Martino screamed and darted towards the sofa but Pickrang flung Rocco aside and swooped on the pistol. Martino turned and lunged for the door but Pickrang caught him by the back of the shirt, jerked him up short, then rammed him face first into the wall. He whirled Martino around and flung him onto his back on the sofa.

Pickrang placed his left knee on Martino's chest and loomed over him.

"If I wasn't in a hurry," he said conversationally, "I'd stick your head in the oven till it melts."

He picked up a cushion with his left hand and placed it over Martino's face. Perfumo flailed his legs unavailingly, like a beetle flipped on its back. Pickrang thumbed back the hammer and pressed the muzzle against the cushion. He fired three times, moving the muzzle slightly each time. The first shot missed altogether; the second clipped the point of Perfumo's cheekbone and ploughed a furrow up the side of his head, removing part of his left ear; the third entered his face just below his nose, precisely where previously the left and right halves of his mustache had met. After the pizza oven incident, Martino had found it difficult to cultivate hair on his upper lip; eventually he'd decided that a moustache which sprouted unevenly in the style of a moulting chicken's neck was worse than no moustache at all. Thus he died clean shaven, breaking a family tradition, by no means confined to the menfolk, that went back many generations.

CHAPTER *18*

Caspar Quedley lay on his back, snoring faintly. At intervals of approximately 90 seconds his mouth fell open and a fresh globule of saliva emerged to join the thin trail of dribble running down his chin, under his ear, and into the little pond of drool which had formed on his pillow. There was a whitish wedge of coagulated spittle in the other corner of his mouth and the inner corners of his eyes, on either side of the bridge of his nose, were likewise gummed with nocturnal emissions. All in all a big night for discharges, thought Louise Appleyard.

Having completed her slightly disillusioning inspection, Louise got out of bed. She paused to look at herself in the mirror above the chest of drawers. Satisfied that she could withstand early morning scrutiny at least as well as her bedmate, she put on Quedley's towelling robe, and went downstairs. She was sitting at the kitchen table drinking her second cup of tea when Quedley appeared half an hour later. He wore jeans and an old sweatshirt; his hair was damp and his collection of encrustations had been rinsed away.

He halted in the doorway and studied Louise warily.

"Hello," she said.

Quedley's expression grew even more dubious. Finally he asked, "Do I know you?"

Louise sipped her tea. "I think I come under the heading of a barge that passed in the night," she said. "Give it a little while, it'll probably all come back to you – the tedious dinner party, too much to drink, latching onto a bit of stray. Perhaps you should keep a visitor's book by the front door and get your pick-ups to sign in as they enter. Might help you to keep track."

Quedley nodded gravely. "Not a bad idea."

He switched on the coffee machine and took a packet of coffee out of the freezer then sat down opposite Louise.

"So how'd you be?"

Louise smiled back. She hadn't been sure what to expect from Quedley in terms of his morning-after manner although a marriage proposal would have surprised her. Above all she'd dreaded a review of the events of the night before or even, God forbid, an appraisal of her performance.

Quedley insisted on cooking breakfast. Louise estimated it had been at least five years since she'd eaten bacon and eggs; she'd forgotten what a satisfying meal it could be.

As she cleared away the plates, Louise said: "I seem to remember you were going to tell me about this communication from beyond the grave? Or was that just part of the seduction process?"

Quedley raised his eyebrows. "Excuse me? I seduced you?" He sat back in his chair and assumed the air of a raconteur. "Yes, I was going to tell you about poor Julian. You've heard the line about the practising homosexual who believed that practise makes perfect? That could be Julian's epitaph. You know they're always arguing about whether someone is born gay or goes that way because his mother made him play with dolls or because he was groped in the pup tent by a scoutmaster? If ever anyone was born bent, it was Julian Gage. By the time I got to know him – he would've been 15 I guess – he knew he was gay; what's more, he was pretty open about it which took a bit of nerve in those days."

"I'm trying to picture him," said Louise. "What did he look like?"

"Oh he was a handsome youth, all right – good looking,

175

olive skin, big brown eyes – and promiscuous. It turned out to be a fatal combination – he ended up getting AIDS."

"Oh no. The poor, poor man." After a pause, she said: "Some might find the accusation of promiscuity a bit rich coming from you, in view of your reputation." Quedley started to protest but she continued: "So Caspar, is all this leading up to a confession; did you fall victim to his charms?"

"I didn't as a matter of fact but not for lack of effort on Julian's part. Despite that – or maybe because of it – we ended up being quite good friends. I saw a lot of him after we left school and even after he moved over to Sydney, we kept in pretty close touch. Then, a few years ago, he was diagnosed HIV positive. I did what I could: went over and saw him, lent him – gave him – some money so he could do a bit of travelling and whatnot. But it wasn't enough. He became more and more demanding; he'd want me to drop everything at a moment's notice to spend time with him or shell out a small fortune so he could get the miracle cure at some clinic in Bermuda or Turkey or somewhere. Eventually I drew the line, I said 'Sorry Julian, that's it pal, no more'. Well fuck, overnight" – Quedley snapped his fingers – "I became the Anti-Christ. He accused me of abandoning him and started making these threats – he was going to expose me, destroy my reputation, God knows what. I didn't take too much notice, I just thought the poor bastard's going a little crazy. Jesus, I could understand that; who wouldn't? And he might've had a point – maybe I should've done more for him; I'm not one of nature's good Samaritans, I'd have to admit. But you know, I don't have unlimited funds plus I had a business to run. The way my business works, if I'm not there, the revenue dries up pretty quickly. My staff can handle the day-to-day stuff but the key relationships are between me and the top people in the client companies. And what they're paying for is seven days a week, 24 hours a day access to me.

"So anyway, just before he died, Julian sent me this letter

saying he'd make me pay for turning my back on him by exposing all the terrible things I'd done at school – cheating, blackmail, driving people round the bend, you name it." Quedley shook his head wearily. "He said he'd written it all out and was going to send it to an interested party – enter, stage right, your late husband."

"Yes, Vic saw him in Sydney."

"Oh well, there you go – perfect timing."

"Are you really worried about it? I mean, who would believe it?"

Quedley shrugged gloomily. "I guess it depends what he's said but people love scuttlebutt don't they? The thing is, reputation counts for a hell of a lot in the PR game but there are a few people out there who'd just love to see me on the back foot and would be only too happy to spread the dirt around. What really scares the shit out of me is the thought of *New Nation* getting hold of it – that bloody Jackson Pike would have a field day."

Louise walked round the table and stood behind Quedley, brushing the hair off his forehead. "Don't worry your little head about it, sugar. Whatever he's said about you, no one's going to see it. It'll go straight into the fire."

That Sunday morning Reggie Sparks and Dean Delamore caught the 10.25am Air New Zealand flight to Auckland. Delamore had announced during the drive in from Palm Beach that he'd also be going to Auckland; he said he'd been planning a trip for a while and now seemed like a good time to get out of Sydney. That suited Sparks. Delamore, he felt, could contribute a lot to his story.

They boarded the aircraft at 9.50am. At 9.55am Herman Pickrang entered a departure lounge elsewhere in the terminal where passengers on the 10.40am Qantas flight to Auckland were waiting to board. At 10am, when the business class passengers on his flight were called, Pickrang went over to a bank of pay phones. He inserted a few coins and dialled the number for the Ristorante Vesuvio in Leichhardt which he'd got off a card in the late Martino Perfumo's wallet. Pickrang had simply been helping himself to the dead man's cash but the card, which identified Martino Perfumo as the manager of the Ristorante Vesuvio, had given him an idea.

A woman answered the phone.

"Martino Perfumo's the manager of your joint, right?"

"Yes he is. He's not here at the moment though. He should be in around 11."

"No he fucking won't because he's dead; dead as a dodo. So's his brother."

"There must be some mistake . . ."

"How about I talk, you listen? You got a pen? You'll want to write this down. The pair of them are in the boot of a green Ford parked in the garage of number 14 Clifftops Road out at Palm Beach. Right? The garage door's down but it ain't locked. Now this bit's really fucking important. They're dead because this Kiwi guy Barry Plugge put a contract out on them – that's P,L,U,G,G,E. He's over in Auckland. You pass this on to the right person, he'll know who Plugge is. You got all that?"

"I think so."

"What's the guy's name?"

"Plugge. Barry Plugge."

"Good on you."

Pickrang replaced the handset and strolled back to the lounge. Most of the other passengers had boarded which suited him down to the ground because he was not fond of queuing.

Steven Perfumo, the lawyer, sneaked another furtive glance at his watch. It showed the time as just after 1pm. Perfumo was fretful because he had planned to have lunch with his third best friend's wife with whom he very much wanted to go to bed. Her husband was due back from Ho Chi Minh City, where he'd been setting up a pet food business, early the following morning. After that, such an illicit liaison became an undertaking requiring more boldness than Perfumo possessed.

The lunch was to be the final move in a delicate and patiently conducted campaign and Perfumo had been confident of success. It was, he felt, unbelievably if characteristically inconsiderate of his clownish cousins to get themselves murdered on this particular day; it was always on the cards that they'd end up full of holes and stuffed in the boot of a car but why the fuck did it have to be today? Not that he dared give voice to these thoughts in the presence of his father, the head of the Perfumo family, who sat on the other side of the desk, his face twisted with grief and remorse.

"This is my fault," said his father for the fourth or fifth time. "I should've acted when Martino's face was burned. I should've allowed Rocco to take revenge."

He would've only fucked it up, thought Steven, staring at the ceiling. He decided to make one last effort to bring the discussion to some sort of conclusion. "Dad, we went through all this at the time," he said, leaning forward, elbows on the desk. "You know why we didn't respond and you know it was the right decision. The strategy was to set Plugge and the Asians at each others' throats and to stand on the sidelines looking good by comparison while they fought it out. We talked about how it was different over there and that we simply couldn't afford headlines about the Italians coming in; it was a sound business decision. The real question is, how do we deal with this?"

His father ran his fingers through his silver-streaked hair then shrugged and gestured in the Latin manner to indicate that he was unconvinced by his son's argument. Not for the first time it occurred to Steven Perfumo that perhaps his father watched too many gangster movies.

"Explain it to me," said the old man. "How did this terrible thing happen?"

Steven breathed deeply. Maybe they were finally getting

179

somewhere. "As I was trying to say, it looks like a payback that went wrong. I've just been on the phone to Gino over in Auckland; Rocco told him he was coming here for some unfinished business. Gino made a couple of calls and it turns out that Pickrang – the guy who shoved Marty's head in the oven – was in Sydney this weekend, right? So it's pretty obvious what the unfinished business was. Secondly, Pickrang was working for Plugge – he's the established operator in the Auckland market – but Gino's heard they've had a bust-up. My guess is that Plugge wanted Pickrang taken out so he tipped off Rocco that Pickrang was coming to Sydney, hoping we'd do his dirty work for him. You know Rocco – he always took things so personally. He would've decided to do Pickrang himself and Marty would've just gone along with it." He shrugged. "They must've bitten off more than they could chew. Obviously it was Pickrang who called the restaurant this morning; he's trying to work the same number as Plugge."

His father digested the summary solemnly. "So they're both responsible?"

"Well yes. If Plugge hadn't tipped off Rocco in the first place, I guess none of it would've happened."

"And this man Pickrang – do we have any idea where he is now?"

"It looks like he's gone back to Auckland. We've got someone out at the airport checking it now."

The head of the family rose. He put his palms on the desk and looked down on his son. "I want this taken care of by the time the boys are buried, Stefano," he said in a voice trembling with emotion. "I want you to supervise it personally."

Fucking wonderful, thought Steven. Your honour, could we adjourn for a few days? I've just got to jack up a couple of hits.

"I still recommend that we stay at arm's length," he said. "I just don't think it would be a good idea if our people are involved."

"You have someone in mind?"

"Remember that Maori gang we distribute through over there, the Blood Drinkers? Why don't we get them to do it?"

"Are they capable?"

"Well they're the scariest-looking people I've ever set eyes on which isn't a bad start," said Steven with some feeling. He'd personally negotiated the distribution deal with the Blood Drinkers' collective leadership, four scarcely human men-mountains who smelt like a third-world zoo in a heatwave. He shuddered at the memory. "They're animals. They'd scalp their grandmothers for a crate of beer and a Big Mac. The thing is, it would muddy the waters – the police'll see it as a turf battle."

"I'm leaving it to you, Stefano. Do it anyway you want but see to it – make sure it happens. I won't be able to look my sister in the eye until this is settled."

Steven nodded and started to leave.

"By the way," said his father, "what will the police do about Rocco and Martino?"

Steven shrugged. "They'll be a pain in the backside for a week or two. It gives them a good excuse to hassle us but in the end it'll be the same old story – just another wog vendetta."


Caspar Quedley dropped Louise Appleyard off at her house at 9.30pm that Sunday night. He declined her offer of coffee and a nightcap, pleading an early start the next morning. He suspected that she had more than coffee and cognac in mind and that, after the exertions of the afternoon and early evening, he would struggle to rise to the occasion if called upon to do so yet again. The widow, he thought, has taken to it like a stallion just out of quarantine.

By 10.15pm Quedley was in bed. After two late nights in a row and a physically demanding day, he was looking forward to nine hours' uninterrupted sleep. However when the luminous dial on his bedside alarm clock was showing 4.21am, Quedley sat bolt upright.

"I must be out of my fucking mind," he said out loud. "I actually believed the bitch when she said she'd throw it straight in the fire."

aspar Quedley was at his desk by 7.45 the next morning, quite chipper despite his fitful night's sleep. As he set up the coffee machine he sang "Oooh-ooh Brown Sugar, how come ya dance so good? Oooh-ooh Brown Sugar, just like a black girl should", concluding his recital with a violent pelvic thrust. Quedley was cheerful because he saw light at the end of the tunnel. He'd tossed and turned for over an hour during the night, castigating himself for his childlike faith in Louise Appleyard. Eventually he succeeded in stirring his mind into a buzz of erratic activity which made slumber impossible. Finally however, there came a flash of inspiration among the random and unconnected images which cannoned around inside his head like dodgem cars. He'd got out of bed, gone into his study and written three words on a piece of adhesive notepaper which he'd stuck to his briefcase. Five minutes after getting back into bed, he was sound asleep.

The three words he'd written were "Dr Carl Plews". Dr Plews was an American, a graduate of Yale and the London School of Economics, who was often described in the media as a "world expert" in the new-fangled discipline of managing cultural change within large organisations. Quedley tended to doubt this; he reckoned that an American who really was a world expert would be back in the US of A where he could make a hell of a lot more money from transforming the completely fucking obvious into some sort of profound insight by dressing it up in a lot of new-age management-speak bullshit than he could in little old NZ. That wasn't to say that the doctor hadn't done pretty well for himself in New Zealand. He'd certainly earned some juicy consulting fees from advising government departments during their transitions into state-owned enterprises. There were three reasons for Quedley's conviction that Dr Plews would solve his problem: the first was the fact that Dr Plews' most recent client was New Zealand Post; the second related to the doctor's passion for gardening which was always mentioned in the profiles, usually just after the bit about how he was renowned for his volatile temper. That was the third.

Early one sultry evening the previous summer, Dr Plews, satisfied that his bow tie was symmetrical, had picked up the jacket of his tuxedo and called out to his wife Estelle that if they didn't get going within five minutes, they'd miss the start of the show. She'd hollered from her ensuite bathroom that she'd almost finished doing her make-up. Dr Plews smiled, a trifle smugly, and shrugged into his jacket. There was no need to leave for at least a quarter of an hour but his little pretence would ensure that Estelle was ready on time. Dr Plews liked things to go according to plan – his plan.

It occurred to Dr Plews that he had time to potter in the garden. He went downstairs and out through the drawing room French doors which opened onto the upper lawn. It was a beautiful evening; the light was starting to fade and assorted floral scents floated by on the soft sea breeze. Dr Plews closed his eyes and breathed in deeply. Halfway through his exhalation, he froze: a low, snuffling sound was coming from across the lawn. Although a squat bush obscured the source of the snuffles, Dr Plews knew instantly what they signified – there was a god-damn dog in his garden. He bounded across the lawn, swerved around the bush, and was confronted with a scene which caused the worm-like vein in his forehead to judder like a high pressure hose: the bed of delphiniums, which he'd nursed through the squalls of spring and early summer from seed to glorious blossom, was in ruins, the blooms uprooted, scattered and trampled. The devastation couldn't have been more complete had a wild pig wallowed in the flowerbed. The culprit was in fact a young bulldog, scarcely more than a puppy, which stood there panting lightly and regarding Plews placidly through oyster eyes.

"Here boy," said Plews speaking in a strangulated croak.

The bulldog obligingly padded towards him. When it was within arm's length, Plews released a howl of rage, dropped to his knees, seized the dog by its collar, spun it onto its back, and began to throttle it. The dog took two long minutes to die. When it was over, Plews' lips were flecked with foam and his well-pressed trousers were smeared with dirt from the clods which the dog's excavations had left on the grass. Plews stood up; his chest heaved and he was sweating furiously. He mopped his face with a handkerchief and reviewed the situation: he knew the dog – it answered to the name "Rumpole" and belonged to his next-door neighbour, Mr Justice Smout, a High Court judge of flinty disposition. Only a few days before, Plews and the judge had discussed Rumpole over the picturesque if somewhat ramshackle lattice fence which separated their properties, after Estelle had placed her expensively shod right foot on one of the wee fellow's steaming fresh turds. The judge had been apologetic and promised to keep Rumpole on a tighter leash but his fondness for the ugly little brute was obvious. As Plews gulped in air in the gathering twilight, it occurred to him that convincing Justice Smout that his mutt had got its just desserts would be a tough assignment.

Plews reached a decision: he didn't want a vengeful and possibly litigious judge as his next-door neighbour, nor did he relish the prospect of becoming a hate figure for pet lovers and animal rights activists. He got a spade from the garden shed, carried the dead dog to the very bottom of the garden where the compost heap was located, and buried it. Having witnessed Rumpole's fate from an upstairs window, 17-year-old Kirsty Bolton decided that it didn't matter how well the Plews paid, there was no fucking way she was ever going to babysit for them again.

When Quedley heard the story of Rumpole's demise, he laughed so hard he fell off his chair which was not quite the reaction his informant, Kirsty Bolton's mother, had expected. He made no conscious effort to commit the incident to memory. He didn't have to: Quedley never forgot anything which cast someone else in a deplorable light.

At 8.15am Quedley rang Plews and effortlessly talked the doctor's secretary into putting him through.

"Dr Plews? Caspar Quedley here. We met in the PM's office last year."

"I remember it well Caspar. How're you doing?"

"Well I've got a little problem, I was hoping you might be able to help me out with it."

"Shoot."

"It's to do with the postal service . . ."

"Let me tell you Caspar, I know that outfit like the back of my hand. If a postie breaks wind, I get to hear of it. Tell me what the problem is and I'll put you onto the guy or gal who can set it to rights."

"Okay. Right now there's a piece of mail in the system which was posted in Sydney last week to a Mr Victor Appleyard in Takapuna. I want to get my hands on it."

"Excuse me?"

"I don't want that letter to be delivered; I want it intercepted and passed to me."

"This is a joke, right?" said Dr Plews in a tone which suggested he was going to get very cross if it wasn't.

"Carl, if I make a joke, you won't need to ask."

"Well buddy, you've come to the wrong guy," said Dr

Plews frostily. "I wouldn't even contemplate doing that for a friend and you sure don't qualify as one of them. Now if you don't mind, I got things to do."

"What, like strangle a dog?"

"What did you say?"

"Strangle a dog. That's what you did to Judge Smout's little pal, wasn't it – throttled the bugger with your bare mitts? All dressed up in your penguin suit too – Christ, it must've been a sight."

"I don't know what you're talking about and I'm terminating this conversation right . . ."

Quedley cut in, brisk and businesslike: "Carl, here's the deal: either you do this thing for me or I get on the phone to old Smout and tell him how you choked the living shit out of his precious puppy and planted him under your compost heap. It's your call – buddy."

Thirty seconds passed. Finally Dr Plews said: "Who'd you say the letter was addressed to?"

One hour before Caspar Quedley and Dr Carl Plews discussed tampering with Her Majesty's mail, a taxi pulled up outside a central city hotel. The taxi driver, a middle-aged Samoan, insisted on carrying his passenger's heavy suitcase into the hotel lobby; had he known that what appeared to be an attractive young blond woman was in fact a man, he would've left it to the bellboy.

Dean Delamore had left the Sparks residence in St Heliers without forewarning or explanation and while Reggie Sparks and his mother were still asleep. He registered under the name Lesley Gore and took the lift to the 14th floor, affecting not to notice the admiring appraisal of the 18-year-old bellboy. Once the bellboy had departed a dollar richer, Delamore undressed, removed the blond wig, and carefully hung his outfit, a smart lime-green suit, in the wardrobe. He then got into bed and slept for three hours to make up for the sleep he'd missed out on due to the time difference between Australia and New Zealand and by getting up so early.

At 11am Dean Delamore clicked through the hotel lobby in high-heeled shoes which nicely complemented the green suit. He left his room key at reception and got into a taxi which he directed to the office building in Parnell housing Quedley Communications. He checked the directory in the foyer then took the lift to the fourth floor.

Delamore got out of the lift and looked around hesitantly. The receptionist behind the large desk smiled at him brightly.

"Can I help you madam?"

"I think I'm on the wrong floor," said Delamore. "This isn't Deco Design?"

"Next floor up. This is Quedley Communications."

"Oh I've heard of you. You do public relations, right?"

"We sure do."

"We could be in the market for some PR. Do you have a company brochure or anything like that?"

"Yes we do. Let me get one for you."

The receptionist went away and returned a minute later with a glossy brochure which Delamore put into his large black leather handbag. He thanked the receptionist, pressed the lift button, and got into the lift. The receptionist watched the lift panel lights and shook her head. What an airhead, she thought; I just told her Deco Design was the next floor up and what does she do? Goes down.

The letter-sized envelope postmarked Sydney, dated the previous Thursday and addressed to Mr Victor Appleyard, was delivered to Quedley's office shortly before five o'clock that afternoon. Quedley weighed it in his hand. That's odd, he thought; there can't be more than a single page in here. He tore open the envelope; it contained a note, in the same hand-writing as his recent letter from Julian Gage, which said:

Although this letter was sent to Victor Appleyard, I suspect that it's being read by Caspar Quedley.

If not, Victor, some explanation is required: not long ago, I wrote to Caspar to tell him that I'd written what I described as a little memoir of our school days. I was feeling particularly sorry for myself at the time and warned Caspar that unless he made contact with me before it was too late, the document would be sent to an interested party – your good self. In fact it was always my intention to tell the real story of what happened at Prince Albert in 1970; I have enough on my conscience without taking the truth to my grave as well. Thinking about it afterwards, I realised it was a mistake to forewarn Caspar; he is not the sort to sit back and do nothing. He would've set out to throw a spanner in the works and, given his talent for that sort of thing, he'd probably succeed.

I've therefore arranged for the material to be hand-delivered to you. If I've over-estimated Caspar's ingenuity, there's no harm done. If I haven't – well Caspar, for once you've been out-smarted.

Of course, whichever of you is reading this, the fact that it's being read at all means that I'm dead and gone. But not quite forgotten, eh Caspar?

Julian Gage


Quedley read the letter three times then laid it aside. He sighed and rubbed his eyes; he inspected his fingernails; he picked his nose absent-mindedly; finally he sat back in his chair and clasped his hands behind his head. After several minutes' reflection, Quedley reached the conclusion that something extremely shitty was about to happen. As usual, he was right.

Quedley was pouring his second bourbon when he got the message that there was a Mr Dean Delamore on line one.

He picked up the handset, pushed the button and said: "You've got it, haven't you?"

"Got what Caspar?"

"You know fucking well what I'm talking about," snarled Quedley. "The Julian Gage story – 'I was a Teenage Cocksucker'."

"Hmm, that's got a ring to it," said Delamore. "No wonder you're in PR. So Julian was right – you did get hold of the letter? How'd you manage it?"

"What the fuck does it matter? Why don't you get to the point? This whole thing's become balls-achingly tedious."

Delamore clicked his tongue and put on a posh accent. "Oh dear, one does dread being thought a bore. Okay; the point, Caspar, is that yes, I have got it and I'm taking offers for it."

"You're offering to sell it to me? I don't think that's quite what your sugar daddy had in mind."

"Appleyard's dead. As far as I'm concerned, that frees me from my obligation. Besides, you're a fine one to talk about respecting Julian's wishes – if you'd shown an ounce of common decency, we wouldn't be having this conversation."

Quedley grunted derisively. "I could've shown more compassion than Mother Teresa at a train crash and we'd still be having this conversation. Sorry to disappoint you, but I'm not interested. You see, I don't really think that what you're selling is worth buying. Why should I care? In the first place, it'd be my word against what – the lurid ramblings of a bitter and probably deranged man on his deathbed? Secondly, what are you going to do with it if I won't play ball? Give it to the newspapers? Give me a break – no newspaper here would print a word of it."

"That's not the impression I got from Reggie Sparks," said Delamore imperturbably. "And if you're so blasé about it, why did you send that animal Pickrang over to Sydney? Anyway, who said anything about the newspapers? Somehow I don't think your clients would be totally comfortable with some of the things you got up to as a lad. I've got one of your brochures in front of me as a matter of fact; goll-y, that's an impressive client list. Now, do you want to talk or should I go find myself a photocopier?"

"Is Sparks in on this?"

"Don't be silly."

"Oh well, no harm in talking I guess. Where are you staying?"

"Come now Caspar," said Delamore reprovingly. "That's unworthy of you – Julian made you out to be so clever. I went for a little wander today and Albert Park seemed a nice spot, especially at lunchtime with all those pretty young students around. Let's say tomorrow at 12.30."

"How will I know you?"

Delamore chuckled. "Don't you worry about that. I've got your brochure remember? God, what an ego trip – there must be at least a dozen photos of you in it. Not that you don't take a nice picture . . ."

Quedley told Delamore to get fucked and put the phone down with a clatter.

CHAPTER *20*

*A*t 11am the following day, Tuesday, Dean Delamore walked through the lobby of his hotel and out onto the street. He was unshaven and wore jeans, sneakers, and a voluminous sweatshirt over a polo shirt; he didn't wear earrings or a blond wig or make-up. No-one gave him a second glance. He didn't leave his room key at the reception desk. As far as the hotel staff were concerned, the guest in room 1414 was a young blond woman and Delamore was anxious not to disturb that impression.

He had a cappuccino in a High Street cafe, bought a newspaper and a tuna, tomato and alfalfa sandwich, then strolled up through Albert Park towards the university. It was a mild spring day; clusters of dirty-grey cloud were blowing in from the west every half-hour with metronomic regularity and the smell of rain rose from the pavement when the sun broke through.

At 12.15pm Delamore sat down on a park bench opposite the university clock-tower and began to read his newspaper. There were plenty of people around, mainly students plus a few office types who'd come up from town to escape their colleagues, eat lunch, and enviously eye the students who canoodled and smoked cigarettes with an abandon suggesting they were unaware of the risks attached to both activities. At 12.25 Caspar Quedley walked up Princes Street and turned into the park. He stopped and looked around expectantly then shoved his hands in the pockets of his raincoat and pretended to take an interest in the large clock-face flowerbed. Delamore studied him from behind his sunglasses for a minute or two; having decided that the photos in the brochure didn't do Quedley justice, he turned his attention to the tuna sandwich.

At 12.45 Herman Pickrang got out of the red Mitsubishi which was illegally parked in a bikes-only zone on the other side of Princes Street and crossed the road. He walked towards Quedley, his gaze tracking slowly right to left through 180 degrees and back again. As he passed Quedley, he shook his head. Quedley shrugged. Delamore dabbed his mouth with a tissue, threw the tissue, sandwich wrapper and newspaper into a rubbish bin, got up and set off across the park. There were better ways to spend the afternoon than looking at microfiche in the city library but, he reminded himself, he was in Auckland on business, not on holiday.

Delamore got back to his hotel at 4pm. He thought about ringing Quedley but decided to soak in the bath first. Let him stew a bit longer, he thought. Delamore was enjoying the game of cat and mouse, all the more so because he was sure Quedley would hate being cast in the role of rodent. That was emphatically borne out when, shortly after five, Delamore finally made the call.

"What the fuck are you playing at?" the public relations man screeched down the phone. "I stuck around in Albert Park like a shag on a rock for half an hour . . ."

Delamore cut in: "Caspar, I've got to say you've been a big disappointment. All I used to hear from Julian – until he went off you – was Caspar this, Caspar that, Caspar's so smart, what an operator you were, Mr Cool. I mean, am I missing something here? I keep expecting class and style but, to be frank, all I see is clumsiness. I was in the park today, on time, ready to do a deal. If you'd just played it straight, you'd have Julian's stuff right now."

"What d'you mean, you were there? Where were you?"

"Well you'll just have to take my word for it. I saw you – you were in an ivory-coloured trenchcoat over a navy-blue suit. For what it's worth, I thought the coat was a shade . . . well, theatrical. I'm not sure that Humphrey Bogart look is really you."

Quedley's tone of shrill exasperation grew more pronounced: "If you were there, why the bloody hell didn't you show yourself?"

"Why the bloody hell do you think? I guessed you'd try something and I guessed right, didn't I? As I was saying, it was very clumsy Caspar. Jesus, you can spot that pet gorilla of yours a mile away."

"Okay," said Quedley sounding flat and tired. "You win. You're way ahead of me. Name a time and place and I'll be there – just me, no tricks, no frigging around."

"Uh-uh, not so fast, sugar," said Delamore in what he thought of as his southern belle voice. "I offered you first bite at the apple and you didn't take it. Now you've got to go to the back of the queue."

Delamore hung up in the middle of Quedley's protests and collapsed laughing on the bed, drumming his heels. When he stopped laughing, he went to his suitcase and retrieved the page he'd torn out of Reggie Sparks' notebook. On it was a list of names and phone numbers, one of which he dialled. The phone was answered on the second ring.

"Dermot Looms speaking."

"Hello, my name's Dean Delamore. I was a friend of Julian Gage's – a very close friend."

"Julian Gage – there's one out of the blue. I'd pretty well forgotten that name."

"You surprise me – I mean, considering what you've got in common."

"I think you've got the wrong end of the stick, my friend. You could cover all the stuff Gage and me have got in common without having to draw breath."

194

"Well Dermot – may I call you Dermot? – I'd have to disagree. Julian, you'll be sad to hear, passed away last week. Not long before he died, he sat down and wrote an account of his schooldays at Prince Albert College. When I read it, it struck me what a strong link there was between the two of you, a bond almost. I suppose you could say I've inherited that fragment of autobiography but it occurred to me that it might have some emotional value for you. It also occurred to me that you might be able to put a figure on that emotional value."

There was a very long silence which didn't surprise Delamore and which he made no effort to break. Eventually Looms said that yes, he supposed he might be able to do that.

"Good," said Delamore. "I felt sure you'd be interested. Well I guess the next step is for us to get together and toss a few numbers around."

Never again, thought Steven Perfumo. I don't give a fuck what happens or what the old man says, I'm never doing anything like that again – full stop.

He was sitting in the business-class cabin of an Air New Zealand Boeing 767. The aircraft was only an hour out of Auckland but Perfumo was already drunk. He took another noisy gulp of his Scotch and leaned back, closing his eyes. The scenes ran through his mind like frames from a favourite movie. He was living in a little country town or maybe somewhere up the coast – somewhere where the weather was good and everyone knew everyone else and you could go out at night and leave your place unlocked. He'd be in a little one-man legal practice, working nine to five then going home to the wife and kids, have a couple of beers, throw a few steaks on the barbecue in the backyard, maybe even wear a hat and an apron with one of those dumb sayings on it – 'Don't blame the cook, he's doing his best', some shit like that. Life would be simple and safe: no "family matters" to attend to, no looking over his

195

shoulder, no hassles from the cops. Most important of all, there would be no 25-stone Maori sociopaths with yellow-rimmed, blood-streaked piggy eyes and obscene tattoos on their stupendous arms and dreadlocks down to their arses and filthy clothes stained with what looked like every type of fluid and waste matter the human body is capable of producing.

Perfumo had known from the outset that negotiating the terminations of Herman Pickrang and Barry Plugge with the Blood Drinkers would be a nerve-wracking and unpleasant experience. It had turned out to be far worse. As Gino, the acting head of the family's New Zealand operations, had explained on the way back to the airport, the Blood Drinkers Perfumo had met on his last visit were the gang's businessmen; the guys they'd just talked to were the shock troops.

What had been truly frightening about that hour in the Otara hovel was the knowledge that he was completely at the mercy of people to whom, quite clearly, the concept of mercy was as irrelevant as last month's balance of payments figures. Sure, Perfumo knew some cruel and vicious people; he was related to a few although their number had decreased by two at the weekend. But most of the bad things those people did, they did for a reason. They could be vicious when they had to be for business reasons. When they didn't have to be, they could and did behave more or less like human beings. But the Blood Drinkers – who could imagine what atavistic instincts they followed? Who knew what savage pagan gods they worshipped? How had he felt, an 11-stone Italian-Australian lawyer in a Giorgio Armani suit and little tassles on his beautifully polished loafers, being glowered at by a quartet of those cavemen? He'd felt like a bobby calf in the slaughterhouse pens, sniffing death in the wind; Holy Mother of God, he'd felt like dinner!

Christ alone knew what insane impulse had prompted it but he'd actually asked them where they'd got their name from. The leader, a pot-bellied colossus with a mangled ear and Maori markings on his chin, had chuckled, a sound like an underground bomb test.

"Our ancestor Te Kooti was a great warrior. He and his men killed some pakeha in a church one time and drank their blood, eh." He shifted on the burst and tattered couch, releasing a pocket of fetid air which made Perfumo's stomach lurch. "We don't do it, eh." He looked slyly at his companions. "Maybe if we ran out of piss." As the four Blood Drinkers bellowed with laughter and shunted one another like Sumo wrestlers, Perfumo made a snap decision to increase his opening offer by $10,000. He wasn't up to haggling.

Perfumo shuddered and signalled to the stewardess for a refill. At least his father would be happy; Pickrang and Plugge were dead men, utterly doomed. They had less chance of saving their skins than a cat in a Chinese takeaway.

Caspar Quedley had two couches in his office, one of them a massive affair which he'd installed following a painful experience involving a supple and adventurous secretary, some whipped cream, a bunch of grapes, and the corner of his desk. But that Tuesday evening he was simply grateful that the couch was long enough for him to stretch out full-length, collar unbuttoned and tie askew, as he sought to regain his composure and find a way out of the quicksand into which he was sinking.

How could they possibly have missed Delamore in the park? That moron Pickrang – he'd actually seen the little shit in the flesh; it defied belief that Pickrang wouldn't have recognised Delamore if he'd been there. He was there all right; he'd just been one step ahead of them. A disguise maybe?

Quedley groaned as it dawned on him how he'd been played for a fool. Pickrang had been adamant that Delamore was a transvestite; it seemed thoroughly unlikely but when his receptionist had said that yes, someone had been in to collect a brochure that day, a blond woman in a lime-green suit . . . well

197

it all appeared to fit. Pickrang hadn't spotted him in Albert Park because he hadn't been in drag.

Back to square one. How do you track down someone when you don't know where they hang their hat or what they look like? You start with what you do know which amounts to two fifths of fuck all: he's a 20-something gay Australian man with a flair for cross-dressing. That's it.

Quedley had an idea; it was long shot but it was all he had. He went to his desk and rang a number he knew by heart. It was the number of his favourite restaurant, a brasserie in Ponsonby, whose owner was an identity on the local gay scene.

"Do me a favour Jerry – I'm trying to track down a character called Dean Delamore. He's gay, an Aussie, mid-to-late 20s, slim build, just come over from Sydney. He claims to be some kind of drag artist although I doubt he's wandering around the place in costume. He's probably staying in a hotel or motel; at a guess one of the better ones in the city – I'd say he's got a taste for the high life. Can you check around the traps and let me know if you hear anything?"

# CHAPTER 21

*I*t was a new-look Louise Appleyard who opened the door to Reggie Sparks. She was barefoot and wore large gold hoop earrings and a long, clinging floral dress with buttons all the way down the front; it looked like she'd started buttoning up at the waist and got sidetracked before she'd got too far in either direction. Her hair was tousled and unruly, the fringe cascaded down her face prompting frequent horsy head movements which Sparks found distracting. The lights were back on in her eyes and shining so brightly it was hard to believe they'd ever been dimmed. His phone call from Sydney had left Sparks apprehensive, sensing that unwelcome developments were in the wind; as he followed her inside, that vague uneasy feeling returned.

They were sitting at the kitchen bench.

"New look?"

She grinned happily. "Not really. I just felt it was time to loosen up a bit. What do you think?"

"I like it. It's sort of the gypsy look without hairy armpits."

Louise snorted with laughter. "Bloody hell Reggie, I'm not sure about that. Is that meant to be a compliment?"

The conversation moved along easily until Sparks brought up Julian Gage's posthumous dispatch. Then he discovered that Louise Appleyard had changed her mind along with her appearance.

"Hasn't arrived," she said, dropping her eyes.

"What? That's crazy. Delamore – Gage's boyfriend – posted it a week ago. You should've got it yesterday or the day before."

"Oh well, I guess it'll turn up," said Louise disinterestedly. Sparks tried to catch her eye but she examined the contents of her coffee mug. Neither spoke for a while. Finally she said slowly: "Look Reggie, I've been having second thoughts about this."

Sparks cupped his chin in his hand and stared at her unblinkingly.

"Oh yeah? What brought them on?"

Louise shrugged diffidently. "Oh I don't know. It's just that the more I think about it, the less likely it seems that one person's version of events that happened 20 years ago is going to prove a hell of a lot. Apart from anything else, who's to say he's telling the truth?"

"Who's to say he's not? The bloke was dying – why the hell should he lie?"

Another shrug. "Well, we don't know what his motivation was, do we? Maybe he was playing Vic along, pretending to know something about the girl's death. Maybe he had a grudge against someone and wanted to, you know, blacken their name."

Louise glanced up, caught Sparks' frown, raised her eyebrows defiantly as if to say "well, it's possible". She looked down again and continued: "Anyway, what I'm leading up to is that I can't guarantee that you'll get to see the letter. You're just going to have to trust my judgement, okay?"

Sparks sighed and turned his head, running his fingers through his hair. He found himself looking at a small blackboard on the wall next to the fridge. In the middle of the blackboard, surrounded by *aides-mémoire* – "pay phone bill", "new leotard" – boxed off, underlined and written in capital letters was the name "CASPAR" and a pair of phone numbers. One of the numbers had "home" in brackets after it.

Sparks spent 30 seconds considering the implications of this discovery and deciding they were all extremely negative. He picked up a packet of cigarettes that was lying on the bench.

"May I?"

"Help yourself."

He lit the cigarette and inhaled. It made him feel even more nauseous. What the hell, he thought. Let's get it over with. He cleared his throat and said, "Are you going out with Caspar Quedley?" He wanted it to come out casually, oh-by-the-way, but, to his ears, it sounded blunt and inquisitorial.

"What makes you think that?" she said, surprised.

Sparks took another drag on the cigarette and spoke through the smoke. "Just the thing on the blackboard there. Only thing missing is a heart with an arrow through it."

She smiled wanly. "Very droll. As a matter of fact, yes; we've been out a couple of times."

"And?"

"And what?" she said, her voice rising. "You want to put that in *New Nation* too?"

"I just meant how did it go," said Sparks stiffly. "None of my business obviously." He got up. "Thanks for the coffee – and the cigarette."

Louise Appleyard followed Sparks to the door thinking that she could have handled it worse – like she and Quedley could've been entwined on the front lawn when Sparks arrived. Sparks half-turned at the door, gave her an expressionless nod, and walked to his mother's car which was parked at the top of the drive, next to the letterbox. As he reached the car, a post-woman cycled up and slipped a bundle of letters in the box. Sparks looked around; Louise had gone back inside and closed the door. He retrieved the mail from the letterbox and shuffled through the envelopes; there was nothing from Sydney.

He walked back up the path to the house and knocked on the door. When Louise opened it, he handed her the mail.

"Is it there?" she asked. "Don't tell me you didn't look?"

"No it's not. If it's not a gross impertinence, can I ask you a personal question?"

Louise checked to see if there was a trace of irony behind Sparks' formality but found no evidence of it.

"Feel free."

"Did you tell Quedley that Gage's letter was coming here?"

She nodded.

"Could I use your phone?"

Sparks rang Jackson Pike and asked him if he thought Quedley had the clout to intercept other people's mail. Pike said he was buggered if he knew but he'd ask someone who would and call straight back. Sparks gave him Louise's number.

"Aren't we getting a tad paranoid?" she asked when he hung up.

"We'll see."

After that, they waited for Pike to call back in strained silence.

Pike called Garth Grimes and put the question. Grimes laughed. It wasn't his usual throaty wheeze; it was a full-blown cackle and it went on for a full minute. Then he said: "Jackson, you really shouldn't do that to an old man. I'm hanging up now; I have to go and lie down."

I guess that's a yes thought Pike and rang Sparks. Sparks listened to Pike, thanked him and hung up.

"Well?" said Louise.

Sparks gave her a long look which bordered on the unfriendly. "A guy who knows a lot more about your boyfriend than we do doesn't think I'm paranoid."

When Sparks had gone, Louise Appleyard went out onto the deck overlooking Lake Pupuke to reflect on the look Reggie Sparks had given her when he'd got off the phone. It took her the time it takes to smoke a cigarette to establish that the look bothered her. Working out why took a little longer.

As Reggie Sparks sat beside the pool at the Mon Desir Hotel drinking beer and thinking bitter thoughts about Dean Delamore, Louise Appleyard and Caspar Quedley, the latter was receiving good news.

"I think I might've found your lad," said his restaurateur friend. "The barman at the Rococo says an Australian calling himself Dean has been in the past couple of nights. He fits the description – right age, slim build and so forth. The barman and he got chatting and this Dean chap mentioned he was staying at the Regis. I didn't bother to ask if it was in the context of your place or mine; I didn't think it was germane."

The Regis, thought Quedley as he hung up. About time I got a break. They owe me for all the business I've put their way over the years. He rang the Regis' banqueting manager who was pleasingly servile and only too happy to check if there was a Dean Delamore staying in the hotel. There wasn't. Any name that was vaguely similar? Strike two. Quedley racked his brains; maybe Delamore registered as a woman? Why not? He was tricky enough and he could get away with it. Look how he fooled his receptionist.

Quedley asked the banqueting manager to run a check on the young, single women staying in the hotel. The one he was looking for would've been there for the past few days; she was slim, blond and she'd been seen around in a – what was it? – yeah, a lime-green suit.

The banqueting manager called back half an hour later to say that there were only three single woman guests; the one who fitted the bill most had checked in first thing Monday morning under the name Lesley Gore.

Lesley fucking Gore? thought Quedley. Wasn't she a pop singer? Christ, years ago. Did she do *C'mon baby, do the Locomotion*? No, that was Little Eva. *It's my party and I'll cry if I want to*? Something like that. Lesley Gore's got to be a little in-joke. Just like a faggot – too clever by half.

"All right," said Quedley. "Now we're getting somewhere. What's Ms Gore's room number?"

Delamore and Looms had arranged to meet in the Gateway to the North Tearooms in the foothills of the Brynderwyns, north of Wellsford, at 2.30pm. Delamore set off in a hired car just before midday. The concierge at the hotel had said it was about a 90-minute drive but he wanted to take his time and see some countryside.

The tearooms were a white-painted weatherboard box with a red corrugated iron roof and a glass frontage enabling customers to watch the lorries they'd overtaken with great difficulty 50km back down the road trundle past. Alongside was a scruffy little repair garage with a couple of petrol pumps. The tearooms were strategically located, just about the exact driving time from Auckland that it took the average family going north on holiday to start bickering. Just when the kids in the back seat would begin agitating for a comfort stop and an ice cream and Dad would be feeling like a break and a cup of tea before tackling the climb over the Brynderwyns, they'd spot the sign saying "Tearooms 200m ahead." Summer was the busy time; apart from the holidaymakers, the truck drivers and travelling salesmen would linger over a second scone and instant coffee to ogle the teenage girls in their shorts and tank tops.

There were only two cars in the parking area when Delamore pulled in five minutes late – a white station wagon with a car phone aerial and a Volvo. He parked and went in. A young man with frizzy red hair, densely freckled forearms and a row of cheap ballpoints in the breast pocket of his short-sleeved white shirt was debating the merits of ordinary milk versus the low-fat variety with the woman behind the counter. An older man, heavily tanned and mostly bald, was sitting by himself with his back to the wall at a table in the far corner. He observed Delamore over the rim of his cup. Farmer Giles I presume, thought Delamore.

He bought a Coke and walked over to the table in the corner.

"Mr Looms?"

"That's me. Sit yourself down."

Delamore pulled out a chair and sat down. Looms put his elbows on the table and hunched forward. His sleeves were rolled above the elbow and ropey veins ran down his forearms and wrists, branching off into tributaries which laced the backs of his thick, powerful hands. Looms' jaw jutted aggressively and his hard grey eyes stared out stonily from beneath bushy brows. This is a tough hombre, thought Delamore; not that you didn't know that already.

"So Gage wrote a little story, did he?"

Delamore nodded. "I'd describe it as a hair-raising tale – well, for those of us with hair."

"You're a funny little fellow aren't you?" said Looms without a twitch of reaction showing on his granite features. "How come you've got it?"

"Julian and I were friends."

"Bum chums?"

Delamore shrugged. "I've been gay-bashed three times so being called names doesn't bother me too much. But you go right ahead if it makes you feel better."

"I started losing my hair when I was 19; can't recall too many people taking the piss about it."

"Well there's a surprise," murmured Delamore. "Now that we've defined our respective areas of sensitivity, can we get on with it?" He looked around. "This is very cosy but it's not really my scene."

Looms raised his eyebrows as if amazed that anyone could find fault with the surroundings.

"Okay. You got it with you?"

Delamore tilted his head to one side. "Get real."

"Where is it?"

"In Auckland. In a safe place."

"It's not worth shit, you know?"

"I disagree," said Delamore confidently. "I can think of a number of people who'd be riveted by it – Mr and Mrs Ticehurst for instance. I checked them out; they're still around, still living in Auckland. He's a partner in one of those big accountancy practices – a man of substance as they say; the sort of man who could get the authorities to sit up and take notice. I think they'd find Julian's recollections convincing. Let's face it, deathbed confessions do have a certain credibility."

Looms frowned and rubbed his chin. "Maybe. So what's your angle?"

"This is my offer and it's non-negotiable: I get $100,000 Australian; you get Julian's rave from the grave and never hear from me again. You've got till the weekend to organise the money. I'll call you then and tell you where it's to be deposited. As soon as the bank confirms the transfer, I'll hand over the document."

"A hundred grand? You're off your fucking head."

Delamore smiled. "You can get help, split the cost. You're not the only one at risk so why should you bear the whole cost?"

Looms nodded dubiously. "Even if I could raise the money, what's to stop you making photo-copies and coming back for another bite?"

"Now that you mention it, nothing really. You're just going to have to trust me. The reality is, you're paying me to keep my mouth shut and go away. Which I'll do. Take it from me, I don't want to make a career out of this."

"Why not?" said Looms sourly. "You seem to have a talent for it."

Delamore stood up. "You're too kind. I'll be in touch."

Delamore hurried to the hired car and got in. As he put the key in the ignition, he felt something cold and metallic on the back of his neck. He looked around. A plump, moon-faced man with a ponytail and bushy white sideburns and wearing serious spectacles lay across the back seat. He cradled a single-barrelled shotgun pointed at Delamore.

Basil Batrouney smiled his other-worldly smile and said: "Just drive man – I'll tell you where."

# CHAPTER 22

*T*here was nothing sophisticated about the way Dermot Looms interrogated Dean Delamore. Directed by Basil Batrouney, Delamore had driven his hire car to Looms' farm and into a lock-up garage. When Looms arrived a few minutes later, Delamore was herded at gunpoint to the woolshed which was 100m or so beyond the farmhouse, down a gentle slope. The woolshed was the size of a single-storey house. There were half-a-dozen holding pens, a massive wooden bench for wool sorting and a large space where the shearing was done. Even though Looms kept a clean shed, the devoutly urban Delamore found the smell – a blend of one part blood, several parts sweat and many parts sheep droppings and urine which had been stewing gently for three generations – almost overpowering. There was a rickety old highback wooden chair against the wall. Looms moved it to the centre of the shearing area and made Delamore sit on it. He pulled Delamore's arms behind him and around the back of the chair, tied his wrists together with twine then lashed his ankles to the chair's front legs.

Preparations complete, Looms stood in front of Delamore with his large, lumpy hands on his hips. Batrouney hovered in the background, humming to himself.

"Now then Sunshine," said Looms. "Where've you got this thing of Gage's hidden away?"

During the drive from The Gateway to the North

Tearooms to Looms' farm, Delamore had reached the conclusion that his best – if not only – chance of avoiding serious
injury or worse was to refuse to divulge the whereabouts of
Gage's letter. That in turn, he felt reasonably sure, would
require him to withstand a considerable amount of pain.

As he'd told Looms, Delamore had on three occasions
been a victim of the young men who, on Friday and Saturday
nights, drive in from Sydney's working-class west to its trendy
inner east – Oxford Street, Paddington, Darlinghurst – with
the express purpose of beating up homosexual men. Delamore
had taken his beatings fatalistically, assuming that there must
be a genetic link between male heterosexuality, low IQ and the
urge to consume huge quantities of cheap beer and gang up on
gays. The third time it happened he'd tried to reason with them,
pointing out that if it wasn't for all the queers, they'd have even
less chance of getting girls. Perhaps it hadn't come out quite
right because they just went ahead and gave him a kicking
anyway.

While these experiences had left him less fearful of
physical assault than the average person, he suspected that what
he'd be subjected to in Looms' woolshed would be far worse: it
wouldn't be drunken youths, half-mad with some sort of mob
hysteria, flailing and hacking wildly and getting in one
another's way; when it came to dishing out punishment,
Looms, he felt pretty sure, would be both vigorous and
methodical, a formidable combination. As long as that fat freak
with the ponytail doesn't join in, thought Delamore. He's a
psycho if I ever saw one.

So Delamore swallowed hard, licked his dry lips and said:
"I'm afraid that's got to remain my little secret."

Looms tut-tutted and stepped forward to position
himself within easy reach. He planted his feet.

"Sure about that?"

Delamore braced himself and gave a slight nod.

Looms swayed back, gathered himself, then drove his

right fist into the side of Delamore's face. The chair was flung over. Delamore lay on his side with his undamaged cheek on the floor. The stench of sheep droppings wafting up through the spaces between the floorboards was several times ranker than the general atmosphere. Batrouney was shadow-boxing, hopping from one foot to another, chirping: "Pow! Biff! Whacko! Take that Mr Bad Guy!"

Looms hauled the chair upright and let fly with a roundhouse left which caught Delamore just under the eye and knocked him sprawling again. As he propped up Delamore, he cocked an eyebrow.

"Well?"

Delamore could feel swelling coming up around his right eye. His upper lip on one side felt mashed and he could taste blood in his mouth. He shook his head.

"I can do this all afternoon if I have to," said Looms with a shrug. "You're not going to be a pretty sight."

Delamore closed his eyes for a few seconds. He opened them in time to see a big, brown, gnarled fist heading straight for the centre of his face. His nose was shattered and flattened in an explosion of blood and gristle and the chair pitched over backwards.

Delamore lay on his back with his bound legs in the air. He could hardly see and his entire face was ablaze with pain. He heard Batrouney's high-pitched scream: ". . . and the challenger hits the canvas for the third time. And here's the count: a-one, a-two, a-three, a-four . . ."

"Baz, you mad bugger, pipe down," said Looms amiably and walked over to Delamore. Then: "Hello, what've we got here?" Delamore, twisting his head to spit out blood, saw Looms stoop to pick up his hotel room key which had been jolted out of the back pocket of his jeans.

"Room 1414 at the Regis Hotel," said Looms. He hauled the chair upright again and peered into Delamore's face. "I'll bet that's where it is. Save it, Sunny Jim – I can see it in your eyes. Well the one that's still open anyway." He sighed and shook his head. "Christ, I told you – you could've saved yourself a few smacks in the scone by just giving me the bloody key in the first place."

Looms hitched himself up onto the bench. He flexed his right hand a couple of times. "I take my hat off to you, mister – I wouldn't have credited it in a blue moon. I thought one decent thump and you'd be howling the roof down." He looked at the key. "If this hadn't dropped out of your pocket, I probably would've been hammering the buggery out of you till teatime. Oh well, fat lot of good it did you. I'll shoot down to Auckland later on and find that fucking thing of Gage's. Then we'll have to decide what to do with you. What d'you reckon, Baz?"

"I do declare, hanging's too good for that varmint, marshal," said Batrouney in a hillbilly twang. "I say we do what the Injuns do – string him up by his nutbag and skin him alive with a red-hot knife."

At 9.10 that Wednesday evening Herman Pickrang, wearing his best suit and tie and carrying a briefcase, strode purposefully through the lobby of the Regis Hotel. The outfit and the briefcase, which he'd bought that afternoon, were intended to make him look like a businessman. In fact he looked exactly what he was: a thug in a five-year-old suit carrying a cheap plastic briefcase. Since the lobby was almost deserted, the thinness of his camouflage hardly mattered.

Pickrang took the lift to the 14th floor and found room 1414. The corridors were empty. He donned a pair of tight-fitting rubber gloves. As Quedley had promised, getting into the room wasn't difficult; the banqueting manager had been by a few minutes earlier to make sure of that.

Pickrang was not what could be termed a tidy burglar, one of those who pride themselves on leaving no trace of their visit apart from the absence of the stolen items. He violently stripped the bed, wrenched the mattress off the base, and scattered the contents of the drawers and wardrobes without finding anything.

The suitcase was locked. It had been a long time between knifings for Pickrang but impaling Rocco Perfumo had brought back to him just how satisfying knifework could be. On his return to Auckland, he'd procured a razor-sharp flick knife which he wore taped to his right calf as he'd seen Clint Eastwood do in a movie. He popped the blade and plunged it through the suitcase's canvas exterior. He ran the blade round the frame of the suitcase, cutting out the whole of one side. As he went to discard the material, he felt the envelope which had been sewn in between the canvas and the cloth lining.

Pickrang opened the envelope; it contained several typed pages. A quick scan satisfied him that it was what Quedley wanted. Pickrang replaced his knife, put the envelope in the briefcase, checked there was no one in the corridor, and left the scene.

He came out of the hotel, turned right and headed for his car which he'd left in a side street a couple of blocks away. As was usually the case at 9.30 on a Wednesday night, the city was near-empty and quiet.

Luther "Bad Louie" Potau awoke with a start when his mobile phone rang. He was sitting in the driver's seat of a 15-year-old Ford Falcon parked in the one-way inner-city side street directly opposite Pickrang's Mitsubishi. The caller was a fellow member of the Blood Drinkers who'd been stationed in the bus shelter across the road from the Regis Hotel waiting for Pickrang to come out; he was ringing to report that Pickrang was on his way.

Potau sat up and rubbed his eyes. He screwed the top back on the half-empty litre bottle of dark rum which was propped up between his massive fleshy thighs and slipped the bottle under the seat. For the third time that evening he broke open the sawn-off shotgun to check that it was loaded.

Just as he snapped it shut, he saw, in his rear view mirror, Pickrang round the corner. Potau laid the gun on the passenger's seat and wound down the window on that side. Pickrang walked a little way up the footpath on Potau's side of the road then crossed over to his car. He set down the briefcase and fumbled for his car keys. As he inserted the key, he heard a car door open behind him. He looked around. A huge Maori wearing a woolly cap and wraparound sunglasses got out of the beat-up Ford on the other side of the street and walked slowly around the front of the car. He leaned against the passenger door, folded his arms, and looked at Pickrang without speaking.

Pickrang picked him straightaway as a gang member, a species he despised despite the many things they had in common. After a few seconds' silence, he snapped: "What the fuck do you want, you big fat cunt?"

When Luther Potau reached in the open car window and brought out a sawn-off shotgun, Pickrang decided that a less confrontational approach might be in order. Because such an approach didn't come naturally, he was still trying to think of the appropriate words when Potau raised the shotgun and gave him both barrels. The blast hurled Pickrang onto the bonnet of his car. He rolled off the bonnet onto the road where he lay with his head in the gutter.

Potau, who didn't believe in looking gift horses in the mouth, walked across the road and picked up Pickrang's briefcase. He got into his car, threw the briefcase and the shotgun into the back seat, and drove off. As Potau turned out of the street, Pickrang lifted his head a few centimetres out of the gutter and coughed wetly. His chest hurt horribly. Perhaps, he thought, he should call for help. It went against his code of stoicism and self-reliance but, then again, he'd never found himself face down in a gutter with a chest full of buckshot before. When he tried to shout, he found he simply didn't have enough breath to make a sound. Before Herman Pickrang had

213

a chance to get to grips with the implications of his extreme shortage of breath, he died.

Cec Gilpin considered that he was extremely lucky to have a friend like Barry Plugge. Even though Plugge had made it – really made it – in life, he hadn't forgotten his boyhood mates. So when, at the age of 50, Gilpin had been made redundant by the city's parks and recreation department for which he'd worked for the whole of his adult life, Barry Plugge had put him on his payroll.

Plugge called him his "chauffeur and gofer". Gilpin didn't know and didn't care what a gofer was; he just did whatever Barry wanted. Sure, the pay was pretty ordinary – not much more than the dole if the truth be told – but the main thing was that he was occupied; he had something to do with himself, somewhere to go of a morning rather than moping around at home and having a blue with the missus. There was one other great benefit: he got to drive Plugge's cherry-red Jaguar Sovereign with the personalised number plate FLASH. Since he was a boy, Gilpin had regarded Jaguars as the ultimate in automotive excellence and style. If anyone had ever suggested that one day he'd be driving a Jag on a regular basis, he would've dismissed the notion out of hand. Yet here he was most days of the week, cruising the streets behind the wheel of this majestic machine.

Gilpin might've been less positive about both Plugge and the Jaguar if he'd been aware of the background to the Sultan of Sleaze's out-of-the-blue announcement a few months previously that Gilpin would henceforth chauffeur him around. It was to do with the threat from the Italians from Sydney. On the basis of the occasional television news reports from Sicily about prosecuting magistrates being blown to smithereens by car bombs, Plugge was of the view that the car bomb was once again the preferred assassination method of the Italian criminal fraternity. As any moviegoer knows, most car bombs were rigged up to go off when the car was started. Guarding against this eventuality meant going through the tiresome procedure of getting down on your hands and knees and inspecting underneath the car every time you wanted to go anywhere. The thought of a constantly cricked neck and soiled trousers didn't appeal to Plugge; furthermore, he was so ignorant of the workings of a car and things mechanical that he could conceivably have looked straight at a bomb without recognising it as such. A much better idea was to insure the hell out of the Jag and let someone else take the risks.

Thus it was that at 9.53 that Wednesday night, Cec Gilpin drove Barry Plugge's Jaguar out of the carpark, around the block, and double-parked it out in front of the Blue Angel strip club to await his employer. Knowing the wait could last anything up to half an hour, Gilpin turned on the car radio which he had tuned to a classic hits station. The first song to come on was Gene Pitney's *The Man Who Shot Liberty Valance*. Gilpin gave a grunt of delight and turned up the volume. In Cec Gilpin's pantheon of heroes, Gene Pitney ranked a close second to Barry Plugge. Sitting back in the soft leather and singing along to Gene with his eyes shut tight, Gilpin didn't see the battered Ford Falcon which came up Karangahape Road from the opposite direction, stopped a few metres away to allow a car to go by, then swerved across the middle line to pull up alongside the Jaguar.

Gilpin was doing his inadequate best to stay with Gene Pitney through the descending cadence of "He was the bravest of them all", when Luther "Bad Louie" Potau bellowed at him from less than three metres away: "Yo, white bread mother-fucker."

Gilpin swivelled his head towards the source of this unwelcome interruption. Potau poked his sawn-off shotgun through the car window, waited till Gilpin's expression changed from puzzled annoyance to eye-popping terror, and pulled the trigger. He gave him one barrel only but it was quite enough. As Bad Louie told himself as he roared down Karangahape Road towards the Symonds Street motorway ramp, he was only half the size of the other cunt, so why waste a second cartridge on him?

CHAPTER *23*

*D*ean Delamore's evening meal consisted of two slices of slightly stale bread, a lump of cheddar cheese, a glass of water and a handful of aspirins. He was then locked up for the night in the cellar under Looms' house. It was chilly and pitch-black and each creak and rustle caused him to wonder what other forms of life inhabited the cellar. After midnight the aspirins wore off and his wrecked nose set up a fiery throb which intensified as the night dragged on. The pain was enough to make sleep difficult; the combination of pain, the expectation of being scampered over or even gnawed by foraging rats, and dark thoughts of what the morning might bring which, try as he might, he couldn't block out of his mind, made it impossible.

At eight the next morning Looms let him out of the cellar to go to the bathroom. He examined his bruised, yellowing, misshapen face in the mirror. He decided it wasn't really the Rexette look. Suddenly he felt the delayed effect of all the pain and shock and fear which he'd gone through and he began to shake violently. When the shaking died down, he took a last look in the mirror. Remember, he told himself, big girls don't cry.

He came out of the bathroom. Looms, who'd been waiting outside the door, gripped him by the arm and pushed him down the corridor.

"I suppose you're wondering what's happening?" he

said. "Well I would in your shoes. I drove all the bloody way to Auckland and couldn't get within five blocks of the hotel. I don't know what the hell was going on but there were police everywhere, roadblocks, the works. So I'm going to have to do it all over again tonight. I should charge you petrol money." He stopped Delamore by the kitchen door and breathed in heavily. "Smell that? Bacon, eggs, tomatoes, fried bread and farm mushrooms – Baz's speciality. What did they used to say – 'the condemned man ate a hearty breakfast'?"

Having reviewed the events of Wednesday night, Detective Sergeant Tito Ihaka felt that, on the whole, it had been one of the better nights for the forces of law and order.

True, there was a shotgun killer on the rampage who didn't appear to draw the important distinction between legitimate targets and law-abiding taxpayers. But even then, Cec Gilpin hadn't died in vain: the shocking sight of his chauffeur's face plastered across the windscreen of his Jaguar had put a hurricane-strength wind up Barry Plugge. He'd drawn the obvious conclusion – that he, rather than his employee, had been the intended victim – and immediately sought sanctuary at the Central Police Station, the only place in Auckland where he felt safe. To ensure that the police didn't throw him back on the street, Plugge had demanded a tape recorder and started owning up. When Ihaka switched off the tape recorder four hours later, he estimated that Plugge would be eligible for parole sometime around the year 2015.

Plugge began by outlining the ingenious scam he'd cooked up with the jailed lawyer Trevor Lydiate. Then he'd explained the circumstances surrounding the demise of private investigator and candid photography specialist Wallace Guttle. No sooner had Plugge confirmed that Herman Pickrang had done for Guttle than the news came through that Pickrang himself was past tense; he'd been the first of the unknown shooter's brace of victims.

Although Ihaka felt the shooter deserved society's heartfelt thanks for getting rid of Pickrang and couldn't suppress a twinge of admiration for his industry and no-nonsense approach, the pressure was on for a swift arrest. While Ihaka took a detached view of the previous night's events and, as always, was unable to get too worked up about what civilians did to one another – as far as he was concerned, the only sensible attitude for a policeman to adopt – the media were busy scaring the daylights out of the citizenry with its coverage of the double slaying. Ihaka didn't think the manhunt would be a long one. The way this merchant operates, he thought, he ain't exactly the Scarlet Pimpernel. The only question was how many people would be wiped out in the process of taking him out of circulation. Keep your wits about you, fat boy, Ihaka told himself; whatever happens, don't you be the first poor bastard through the door.


Detective Constable Johan Van Roon hovered nervously in front of Ihaka's desk, waiting for the sergeant to acknowledge his presence. Van Roon, who was 24, was a first-generation New Zealander, the son of Dutch immigrants whose fair northern European complexion he'd inherited. Ihaka had a sharp eye for others' distinguishing features or physical peculiarities and Van Roon's milky skin had immediately caught his attention. Van Roon, he'd announced to a crowded station room on the constable's first day at Central, was the whitest white man he'd ever seen.

Eventually Ihaka looked up.

"Well if it ain't the Milky Bar Kid. What's your problem?"

Van Roon tried to smile but didn't quite get there. "Sarge, there's something a bit odd about this Pickrang thing; it looks like he might've pulled a burglary at the Regis hotel just before he got hit."

"Oh yeah?" said Ihaka disinterestedly. "I'll bet it wasn't the only thing he pulled."

Van Roon soldiered on. "Pickrang copped it about 9.30. A bellboy saw him in the lobby just after nine and some time around then a guest's room got really turned over."

Ihaka sniffed noisily and looked at his watch. "Is this going to take long, constable?"

The constable, who'd heard that Ihaka's bark was worse than his bite but didn't believe it, swallowed hard. "Sure Sarge, I'm just about there. The guest whose room got done over is a Ms Lesley Gore from Sydney but immigration has no record of anyone of that name entering the country. There was an Aussie passport in the suitcase which the burglar took to with a knife – Pickrang had a knife on him by the way . . ."

"Hold it, what did he take to with a knife – the fucking suitcase or the fucking passport?"

The constable nodded hurriedly. "Sorry, sorry – the suitcase. He cut one whole side panel out of it. Anyway, that's a bit beside the point . . ."

"What is the point, son?" said Ihaka with quiet emphasis.

"The passport belongs to a 27-year-old man called Dean Delamore who flew in from Sydney on Sunday; the guest registered as Lesley Gore, and there were men's and women's clothes and toiletries in the room. The women who make the beds and that say they never saw any bloke's gear – it must've been kept in the suitcase – and they're certain there's only been one person in the room."

Ihaka said "Hmmm" and stood up. "How do they know that? They sniff the sheets or something?" He walked around and sat on the edge of the desk in front of the constable. "Have we tracked down the mystery guest?"

"No. There's no sign of him – or her. The staff at the front desk say they haven't seen Ms Gore for a couple of days. She always hangs out the "Do not disturb" sign when she's in the room. We showed Delamore's passport around and a couple of people seem to think Delamore and Gore are the same person but they wouldn't swear to it. Yesterday morning a guy the concierge identified as Delamore from the passport photo was asking about driving up north, somewhere round Wellsford."

"You check the car hire companies?"

"Yeah we did. Delamore picked up a Honda Civic from the Hertz place in town around midday yesterday. He used a New South Wales licence and said he'd have the car back by the weekend at the latest. I sent the number up to Wellsford and asked them to keep an eye out for it. We also faxed Sydney but haven't heard back yet."

"So Herman Pickrang burgled a man who's pretending to be a woman; then a few minutes later, a party or parties unknown spread his lungs over half of downtown. You seem to be right on top of things, son – what's your theory?"

"I haven't really got one, sarge. I just thought it was all a bit strange. If Delamore and Gore are one and the same – and it sure looks that way – you kind of think he must be up to something to go through all that carry-on. Oh by the way, we found this in the suitcase too."

He passed Ihaka a folded sheet of notepaper. Ihaka opened it. On it was a handwritten list of names, addresses and phone numbers; some had a line through them, some had ticks beside them, some question marks. It was the second time Ihaka had seen these particular names; the first time was on the long-dead Bronwen Ticehurst's dance card.

Ihaka stared at the list for a full minute.

"Son, you're absolutely right. This is definitely strange. You've got something else to tell me, haven't you?"

Van Roon racked his brains. "I think that's it, Sarge," he said uncertainly.

Ihaka looked at him wide-eyed, shaking his head. "Uh-uh. If Pickrang did the break-in, what'd he nick and where is it?"

221

"Nothing as far as we can tell. I mean, we didn't find anything on him or in his car. Oh shit, hang on – the bellboy said Pickrang was carrying a briefcase."

"But you didn't find a briefcase, right? So it's reasonable to assume that A, whatever he nicked from Delamore's room was in the briefcase and B, whoever pinged him took the briefcase."

Van Roon was so angry with himself for having overlooked the briefcase that he almost forgot to pass on his final piece of information. He had to go back and interrupt Ihaka's paperwork again.

"One other thing, Sarge," he said. "When Delamore filled in his immigration form, he didn't say he was going to stay at the Regis. He put down a private address somewhere in St Heliers – I've got it written down if you want it. It's the home of a Mrs Sparks – Mareena Sparks."

Mareena Sparks and Tito Ihaka greeted one another like old friends. After they'd finished assuring each other that they were in the pink, Mareena escorted the policeman to the downstairs den where her younger son lay on the couch watching TV. When she'd gone, Ihaka asked Reggie Sparks how his story was going.

"Shithouse," he said. "Next question."

"Yeah, it's good to be alive isn't it? I've got some news that might cheer you up – it's about your old sparring partner, Herman Pickrang."

Sparks rolled into a sitting position.

"Hang on – let me guess. Pickrang's body was found somewhere in the vicinity of Palm Beach, a little place on the coast just north of Sydney. He was shot by someone using a handgun, probably in the early hours of last Sunday morning. Am I right?"

Ihaka looked at Sparks as if he'd announced his intention to roller skate to the South Pole. "You quite finished? Pickrang's dead all right. His body was found in a side street in the centre of Auckland, a city situated on an isthmus separating the Waitemata and Manukau harbours. It happened around half past nine last night. And handgun, my black arse – he bought a full load from a double-barrelled sawn-off from as close as me to you. What's all this shit about some place north of Sydney?"

Sparks leaned forward staring at Ihaka. "What? He was killed here? Last night?" He slumped back on the sofa. "Last week I went over to Sydney, for *New Nation*. Pickrang was over there as well. I was at this place at Palm Beach when Pickrang turned up doing his 'I'm going to rip your ears off' routine. Then these two other guys showed up. Don't ask me who they were but they were dirty on Pickrang in a huge way – something to do with he'd shoved one of them in a pizza oven. Anyway, these guys had a gun, a pistol. They told us to get lost; it was pretty obvious what they had in mind."

"What was Pickrang doing over there?"

"I'm pretty sure he was sent by a guy called Caspar Quedley." Sparks told Ihaka about Julian Gage. He finished: ". . . but by the time he got over there, Gage was dead and his stuff was in the mail. Gage didn't know about Appleyard – that's why he sent it to him – but it hasn't arrived; I reckon Quedley's got his hands on it."

"How could he do that?"

"He's an operator, you know, he's got fingers in all sorts of pies, knows everyone who's anyone."

Ihaka nodded slowly. "Well if he's got the juice, I suppose he could. You know a guy called Dean Delamore?"

Sparks sat up again. "Yeah I do. He was a friend of Gage's; he posted Gage's stuff for him. Delamore was at Palm Beach when Pickrang turned up. He came over here with me on Sunday."

"Well that explains that. Where is he now?"

"No idea," said Sparks flatly. "He stayed here Sunday night then shot through without a word."

"Tell me something Sparks, how friendly are you and this character? The reason I ask is that I hear he likes dressing up in women's clothes. You don't have showers together and take turns picking up the soap, that sort of stuff?"

Sparks gave him a sour look. "Yeah, that's us all right."

"Hey, don't get me wrong; I've got nothing against it. Matter of fact, I wouldn't be surprised if the boy I sleep with is a bit that way."

Sparks' lips twitched. It was as close to a smile as he'd got in 24 hours.

"What about Delamore?"

"After Delamore left here, he checked in at the Regis Hotel – as a woman. Called himself Lesley Gore – that mean anything to you?" Sparks shook his head. "Looks like Pickrang's swansong was a B and E on Delamore's room. Typical Pickrang – tore the fucking place apart. Now what do you reckon he was after?"

"The stuff Gage wrote? Doesn't make sense. Delamore posted it in Sydney last week . . ." Sparks stopped in mid-sentence.

"You only got his word for it, right? I think your little mate's playing his own game." Ihaka passed Sparks the sheet of paper with the list of names on it. "We found this in his room."

"This is out of my fucking notebook, the little shit." Sparks put his head in his hands and thought hard. "If Delamore didn't send Gage's letter, Quedley couldn't have intercepted it. So Quedley finds out Delamore's staying at the Regis – how would he even know he's in town?"

"Delamore must've got in touch with him. Quedley must want this letter thing bad to send Pickrang over to Sydney. Why? Because it dumps shit on him?"

"I'm pretty sure it does."

"Well I'd say Delamore's trying to blackmail him."

Sparks thought about it. "I don't know about that. I can't see Delamore as a blackmailer."

"Grow up, mate. You've known him what – a few days? The way he pissed off out of here tells you he's up to something."

Sparks shrugged. "Okay, for the sake of argument, let's say you're right. But if Delamore had it and Pickrang stole it, where is it now?"

"We don't know for sure that he did. I mean, he left the place in a shambles but that doesn't prove he found anything. Pickrang was seen in the hotel with a briefcase which we haven't recovered, so the way it looks, if he did find it, whoever offed him has got it now."

Sparks rubbed his face wearily. "Jesus, this started out as just a story for a magazine."

"So it's a mess, so what's new? It's always this way for cops – nothing's ever simple. It's only you fucking journalists who make out it's ever any different, writing things up like they happened all nice and neat."

"Some journalist – I haven't written a fucking word yet. So where's Delamore now?"

Ihaka shook his head. "Christ knows. He's hired a car and looks like he took off up north. He was talking about going to Wellsford or somewhere."

Ihaka gave Sparks a quick rundown on the Plugge-Lydiate scam and its repercussions for Wallace Guttle then stood up. "Well I'll leave you to it Sparks. You're obviously a busy man, you got TV to watch, balls to scratch. Where do I find this Quedley joker? I'll think I'll go and talk to him about his ex-employee."

CHAPTER *24*

When Herman Pickrang didn't report in that Wednesday night, Caspar Quedley took it for granted that something had gone wrong. It stands to reason, he said to himself; everything else has. Bill Tench rang him in his office the next morning to report that, as he heard it from his police contacts, Pickrang had carried out his assignment in room 1414 of the Regis Hotel; shortly thereafter though, he'd found himself on the wrong end of a sawn-off shotgun. When Quedley wondered out loud who could've pulled the trigger, Tench spluttered with amusement and replied that the police didn't know where to start looking since a gathering of the enemies of Herman Pickrang would fill Eden Park. Afterwards Quedley reflected that if Pickrang hadn't found Gage's letter in room 1414, he was back to square one; if he had, then the likelihood was that at that very moment, Gage's account of life and death at Prince Albert College would be being studied, with some interest he imagined, at the Central Police Station.

Thus Quedley's spirits and shoulders sagged when he returned to his office after an early lunch to find Detective Sergeant Tito Ihaka waiting for him. He recovered himself quickly, pumped Ihaka's hand as if meeting him was the fulfilment of a long-held ambition, and ushered him into his office. Ihaka, however, proved difficult to charm.

"Didn't you used to play in the front row for University?" asked Quedley, examining him closely.

"Me? Shit no. You must be mixing me up with some other big coon."

"Yes, well, a lot of you folk are impressive physical specimens, that's for sure," said Quedley, undeterred by Ihaka's barely disguised truculence. "It's something to do with the bones, isn't it? Now Sergeant, what can I get you – coffee, tea, or something stronger?"

Ihaka shook his head. "I'm right."

"Of course you poor buggers can't drink on duty, can you? Well if you'll excuse me, I've just had a very grim lunch with one of those born-again wowsers who live on salad and mineral water. You know what alfalfa smells like?" said Quedley getting a beer out of the small fridge under the bar. "Get a whiff of it – you'll understand why they call it spunkweed." He poured the beer and raised the tall glass to Ihaka.

"Cheers. Now how can I help you?"

"Herman Pickrang's been working for you, right?"

Quedley's brow furrowed. "Herman who?"

"Pickrang. We have reason to believe you sent him to Sydney last weekend."

Quedley chuckled. "Reason to believe – isn't that what you lot say when you haven't got a shred of evidence? I'd love to know your reason Sergeant, because I've never even heard of the man."

"I suppose you don't know Dean Delamore either?"

Quedley rubbed his chin. "Delamore you say? Now that name does ring a bell. I can check with my secretary but I seem to remember getting a call from a Delamore the other day. I couldn't get rid of him; he was babbling away about Prince Albert College – I couldn't make head or tail of it. I think he was trying to screw a donation to the chapel restoration fund out of me. You never escape them, you know. You spend five miserable teenage years there and they pursue you relentlessly for the rest of your life."

Ihaka nodded. "Yeah I know what it's like. Tamaki

College is chasing me for money to re-lay the croquet lawns. What about Julian Gage – you know him?"

"Well I used to. He's dead. If it's not asking too much, would you mind telling me what this is all about?"

Ihaka stood up. "Seeing you never heard of Pickrang, you wouldn't be interested in the fact that he was shot dead last night."

Quedley drained his beer. "My, is that so?" he said blandly. "Just as well I didn't know him then – funerals make me depressed. Who did it?"

"We don't know yet but we'll find him. The thing is, the shooter took Pickrang's briefcase and we have reason to believe – there I go again – that there was something in the briefcase that a few people around town are fizzing at the bung to get their hands on. I thought you might be one of them. Wrong again, eh?"

Ihaka watched Quedley's expression turn thoughtful. He walked out of his office and got in the lift. On the way down he reflected that if the opportunity arose, he'd get enormous satisfaction from nailing Caspar Quedley to the wall – by his no doubt perfectly proportioned dick.

After leaving Quedley's office, Ihaka drove down through Parnell, up the hill past the university, and across town to Grey Lynn. He parked in Williamson Avenue and got out of his unmarked car. He was wearing jeans, running shoes and a zip-up bomber jacket. He put on a baseball cap and sunglasses and walked down a side street until he reached an old stone building. It was a church-cum-social club for one of the Polynesian communities; he had an idea it was the Tongans. There didn't seem to be anyone around. Ihaka followed the path down the side of the building to the rear where there was a low embankment. There was a two-metre-high wooden fence on top of the embankment which formed the boundary of the church property. Ihaka climbed up the embankment, swore, took a deep breath and hoisted himself up the fence. He squirmed over the fence and came down in a private and well-tended backyard. Ihaka walked up the lawn towards the house, a tidy old wooden villa. He tapped on the back door.

The man who opened the door was in his early thirties. He was tall and thin and had long, unkempt blond hair, an earring, and a little triangle of white fluff under his lower lip. He wore faded jeans, cowboy boots, and a tight black T-shirt bearing the legend "Kill 'em all and let God sort it out" in large white lettering. The man's name was Blair Corvine and he was an undercover policeman. By and large Ihaka was sceptical of the value of undercover police work; it took forever to get undercover men in place and then half the information they provided couldn't be used because it might blow their cover. A lot of them also turned into giant pains in the arse; he suspected it was all the dope they smoked. Corvine, on the other hand, had always been cut out for it; in fact Ihaka used to wonder how someone with such obvious criminal inclinations had ever got into the police force in the first place.

Corvine let Ihaka in. "Hey, it's big chief Ihaka," he said. "You and the bros dispossessed any hard-working honkies lately?"

"Well my man, the fight for justice is never-ending. I tell you what, they wear you down these pakehas, bleating about how their family's been there for 150 years and how they've levelled hills and cleared a thousand acres of bush and all this shit. You wouldn't believe the crap we have to put up with. Christ, we're not unreasonable people; we let you stay here – what more do you want?"

"I'd settle for not having that oily heap of shit with the tiki on TV every other night."

"I'm afraid you'll have to be more specific."

Corvine got two cans of beer out of the fridge and handed one to Ihaka. Ihaka, who hadn't enjoyed watching Quedley savour his beer, drank it in less than a minute.

Corvine took a careful sip of his beer. "Listen, I really enjoy it when you drop in," he said, "the way you trample on my flowers and hoover my piss and that, but is there a reason for it that's got anything to do with, like, our jobs?"

"Yeah I was going to ask you about that. I mean, what is it with you and all these flowers? Why don't you grow some fucking vegetables?"

"That's the Ihaka philosophy is it – if it you can't fuck it or eat it, it's a waste of time? I guess it's difficult for someone whose great-grandfather was a cannibal to grasp the concept of aesthetic pleasure."

"Watch yourself pal, I haven't had lunch. The reason I'm here, those Eyeties from Sydney who stirred up some shit in K Road a while ago . . ."

"The Perfumos."

"Yeah, they operate from a pizza joint, don't they?"

"Sure do – up the top of Queen Street there. They do a fucking good pizza as a matter of fact, lots of anchovies. I love anchovies. You like anchovies?"

"You're a sick man, Corvine. Didn't Herman Pickrang have a run-in with them?"

"The late, great Herman? Did he ever! They sent over these two brothers to run the show for them here; the pizzeria's the front. Apparently Herman barged into the joint and stuck one of them head first into the pizza oven. They reckoned you could hear the cunt scream in Henderson. I forget which one it was, Marty or Rocco. It was the dumb one; man, this fucker's so thick, you'd have to tell him what to do if his wang was on fire."

"That's pretty dumb. So where are they now?"

"The one who got cooked went back to Sydney; the other one's still around last I heard. What's up?"

"I just wondered if they had anything to do with Pickrang getting blown away. I mean, these guys are meant to be the Mafia, aren't they? You'd have thought they'd have been after Herman."

"Yeah you would, wouldn't you?" said Corvine. "The word was they decided to call a truce but maybe they were just biding their time. Why the hell are you chasing whoever did that scumsucker? Guy deserves a medal."

"Wheels within wheels, matey. You talk to the Sydney cops now and again, don't you? Why don't you give them a ring, see if they've heard anything about the Perfumos lately? Thing is, I heard Pickrang was over there last weekend and had a run-in with a couple of guys who sound like them."

"What, make a fucking international call on my phone?"

"Come on Blair, I've seen your expense claims. I bet you make a profit on it."

Corvine made the call. It took 10 minutes, half of which was obscene badinage, and was punctuated by frequent exclamations.

"Hey chief your source is red-hot," said Corvine when he put the phone down. "Martino and Rocco bit the big one last Saturday night: one of them got a third nostril, the other got a knife through the neck. The deal went down in a place called . . ."

"Let me guess – Palm Beach, a little place just north of Sydney?"

"You're on the ball chief, by Christ you are. So now we know who zapped Herman and why. Shit, I just thought of something."

"Must be a leap year."

"You know who moves most of the Perfumo's dope here? The Blood Drinkers. Those hits last night had Blood Drinkers written all over them – drive up with a sawn-off on your lap, boom, no fucking beg your pardons. 'What? We offed the wrong guy? Shit happens, we'll try again tomorrow.' That's them to a T. I'll bet what happened was the family put them on the case when Marty and Rocco got wasted, told 'em get Plugge while you're at it. Tell you what, I pissed myself when I heard how Barry scooted down to Central waving a white flag

231

but fuck, if he's got those guys after him, it's the only way he's going to keep a head on his shoulders."

"The Blood Drinkers," said Ihaka. "That's just lovely."

Shortly after Ihaka got back to Central, he got a call from Reggie Sparks.

"How'd you get on with Quedley?"

"He's a cutie, isn't he? In a word, nowhere – he says he's never heard of Pickrang. He's lying of course. He didn't bat an eyelid when I told him Pickrang was dead and the turd's name hasn't even been released yet. He'd be happy that whoever did Pickrang's probably got Gage's letter; better than us having it and the chances are it'll be thrown away or lost or something. By the way, those guys who turned up at Palm Beach? It looks like they fucked up in the worst possible way." He told Sparks what had become of the brothers Perfumo. "So there you go," he finished. "I guess Pickrang found out what happens when you rumble with the big boys."

Sparks rang Louise Appleyard who said what a pleasant surprise it was to hear from him.

"Let's just say a surprise," said Sparks spurning the olive branch. "Going by what you said yesterday – that stuff about grudges and reputations being blackened – you and Quedley obviously talked about what Gage might've said in his letter?"

Louise decided to ignore the snub. "Caspar said he and Gage used to be quite close but they'd fallen out badly. Gage was all bitter and twisted and had threatened Caspar, more or less to destroy his reputation. He said the letter would just contain a lot of lies about him – he wasn't specific if that's what you mean."

"Did you believe him?"

There was a long pause. "Yes, but I suppose I didn't really think about it too hard."

"What does that mean?"

"It means I probably had other things on my mind at the time."

Sparks cleared his throat. "Look I want to ask Quedley a few straight questions; I'd like you to be there otherwise he'll just give me the run-around. How about it?"

"I think you might be overestimating my influence but all right. When?"

"Now, this afternoon."

They met an hour later in the reception area of Quedley Communications. Sparks, frostily polite, thanked her for obliging at such short notice. She was about to ask him how long she'd have to spend in Coventry when Quedley came out to greet them. He acted as if it was the most normal thing in the world for the two of them to turn up unannounced at his office in the middle of the afternoon. He seated them on the sofas arranged in a V formation in a corner of his office, Sparks on the two-seater, Louise on the larger. He perched on the arm of Louise's in what Sparks interpreted as a proprietorial statement. Louise, wearing snug-fitting dark green leggings and a loose white top, looked slightly anxious. Sparks, in no mood for small talk, got straight to the point.

"What happened at Prince Albert that you're so desperate to cover up?"

Quedley spread his hands and looked from Sparks to Louise with a bemused grin.

"And I thought this was a social visit. Jesus Christ, I don't mind you interrupting my work; I'm not even that bothered by the 'When did you stop beating your wife?' questions. But why drag Louise into it? What's your problem, Reggie? Are you all bent out of shape because of Louise and me so you want to make me look bad in front of her? Is that it?"

"Why stop there? Why don't you throw in my sister-in-law?"

"Your sister-in-law?" said Louise. "Where does she come into it?"

"A while ago Quedley tried to seduce her," said Sparks.

Quedley grinned ruefully. "Yes, that was rather unfortunate. When it comes to married women, I try to operate on the basis that what husbands don't know won't hurt them. How was I meant to know that Gavin was going to mount a room-to-room search?" He wagged a finger at Sparks. "But in the interests of accuracy Reggie, I must pull you up on your use of the word 'tried'. To say I tried to seduce dear old Heather implies that I failed. Now you and I both know that wasn't the case."

Sparks looked at Louise and said, "You can pick 'em." To Quedley: "She's here because I thought there was just the remotest chance that you'd be embarrassed to tell bare-faced lies in front of her."

"You're full of flattery today, aren't you? So are you here in your ace reporter role or what?"

"The chances are there won't be a story. The cops are involved now, shit, people have been murdered. It'll probably all be *sub judice* for months. Anyway, if you've got nothing to hide, what are you worried about?"

"So I have you to thank for the visit from Sergeant Plod do I? I wondered about that." Quedley heaved an exaggerated sigh and looked at the ceiling. "You're persistent, Sparks; you may be obtuse – you're certainly misguided – but you are persistent. Okay, if you really must know." He slipped down onto the sofa beside Louise. "This is strictly not for publication. As I was telling Louise, Julian was a bit of a slut at school. He used to tell me who he was playing doctors and doctors with and if I thought there was some mileage in it, I'd threaten to broadcast it far and wide unless they coughed up. It was hardly extortion on a grand scale – you know, it was hand over your pocket money or, I'll have that cake your mother brought today – but it's not the sort of thing you want written up in *New Nation*."

There was a long silence. Louise looked wonderingly at

Quedley who seemed to be examining his expensive-looking black brogues. Sparks' derisive snort broke the silence.

"Oh right, absolutely," he said, clicking his fingers. "You send a fucking psycho over to Australia because you don't want people to know that 20-odd years ago, you bullied a few spoilt kids out of some chocolate cake. You really think we're a couple of morons, don't you?"

"I can't conceive of any context in which I'd lump you together with Louise," said Quedley coldly. "I've answered your god-damn question; I can't help it if the answer doesn't suit your purposes but that's it."

"That's it huh?" said Sparks. "What about selling the exam papers?"

"Oh the history paper – I'd forgotten about that. I was quite proud of that little stunt; I broke into the master's common room to steal it and then sold copies. Fair cop, guv." He looked at Louise. "Well my sweet, now you know all my guilty secrets," he said, play-acting. "Am I beyond the pale? Does this mean you can never see me again?"

Louise looked uncertainly at Reggie, wondering if it was all over. He was sitting with his elbow on the arm of the sofa, his chin in the heel of his hand, and his eyes on Quedley. She recognised the expression; it was the same angry and disdainful look she'd got the day before.

"You know something?" said Sparks. "There's nobody dumber than a half-smart person who thinks he's really smart."

Quedley went and sat behind his desk. "I don't think that's original is it?" he said off-handedly. He pressed a button on his telephone and asked his secretary if there were any messages for him. Sparks stood in front of the desk and looked down at him.

"You don't know why Pickrang was killed, do you?"

Quedley looked up from his diary. "You still here? You've outstayed your welcome."

"When Pickrang was in Sydney, on your behalf, he killed

a couple of people – two brothers, Martino and Rocco Perfumo. The Perfumo family is involved in organised crime. Shit, why beat around the bush? They're Mafia. Now you know what those guys are like – you kill one of ours, we'll kill two of yours. Revenge is a way of life for them. If the Perfumos find out Pickrang was working for you, you'll be next in line for a shotgun facelift. And if you were going to ask 'how would they find out?' the answer is: because I'd tell them. And I'm pretty sure they'd believe me; I'd tell a good story because, you see, I was there."

Quedley sat back with his arms folded and looked steadily at Sparks who stared back. Then he picked up the phone and dialled.

"Ken? Caspar Quedley. You get *The Sydney Morning Herald* don't you? You got last Monday's handy? You mind having a quick look to see if there's anything about two brothers – someone and Rocco Perfumo – being murdered? Yep, I'll hang on." There was a short wait. "On the front page is it? What does it say?" Quedley listened for a couple of minutes, thanked his informant and hung up. He looked over at Sparks who was standing at the window with his back to him.

He coughed politely. "Sorry Reggie, what was the question?"

Sparks turned round. "Same as before: what would Gage have written that you didn't want people to read?"

Quedley walked over to the bar. "Anyone for a drink?" Louise and Sparks said no. He poured himself one from a heavy crystal decanter, added some ice, then went back to his desk. "The chaplain, a harmless old bachelor called Swindell, was infatuated with Julian," he said slowly looking at no one or nothing in particular. "He was also a masochist. He asked Julian to do things to him – I don't need to spell it out, do I? I blackmailed him. After a few weeks of it, he killed himself – drove his car into a brick wall."

"What about Bronwen Ticehurst?"

Quedley swallowed a mouthful of his drink and shook

his head. "Julian had nothing to do with Bronwen. He probably wouldn't even remember her. It's true, some people said it was my fault but how was I to know what a state she was in? I just told her the truth – that I didn't want to be tied to one girl. Christ, I never dreamt she'd go and kill herself."

"Have you heard from Dean Delamore?" asked Sparks.

Quedley nodded. "He offered to sell me the letter," he said dully. "Then he changed his mind, said he was going to talk to someone else."

"Who would that be?"

"I don't know. I wasn't sure if he was serious. I thought he was just going to make me squirm for a couple of days then come back to me."

Louise Appleyard went over and stood beside Quedley. "Caspar, why on earth did you do those things?"

He looked up at her. "My family . . . we weren't very well off. My father was a vicar and earned next to nothing. I only went to Prince Albert because clergymen's sons got a big discount. I saw how other families lived, the families of the boys I got friendly with. It was a different world, I mean money simply wasn't an issue for them. Say if little Simon wanted to go and stay with his friend in Fiji in the holidays? 'Well of course you can dear. Si-Si needs some spending money? Will $1,000 be enough? Let's make it $1,500 to be on the safe side.' When I wanted a new pair of shoes because I felt such a jerk wearing my black ones out of school, it was a major expenditure decision – my parents argued about it for a week. Then my mother died. All we'd ever really had was each other and that was taken away – we weren't even a family anymore. It just seemed like we had nothing and everyone else had too much."

Quedley sat with his head bowed. He reached out and took Louise's hand; she let him do it, neither withdrawing nor responding.

Sparks said, "Boo fucking hoo," and walked out of Quedley's office.

CHAPTER 25

**R**eggie Sparks sat behind the steering wheel of his mother's Peugeot, which was parked a little way up Parnell Rise from Quedley's office, pondering his next move. He'd made up his mind and was about to start the car when he heard his name being called. He looked up. Louise Appleyard was running up the footpath towards him. With her trim form, her dark hair bouncing on her shoulders and, as Sparks couldn't help noticing, her breasts bobbing perkily beneath the loose top, she looked as if she'd stepped straight from the pages of some glossy healthy living magazine. He wound down the car window.

She was panting slightly. "Are you in a mad rush?" she breathed.

He shrugged. "Not especially."

She walked around to the other side of the car and got into the passenger seat.

"That was a charming exit line," she said. "Didn't you feel even the slightest bit sorry for him?"

He looked at her incredulously. "Sorry for Quedley? You've got to be joking. As for the *Little House on the Prairie* routine, Jesus Christ." He shook his head. "How I managed to keep my lunch down, I'll never know."

"Didn't you believe him?"

"The stuff about his family? Yeah, I believed him – it's pretty much what I'd heard. But so what? Most kids feel hard done by at some stage. And what about the hypocrisy of getting his hooks into the chaplain? Presumably the poor bastard was no better off than Quedley's old man."

She raised her eyebrows non-committally. "What about the rest of it?"

"Hard to say. I still think he knows more about the girl's death than he's letting on. Once I'd hit him with the Perfumos though, I didn't have anything else to pressure him with."

"God yes, what was all that about? Did you really see those men get murdered?"

"Well, not exactly. I wouldn't be here if I had've."

"Tell the truth, Reggie: would you've really gone through with it?"

Sparks' mouth curved into a tight, coldly amused smile. Louise Appleyard was no longer in any doubt that Reggie Sparks possessed a mean streak. The only question was how big and for the second time that afternoon she found herself wondering if she'd underestimated the size of it.

"Shit yes," said Sparks. He held the smile for several seconds. "I still might."

She looked back at him, eyes narrowing. "I don't believe you."

Sparks looked away. "Relax Louise, I won't set the dogs on lover boy. You can scuttle back and tell him mission accomplished."

She laughed mirthlessly. "You know, you can be extremely bloody objectionable when you put your mind to it. As a matter of fact, I'm here because I wanted to let you know that that crack he made, implying that you were jealous – I didn't put the idea in his head."

Sparks gave a shrug of indifference. "You didn't need to. That's just the way his mind works."

"You're not a big fan, are you?"

"I actually quite like him in a funny sort of way," said Sparks mildly. "But the guy's an arsehole; it doesn't matter what you feel or I think, that's it." He twisted round in his seat to look at her. "You know how he gets away with it? He doesn't try to hide it; he lets people in on the secret – hey folks, look at me, I'm a walking, talking arsehole. People enjoy it because he's got a bit of style and because he says and does what they'd like to if they had the guts. Because he's upfront, they think it's an act; they think he's putting it on and deep down, he's not half as self-centred and contemptuous of the rest of us as he pretends. In fact, it's not a facade – he really is an arsehole."

Louise would've liked to have continued the conversation but Sparks brought it to a close by starting the car. She got out and held the door open.

"Where are you off to now?"

"I think I'll head up north," he said. "Who knows? I might find a damsel in distress."

What with having to go home and make sure it was okay with his mother to have her car for the evening and getting caught in the rush-hour Harbour Bridge traffic, Sparks didn't get to Looms' farm until just before 8pm. He followed the drive up to the house, parked right by the front door, and got out of the car. Loud rock music was coming from inside the house. Dermot Looms – rock 'n' roll animal, thought Sparks; I wouldn't have picked it. To the right of the house was a double garage. The roller door was raised and as he'd driven up, his headlights had illuminated a car parked inside. He went over for a closer look. The car was a Honda Civic sedan. It was unlocked and when he opened the driver's side door, the interior light came on. A plastic bag with a Hertz logo hung from one of the knobs on the dashboard. The paperwork showing the car had been rented by Dean Delamore was in the glovebox.

Sparks walked up the steps to the front door and knocked. There was no response. The music was incredibly loud. The bugger must be deaf, he thought. When three sets of knocks went unanswered, he began hammering. After 12 heavy thumps which shook the solid wooden door, it was opened by Basil Batrouney who blinked owlishly behind his thick lenses.

The corridor reverberated to Mick Jagger's lubricious screech: "Oh yeah, you're a strange stray cat/Oh yeah, don't you scratch my back/Oh yeah, you're a strange stray cat/I bet your momma don't know you scream like that/I bet your momma don't know you can sweat like that." Sparks found it vaguely disturbing that Batrouney should be listening to a song celebrating sex with minors.

"Could you turn the music down," Sparks bellowed, making a twisting gesture with his right hand.

Batrouney nodded once and ambled off down the corridor. Sparks followed him into the living room. The music was thundering out of a new-looking stereo system set on a sideboard against the far wall. Batrouney turned the volume right down and looked questioningly at Sparks.

"Who are you?" he said finally.

"Reggie Sparks," he said, his voice sounding strident in the hush. "I'm a journalist. I came to see you a while ago on Waiheke. You showed me your comic, what's it called – *Grub*?" he added in the hope the reference might trigger a reaction in the former rock star's burnt-out brain.

There was no indication in Batrouney's large moist eyes that a mental connection was in progress but something must have clicked.

"I remember you," he said, an accusatory note entering his voice. "You didn't like Jack Stack."

"Oh well you know, I guess it's an acquired taste," said Sparks weakly. "I'm sure if I read a few more . . ." Wait a minute, he told himself, you didn't come up here to exchange toilet talk with this anal retentive zombie. He changed the subject. "What brings you up here? I thought you were pretty much a homebody these days."

"Visiting Dermie. My friend."

Dermie and Baz? Talk about the odd couple. "Is Mr Looms about?"

Batrouney shook his head.

Sparks moved closer. "There's someone else here though, isn't there Basil? A man called Dean Delamore?"

Batrouney's large globular head vibrated violently. "No way Jose, no way."

"I know he's here, Baz. That's his car in the garage." He took Batrouney by the right arm, above the elbow. His fingers sank into soft, doughy flesh. "Where is he?"

Batrouney's head dropped and he tried to pull away. Sparks jerked him back and said in a hard voice, "Where the bloody hell is he? I want you to show me right now."

Sparks pushed Batrouney towards the doorway. Batrouney, his head still bowed, led him into the huge kitchen and took a key from a row of hooks by the back door. He went out the back door and down a few steps to a below-ground doorway. He unlocked the door and stood aside.

Sparks peered through the door into darkness. "In here?"

Batrouney nodded.

"Give us the keys."

Batrouney handed them over. Sparks took a couple of steps down into the cellar. Just then he remembered Batrouney saying at their previous meeting that he no longer listened to rock music. It occurred to Sparks that perhaps everything else the former rock star had told him was a lie but before he could advance this proposition, he was struck a fierce blow on the back of the head. He lost his footing, careered down the remaining few steps, and sprawled on the cold concrete floor. As he lay there stunned, jarred and disoriented, he felt the keys being ripped from his grasp and heard receding footsteps and the cellar door being slammed shut and locked, plunging the cellar into utter darkness.

Outside Basil Batrouney thoughtfully hefted the heavy

242

doubled-handed secateurs then dropped them back into the wheelbarrow parked by the cellar door. He said, "Good work, Batman," in a deep Hollywood voice and went back inside to listen to the other side of *Beggars Banquet*.

Sparks rolled onto his back and sat up. Blood trickled over his fingers as he gently prodded the welt which had already come up on the back of his head. As it dawned on him that he'd been out-smarted by someone whom he'd characterised, a few minutes earlier, as a zombie, Dean Delamore's hesitant voice came out of the darkness: "Is that you, Reggie?"

"No it's not," said Sparks with some bitterness. "It's Sir Lancelot."

Basil Batrouney felled Sparks with the secateurs at 8.25 that Thursday night. At 10pm police teams launched simultaneous raids on several premises in South Auckland believed to be occupied by leading members of the Blood Drinkers gang. Tito Ihaka led the team whose target was a flat in Otara, the last known address of Luther "Bad Louie" Potau. However, in keeping with his promise to himself, Ihaka was not the first man through the door; that distinction fell to an extremely gung-ho 26-year-old constable and member of the Armed Offenders Squad. Ihaka wondered if anyone had explained to the constable that his state-of-the-art rifle and flak jacket didn't guarantee complete protection against a sociopath with a sawn-off shotgun.

At the time of the raid Potau was sitting on a sofa watching television in the living room-cum-kitchen at the rear of the flat. He was surrounded by assorted debris including the packaging which had contained his supper – $35 worth of Kentucky Fried Chicken – and the leftover bones. A 19-year-old girl, whose name Potau was pretty sure was Christine but whom he called "woman" or "bitch" depending on his mood and who threw a better punch than any of his four previous de facto wives, sat on his lap. Christine had consumed four large

243

bottles of beer and three stiff bourbon and cokes and was quite drunk. Potau, who liked to begin the day with a couple of bottles of stout but who never drank beer after sundown on principle, was just over halfway through his nightly intake of a litre of dark rum and therefore more or less sober, albeit not by any medical or legal definition.

When Ihaka banged on the door and bellowed "Police, open up", Potau went to shove Christine off his lap. However shifting 110kg of dead weight took some doing and by the time she'd been tipped onto the floor, the door had been breached and he could hear the raiders advancing down the corridor. Potau carefully set down the bottle of rum and picked up an empty beer bottle. He straightened up to find a rifle being pointed at him by a tall figure in a dark boiler suit who instructed him not to fucking well move. Ihaka entered the room just as Potau released an unearthly roar and commenced his charge. Having to negotiate his way over and around the recumbent Christine, two beer crates and the back seat from a 1966 Zodiac, which served as seating when he and Christine entertained, prevented Potau from building up much speed and saved his life. It gave Ihaka time to step around the constable and stop Potau in his tracks by clubbing him ferociously hard across the face with a baseball bat.

The subsequent search of Potau's flat proved productive: the sawn-off shotgun used on Pickrang and Gilpin was found under the bed; Pickrang's briefcase was amid the chest-high weeds in the backyard; and Julian Gage's memoir of Prince Albert College was on the kitchen table, splattered with grease and surrounded by unwashed dishes. Christine had made a shopping list on the back of one page and begun a letter to her mother in Gisborne on the back of another.

CHAPTER *26*

When Luther Potau woke up, he was taken to the Otara police station to be questioned about the murders of Herman Pickrang and Cec Gilpin. His sullen silence was standard Blood Drinkers' practise so it was some time before his interrogators realised that his speechlessness was not a matter of choice. He was ferried, under heavy guard, to Middlemore Hospital where X-rays of his spectacularly splintered facial bone structure swiftly became collector's items. At the Otara station Tito Ihaka re-read Julian Gage's letter before sending it into Central for Inspector Finbar McGrail's attention. Then he found himself a quiet corner and made three calls.

The first was to Reggie Sparks who, he learned from Mareena, had taken off up north somewhere and wasn't expected back till later. Her tone implied that it was already late. Under normal circumstances, Ihaka might've hesitated to ask her to go in search of the list of names and addresses which Dean Delamore had ripped out of her son's notebook but these were not normal circumstances. Because Mareena derived some comfort from Ihaka's interest in her wayward son, she did so. She found the list where her son had left it, in the downstairs TV room, and told Ihaka what he wanted to know, which was where Dermot Looms lived.

Ihaka thought long and hard before he made his next call. The obvious thing to do was to ring the Wellsford cops.

He imagined the conversation with whoever was on duty at the Wellsford station at that hour of the night: let's see, we've got a hanged girl at a private school ball in 1970, a dead witness and a blackmailing transvestite. And that's just for starters. What the fuck would they make of that in Wellsford? Christ, if someone rang him out of the blue at 11 o'clock at night with a story like that, he'd think the guy had been into the confiscated drugs. And assuming he convinced Wellsford to take it seriously, how about if they rousted a few guys out of bed and sent them out to Looms' place and the whole thing turned out to be a load of crap, a malicious fabrication? No two ways about it, he'd be the laughing stock of the entire police force.

So instead of ringing Wellsford, Ihaka's second call was to Blair Corvine, the undercover policeman.

"Mate, I need a gun."

There was a long silence. "Chief, last time I looked, we had more guns at Central than the fucking army so would you mind explaining why you're ringing me at this hour?"

"It's pretty complicated and I'm really stuck for time – let's just say it's a grey area."

"Now chief, think about this. Think about it very carefully. This sounds like it could be one of those fork-in-the-road-type decisions."

"Who wants promotion anyway? Just more fucking paperwork."

There was another silence. "It's your career buddy. What do you want?"

"A revolver will do."

"Oh just a revolver? I can't interest you in an Uzi machine pistol, you know 600 rounds a minute? What about a shoulder-launched missile, you let it go from the top of One Tree Hill and knock down the fucking Town Hall? Really get the job done."

"You're tempting me, you silver-tongued devil, but I'll settle for a revolver. Can you have it for me in an hour?"

They arranged to do the handover at midnight, by the Victoria Park pavilion.

Ihaka's third call was to Louise Appleyard. It was intended as a courtesy call, to let her know that they'd found Julian Gage's letter to her late husband. It turned out to be rather more than that.

"When can I read it?" was her first question.

"I don't know. We have to treat it like evidence so we can't go handing it round to the public."

"I'm not asking out of vague curiosity Sergeant," said Louise in clipped tones, "and I'm hardly just another member of the public."

"I'm well aware of that Mrs Appleyard. That's why I called in the first place."

"Well you've obviously read it; tell me what it says."

"Look I'm very sorry but I just don't have time. I'm a bit worried about your journalist friend Sparks."

"I saw Reggie this afternoon – he was okay. He said something about going up north."

"That's what worries me and that's where I'm off to now which is why . . ."

"What's up north Sergeant?"

Ihaka was wishing he'd never made the call. "A bloke called Dermot Looms."

"He was at the ball, wasn't he? Do you suspect him of something?"

"You could say that."

"I've got an excellent idea Sergeant. I'll go with you and you can brief me – isn't that what policemen say? – about the letter on the way."

Ihaka protested but Louise became very emphatic about how her late husband had started the whole thing and didn't that entitle her to some consideration? Ihaka thought of falling back on the excuse that it was police business but strictly speaking that wasn't the case. And while Ihaka could be an accomplished liar when the need arose, he couldn't think of a single reason – apart from the obvious one of behaving like a responsible police officer – why he should deprive himself of the company of an attractive woman for the midnight drive.

It was 1.15am but the lights were still on in Looms' house when Ihaka pulled in behind Mrs Sparks' Peugeot which was still parked right by the front door.

"That's Reggie's car," said Louise.

Ihaka grunted and got the pistol out of the glovebox. In the deep, rural stillness, the music from the house was quite audible. It was Jimi Hendrix's *Hey Joe*, not that Ihaka recognised it, Hendrix having been a little before his time. "Listen to that," he said. "Sounds like they're having a party." He put the pistol back in the glovebox. "Guess I won't be needing it."

He told Louise, "You stay here – if I'm not back in 10 minutes, take off," and got out of the car. He walked up to the front door and knocked. No one came to the door. After he'd knocked again without response, Ihaka made his way around the side of the house.

The knocking startled Basil Batrouney. His friend Dermie had been due back half an hour before but, late or not, why should he knock when he had keys? Perhaps it was another of the nosey parkers with whom the Looms spread, despite its isolation, seemed to be infested. Batrouney decided to reconnoitre rather than answer the door. The upshot was that as Ihaka rounded the rear corner of the house and entered the rose garden, he trod heavily on the toes of an odd-looking specimen carrying a single-barrelled pump-action shotgun.

The former rock star received the bigger fright but not by much. Batrouney's perceptions of nosey parkers were largely based on Delamore and Sparks, neither of whom could be said to be physically intimidating. The third intruder had physical presence to burn as testified to by the appalling pain in his left

248

foot. For his part, Ihaka had had quite enough of lunatics with shotguns for one night. While this weirdo looked far less savage than Potau, Ihaka's instant impression was that he'd give Bad Louie a decent run for his money in the lunacy stakes.

They recoiled from the contact and eyed one another apprehensively for a few tense seconds.

"Whoa, take it easy amigo," said Ihaka holding up his hands in surrender. "I'm not looking for trouble. Sorry about the hour but I've got an urgent message for Dermot Looms. You him?"

Batrouney tightened his shaky grip on the shotgun and shook his head. Ihaka shifted his focus to a point over Batrouney's shoulder and flashed a bright grin. "You must be Dermot, right?"

The little charade was executed so smoothly that it would've taken in more alert individuals than Batrouney. Furthermore, being left alone to cope with the influx had made Batrouney fretful and therefore more susceptible to one of the older tricks in the book. His head whipped round as if on a spring. Ihaka shot out his right arm and wrenched the shotgun from his grasp. Batrouney looked back at Ihaka, appearing not to notice that he'd been disarmed.

"I can't see Dermie," he wailed. "Where is he?"

"My mistake," said Ihaka. "A trick of the moonlight." He leaned forward and tugged gently on Batrouney's woolly pullover. "Who are you?"

"Baz."

"Basil Batrouney?"

The former rock star nodded nervously.

"Well fuck me, the gang's all here," said Ihaka cheerfully. "Where's Sparks?"

"Who?"

Ihaka tightened his grip. "Reggie Sparks. His car's parked right outside the front door."

"I haven't seen him, I haven't seen anyone," jabbered

Batrouney. "I've just been grooving with Jimi and waiting for Dermie to come home."

Ihaka shifted his grip, gathering a handful of pullover from just below the neck. He jerked violently, hauling Batrouney up onto his toes. He put his face up to Batrouney's. "Do you want a fucking good hiding?" he asked in a tone of mild curiosity.

"Don't hurt me," moaned Batrouney, tears welling up in his eyes. "I'll show you."

He limped to the back door, took the key off the hook, led Ihaka down to the cellar door, and unlocked it. Ihaka stepped in front of him and pushed the door open. "Sparks," he called out. "It's Ihaka. You down there?"

"Look out," yelled Sparks from the darkness.

Ihaka whirled. Batrouney, teeth bared, stood on tiptoe with the secateurs raised above his head. As he began the down-swing, Ihaka reversed the shotgun and jabbed the butt into his face, fracturing the former rock star's glasses as well as his nose. Batrouney shrieked piercingly and buried his face in his hands. Ihaka grabbed him by the pullover and held him at arm's length. "It's okay," he called into the cellar. "Come on out."

Sparks came out first followed by Delamore who had two perfect black eyes and whose badly bruised face glowed eerily in the half light coming from the kitchen window.

"Thanks for the warning," said Ihaka. "He get you that way, did he?"

Sparks nodded and gingerly rubbed the back of his head. "He sure did."

"Well if it's any consolation, I just gave him a fair poke right on the snotbox." He pushed Batrouney towards the door. "Okay pal, your turn in the dungeon."

Batrouney started to whimper and flap his arms but Ihaka shoved him roughly through the cellar door and locked it behind him.

Louise Appleyard was leaning back against the railing which fenced off the paddock to the right of Looms' house looking at the stars. She was getting cold and about to go back to the car when she saw headlights turn into the drive. The car came halfway up the drive but stopped when its headlights picked up the two cars parked in front of the house. The engine and lights were switched off and Louise heard a car door open and close. She moved deeper into the shadow of the garage.

Delamore, Ihaka and Sparks had just found a bottle of Scotch in a kitchen cupboard when Looms walked in the back door. He looked around slowly, took off his jacket and hung it over the back of a chair.

"Help yourself, why don't you?"

"Don't mind if I do," said Ihaka and took a hefty gulp. "You'd be Looms."

"And who might you be?"

"Ihaka's my name, Detective Sergeant out of Auckland Central."

Looms nodded impassively. "You're a ways from home, aren't you?" He walked over to the table, picked up the whisky bottle and took a swig. Ihaka casually dropped a hand on the stock of Batrouney's shotgun which lay on the table in front of him.

"Still, seeing you're here, Mr Detective Sergeant," said Looms, "I'd like to lay a complaint against Nancy Boy over there." He nodded at Delamore. "The cheeky little poof tried to blackmail me."

"Really?" said Ihaka. He studied Delamore who smiled shyly. "He looks as if he's got something to complain about himself." Ihaka turned back to Looms. "You know, there's one surefire way to take the wind out of his sails – just own up that you murdered Bronwen Ticehurst."

Looms frowned and was rubbing his chin as if he was seriously considering the suggestion when Lloyd Chennell slipped in the back door and pointed a .22 rifle at Ihaka.

"I don't think so," he said. "That would mean an awful lot of effort had been to no avail. Now if you'll put up your hands and step away from the table . . ."

They were in the living room, Delamore and Sparks sitting by the window on a large sofa with Ihaka in an armchair to their left. Looms and Chennell were on the other side of the room by the door, Chennell in an armchair with the rifle between his knees, its butt on the floor, and Looms on his feet, handling the shotgun like an extension of his arm.

Looms was speaking. "It's been a shit of a night, I don't mind telling you. First of all, I had to flag the Regis because there was a cop stationed outside the room, then Lloyd's flight was late . . ."

"Yoo hoo, anyone home?" Louise Appleyard's voice floated down the corridor from the back door. Sparks shot a horrified look at Ihaka who gave a short shake of his head, put his chin on his chest and massaged his forehead. Chennell, wide-eyed, turned to Looms who said "I don't fucking well believe this . . ." He held the shotgun down by his side and put his head round the door.

"Hi there," said Louise advancing down the corridor. "Pardon me for barging in but I seem to have mislaid my driver."

"He's probably in here," said Looms. "Half of Auckland is."

Louise entered the room. "Oh there you are," she said brightly, apparently oblivious to the charged atmosphere. "I got sick of sitting in the car so . . ." Her face fell as she noticed Chennell's rifle. "What's going on?"

Looms showed the shotgun. "Why don't you hop over there on that sofa?"

Louise sat next to Delamore, her hands clasped together between her knees but otherwise looking remarkably composed. Sparks did his best to give her an encouraging smile.

252

"Is that the lot?" said Looms wonderingly. "Or are there a few more wandering around out there?"

"You must be Dermot Looms," said Louise. "Is it true what Julian Gage wrote about you?"

Ihaka started to look up, then thought better of it. Looms looked puzzled. "How come you've seen that?" he asked.

"The sergeant showed it to me on the way up here," she said. Everyone exchanged glances. Louise looked at Ihaka. "Shouldn't I've said that?" she asked anxiously. Ihaka looked up, spluttered, and looked back at his shoes.

Looms guffawed. "Well bugger me. Here's me running all over the show looking for that bloody thing and we've got a door-to-door delivery." He stopped short. "Jesus, I completely forgot about Baz – where the hell is he?" He glared at Ihaka. "You didn't shove him in the cellar did you, you lousy bastard? The poor bugger'll be going frantic."

Looms swapped guns with Chennell. "I'm going to let Baz out and get Gage's letter," he said. "If they try anything Lloyd, let 'em have it." He left the room.

Chennell stood up and held the shotgun across his stomach, pointing away from his captives. When Louise heard the back door open and close, she reached under her loose white top and pulled Ihaka's revolver out of the waistband of her leggings. She pointed it at Chennell and told him to put his gun down.

Chennell stood stock still. Louise sat on the edge of the sofa holding the pistol at arm's length in both hands. Her eyes stayed on Chennells' face like a spotlight but she was struggling to hold the pistol steady.

"My dear," said Chennell huskily, "are you really prepared to kill me?"

The back door opened. The pistol wavered in Louise's grip. Chennell breathed deeply and shifted his hands on the shotgun.

"You do realise Louise," said Sparks conversationally, "that these fuckers killed Victor?"

Chennell saw something red flare at the back of Louise's eyes a split-second before she shot him through the fatty deposit above his right hip, the area sometimes referred to as a "love handle". He squealed, dropped the gun and clutched his wound.

Ihaka leapt across the room and snatched up the shotgun. He peered into the corridor. Batrouney was standing in the kitchen doorway fumbling with the rifle. There was no sign of Looms. Ihaka told Batrouney to drop the rifle. Batrouney squinted down the corridor, screamed "You locked me in the dark" and raised the rifle. At that moment Looms, having failed to find Gage's letter in either car and alarmed by the gunshot, opened the front door and received a bullet, meant for Ihaka, in the Adam's apple. He made an horrendous gurgling sound, fell over backwards, and proceeded to die noisily on the front porch. Ihaka hurriedly lined up on Batrouney's legs and fired. His intention was to disable Batrouney without killing him and in that he succeeded. His aim being high, he also put paid to the prospect of there ever being any little Batrouneys, not that the former rock star had shown any inclination towards reproductive activity for the better part of two decades.

# CHAPTER *27*

*T*en days later Reggie Sparks received a letter
from Tito Ihaka. It said:

Kia ora Reggie boy,
Just to let you know where things are at, it looks like
we're going to close the book on the whole thing.
Batrouney hasn't said a word since the gunfight at the
OK Corral – I know he wasn't too flash to start with
but he's just a veggie now.

Chennell's a different kettle of shit: if we really bust
a gut, we might be able to get him on some sort of
conspiracy charge but those turkeys in the crown
prosecutor's office aren't being much help – "in view of
the most unusual circumstances of this case, we
couldn't proceed against Mr Chennell with any real
degree of confidence". You wouldn't believe the mealy-
mouthed crap those characters come up with. Up at
the farm, he didn't actually do that much apart from
giving Calamity Jane a bit of target practice. There is a
school of thought around here (ie me) which feels that
the precise details of what happened up there should be
allowed to fade into obscurity – if you get my drift. As
you'd expect, anything to do with Bronwen Ticehurst
just goes straight into the "too hard" file. We let
Chennell know that, whatever happens, his school in

Sydney would hear all about it – his lawyer reckons he's already resigned – but we'll tell them anyway to bugger up his job prospects. Apart from that he'll probably walk.

Part of the reason we went easy on Chennell, as I guess you've heard from Louise, is that he explained what happened to her husband. After Gage told Appleyard the answer was on the dance card, he starting working his way through the names (and hired Guttle to check out Lydiate). He went and saw Batrouney on Waiheke and apparently coaxed part of the story out of him. When Batrouney realised what he'd done, he went frothing off to Looms. Looms set up a meeting with Appleyard somewhere here in town and pulled the same trick he pulled on Dolores Delamore – Baz in the back seat with a gun. About four in the morning they made Appleyard drive onto the Bridge with Looms in his car right behind, stopped at the top, and Looms just manhandled him over the edge. If they'd been really unlucky, they might've been spotted on the monitor but the cameras don't cover the whole Bridge the whole time and whoever was on duty was probably doing the crossword anyway. Fair go – some of the kids joining the force these days don't even move their lips when they read. He was a hard man, Looms. Good job Batrouney was such a fucking lousy shot.

Anyway, the insurance company has been advised so Louise gets her dough after all. While we're on that subject, a word of advice – strike while the iron's hot. It's obvious that you're keen on her but a woman like that won't be on her tod for long. I didn't realise she'd actually gone a few rounds with Quedley but I gather that's history. She told me you opened her eyes to what a complete cunt he was or words to that effect. That's not a bad start. Wasn't it Mahatma Gandhi who said that if you can open a woman's eyes, her legs will soon follow? Maybe it was Errol Flynn.

Well on that philosophical note, I'll sign off. Seeing there shouldn't be any legal complications, you can go full steam ahead on your story. Just go easy when you reach the bit about unregistered handguns popping up out of nowhere and retards getting shotgun vasectomies etc. Attached is a copy of Gage's letter which I thought might help. I don't ask much in return – just that your story should make it clear that my role in this little saga amounted to the niftiest piece of intuitive policework since the Crewe murder case. I'll also be very dark if you don't expose Quedley as a shiteating swine. You can quote me on that.

Hasta la vista

Chief Inspector Tito Ihaka (only a matter of time after the article comes out).

PS Burn this.

Sparks turned to Julian Gage's letter to Victor Appleyard.

Dear Victor,

First of all, let me repeat how very much I appreciated your gesture in the restaurant that night. I hope I'm wrong but I strongly suspect that very few men in your position would break off from a business dinner to speak to someone whose appearance rather encourages others to assume the worst. I also enjoyed and appreciated your subsequent visits and our chats. Many thanks too for the books. I know it's customary to tell giftgivers that they shouldn't have but I'll skip that fib and simply say I enjoyed them enormously, particularly the Jan Morris book about Venice which brought back some wonderful memories.

To say that your comments about poor Bronwen Ticehurst set me thinking would be a gross under-statement; I've thought of little else. I was deeply moved that you haven't forgotten Bronwen and are still troubled by her death (and deeply shamed by the invidious contrast with my own behaviour).

Once or twice I was on the verge of telling you the whole story but I just couldn't bring myself to do so. I suppose it's just a case that I've suppressed it for so long, I now find it terribly difficult to contemplate, let alone talk about. No doubt you found my coyness aggravating. I dare say my gesture of producing Bronwen's dance card with accompanying hints struck you as self-indulgently theatrical. I apologise. As I say, I have buried the knowledge of that episode so deep within me that it requires an immense, almost physical, effort to dredge it up again and these days my physical resources are limited. I might also say, in mitigation of my coyness, self-indulgence and theatricality, that it's not easy to break the habits of a lifetime.

Anyway so much for explanations and self-justification. Today has been rather a momentous day. I have finally come to terms with the fact of my imminent death. My doctor, bless him, still goes through convolutions to avoid stating the obvious and to find an aspect of my impressive range of ailments about which he can say something remotely encouraging. Like me however, he is fighting a losing battle, the futility of which becomes more pronounced by the day. His whole demeanour delivers an unmistakable message which he can't bring himself to put into words. In the wider scheme of things of course, this is making a drama out of the all-too-mundane; after all, I could hardly expect the laws of nature and medicine to be suspended on my behalf, could I? Nonetheless one lives in hope. Well I no longer do. I shall now concentrate on dying in peace.

The significance of my embracing fatalism is that it has concentrated the mind on the task of clearing out the emotional and spiritual baggage which I either won't need or don't want where I'm going. I have therefore resolved to tell you the full story of what happened at Prince Albert College in 1970. I shall write it down and have it sent to you when I've shuffled off this mortal coil. I know that's somewhat cowardly but it's the only way I can do it. It also has for me the immense attraction that I won't have to live with the knowledge of your contempt, for assuredly that is what you'll feel towards me when you've finished this letter. Your friendship and sympathy have meant a great deal to me and I am selfish enough to want to retain them for the short while I have left.

To begin at the beginning: I'm not sure how old I was when I began to suspect that I was gay but certainly by the time I started at Prince Albert in 1968. Of course, you were a day boy and I'm not sure how much naughtiness went on amongst the day boys. In most of the boarding house dormitories though, there was a constant hum of furtive activity, mostly what we called "mutuals" – tossing off the boy in the next bed after lights out providing he'd return the favour.

If I had to put a figure on it, I'd estimate that at least 50 per cent of boarders indulged in boy-boy sex. It had nothing at all to do with homosexuality in the sense of that being their sexual preference; it was simply a case of deprivation, through being in an all-male environment, on the one hand, and opportunity on the other. Sheer proximity is, after all, the most potent aphrodisiac. I can't say I ever came across anyone who refused to indulge because they had fierce moral objections; most of the non-participants either had extremely modest sexual appetites or were too timid or were so repulsive that no one with an ounce of self-respect would handle them wearing ski mitts.

As I say, there was no particular opprobrium attached to it in one's first and second year but once one reached the fifth form, it was a different matter. To continue from that point was considered to denote a preference; far healthier to satisfy one's urges in privacy with a *Playboy* and a wankie hankie. Those who kept at it were either too ugly or socially inept to get their fingers up during the holidays (excuse the coarseness but the disgusting schoolboy phraseology keeps popping into my head), or were blessed or cursed with excessive randiness or belonged to the tiny minority who just preferred boys and didn't give a hoot for the consequences in terms of being whispered about, sneered at or bullied. With all due modesty, I was the outstanding example of the latter. I have no doubt that I was the most sexually active Prince Albertian of my era; a respectable but nonetheless distant second would have been Caspar Quedley, which is where the tale really begins.

I became infatuated with Caspar in 1969, an easy enough date to remember. He was scarcely aware of my existence; with me being a second year and him a fourth year there were, under the rigid hierarchy of the boarding houses, limited opportunities for contact. Early the following year, however, we were both in the school play, Julius Caesar. Caspar was a thrilling Mark Antony while I had a non-speaking part as one of the friends, Romans, countrymen whose ears he borrowed. In the course of the rehearsals, I managed to inveigle my way into his acquaintance and, at the first opportunity, proclaimed my love and put myself at his disposal. Caspar wasn't in the least embarrassed or perturbed. He said he was flattered but didn't think it was quite his cup of Earl Grey; if he ever changed his mind or felt the inclination to experiment, he'd know where to come, as it were.

We became friends. We were both outsiders, in my case because of my hotly and widely rumoured filthy and unnatural tendencies; in Caspar's because he saw himself as underprivileged – it never ceased to amaze me how someone so well-endowed could feel so deprived – and this drew us together. Caspar didn't give a damn and had a perverse sense of humour so it amused him, being the official college stud, to ostentatiously keep company with the college queer. He also took an intense interest in what I got up to and insisted on being kept fully informed of my dalliances. I thought this was rather promising until I discovered that he was extracting money from some of my partners on threat of exposure. I was furious but Caspar could talk his way out of anything. He was also a very skilful flirt which kept alive the tantalising prospect of my yearnings being reciprocated, in my mind at least.

I was quite a holy boy, believe it or not. I was in the choir, by that stage a light tenor after a stint as the boy soprano – you might have heard me doing the *Once in Royal David's City* solo at the end-of-year carol service. I was also a sacristan which involved helping the chaplain, Padre Swindell, with various little chores around the chapel. The chaplain took a shine to me and was forever inviting me into his flat for a cup of tea and a chocolate biscuit. I thought nothing of this until one night he completely floored me by producing a cane and imploring me to thrash him. Not wanting to seem churlish, I obliged and the poor old thing just about put his back out trying to conceal his erection.

I'm sure you can guess the rest. I told Caspar who straightaway saw the commercial possibilities. The next time I took tea with the chaplain, I left the door off the lock and Caspar just happened to wander in while I was administering the medicine. He pretended to be shocked, horrified, revolted etc – he really was a superb actor – then told me to clear off so he could negotiate the price of his silence. Caspar told me afterwards that the chaplain was as worried about me as about his own position: he said something to the effect that "Julian is innocent in every sense of the word; he has no idea that he was providing me with gratification". That made it even worse when he drove his car into a brick wall a few weeks later.

Although it was presented as an accident, the rumours of suicide were soon rife. I worked myself up into a real state. Caspar eventually gave me a talking to: yes, Padre Swindell had killed himself, he said, but it had nothing to do with us. He claimed the chaplain had told him he had an incurable disease, hence the suicide. It was a lie, of course, as he admitted a few years later. He was worried that I'd break down and confess all and had made up the story to subdue my conscience.

After that you'd think we'd have shied away from these dangerous games but not a bit of it. The next to find his way into the honey trap was Lloyd Chennell, who taught history as you'd remember and was assistant house master in my house. However Lloyd was far from being the passive, guilt-ridden soul that Padre Swindell had been. I began picking up unmistakable signals from him and one night in his study, in the course of reviewing my academic performance, came the inevitable hand on the knee.

Although Lloyd was certainly no matinee idol, he was really my first sexual partner who was more experienced than I – he was about 26 then as I remember. A number of the boys I'd been with were older than me but I was always the knowing one, the one in control. Lloyd was quite adroit; he had the touch. Some do and some don't and, in my experience, it's almost impossible to tell in advance. Nor does having the touch seem to bear much, if any, relation to a person's general sexiness either in terms of their appearance or their ardour. Some of my most handsome and ardent lovers have been the most ham-fisted.

Of course I told Caspar and shortly thereafter he struck terms with Lloyd. It all seemed to be conducted in a very civilised manner. Lloyd certainly never took umbrage with me for telling Caspar although I suppose, in hindsight, he was rather addicted to me. Quite what Caspar got out of it I'm not sure – far more, in various ways, than he let on would be my guess. There was money of course and the famous episode with the exam paper which almost gave Lloyd a heart attack. He slipped Caspar the paper in advance solely for his own benefit, never dreaming that he'd make copies and sell them. Theirs was a curious relationship, not friendship exactly but certainly not the fear and loathing you'd expect under the circumstances. Perhaps Lloyd was bedazzled by Caspar too.

I'm sure you've found all this exceedingly distasteful and boring but I assure you it is relevant. So we come to the 1970 school ball. Needless to say I didn't go. The non-attendees had a free night but I stayed in. I forget why – it mustn't have suited my parents to have me home. Lloyd was one of the masters whose job it was to wander round at the ball and discourage tongue kissing and dry uprights (there I go again) on the dance floor. He suggested to me that if I felt left out, he could slip away from the ball at some point for a quickie. We arranged a rendezvous in the belltower, above the library, at 10.45pm.

I don't know if you ever saw the place but if you went up that spiral staircase from the library floor, you found yourself in this series of little rooms, a bit of a rabbit warren really, which were essentially used for storage. They contained the overflow from the library, books which had been weeded out, old furniture etc. We were in the third or fourth room along, playing with one another in the dark, when we heard approaching footsteps and the murmur of voices, one of which was unmistakably female.

We froze as they advanced through the rooms towards us. They stopped in the one next to ours. There were no doors – just a series of connecting rooms opening into one another – so we could hear every word. There were two boys and a girl and they'd come up for a smoke and a tipple. They debated whether or not to turn on the light; one of the boys, obviously the ring leader, said they wouldn't be able to see what they were doing otherwise and what did it matter anyway, there were no windows and who the hell was going to come up? So they switched on a light and began puffing and swigging and sniggering. Meanwhile Lloyd and I crouched in the dark just round the corner not even daring to put our trousers back on for fear of giving ourselves away. Lloyd, needless to say, was almost paralysed with fear.

After 10 minutes or so of eavesdropping, I'd worked out that the boys were Dermot Looms, a prime example of the large farm-bred louts whom Prince

Albert seemed to attract, and Basil Batrouney, a creepy youth known for his musical pretensions. It was apparent that something was amiss with the girl, whose name was Bronwen. Before long we learned that the agent of her unhappiness was none other than Caspar Quedley. From what we could gather, Bronwen had a major crush on Caspar but he'd just made it plain that it wasn't reciprocated. I couldn't help thinking, welcome to the club, sister.

After what seemed like forever but was probably less than half an hour, the booze – they had a bottle of brandy, Portuguese I think it was – was taking its toll. Bronwen started sniffling. Looms suggested that Caspar wasn't the only fish in the sea and why didn't she forget about him and have some fun. Nothing was said for a little while – I suspect she was sitting there a bit bamboozled by the brandy while Looms nibbled on her. Then the trouble started: Looms tried to force the pace and Batrouney wanted to join in. Whether they lured her up there with the aim of getting her drunk and taking turns or whether it was spur of the moment, I just don't know. Whatever, she was having none of it. She hissed at them to fuck off and leave her alone, that she wouldn't kiss Batrouney if he was the last boy on earth and that if Looms thought she'd take her panties off for him, he was even stupider than he looked. Looms called her a cockteaser; Batrouney accused her of being a stuck-up bitch. Their voices got louder as the violence of their language escalated. She said they could screw each other for all she cared but she was going; Looms roared back, like hell you are; she screamed at him to let her go. There was the sound of a struggle and a sharp slap; Looms called her a fucking slut, and then I heard this indescribable rasping choke. Without thinking about it, I ran in there pulling on my pants and screaming at them to stop it.

Then the four of us were staring at one another, thunderstruck, struggling to make sense of the evidence of our own eyes. The girl lay on the floor between us. At first, of course, none of us believed she was dead – we thought she'd fainted – and our concerns centred on having been caught in the act of considerably lesser crimes although Lloyd was staring professional ruin in the face. For a minute no one said anything. When I broke the silence by asking if the girl was all right, Looms knelt over her and tried to bring her round. Then he stood up and said quite calmly, "I'd say she's dead." She'd slapped him and he'd seized her by the throat and throttled her. It wouldn't have taken much; he was big and strong and Bronwen was quite delicate. Looms looked at Lloyd and said, "Sir, I think it would be for the best if we all forget what's happened here."

He was astonishingly cool. Batrouney was dazed – he was quite drunk and I don't think he really comprehended the situation; I was crying; Lloyd was in a state of shock, looking from Bronwen to Looms and saying "Of course, of course" over and over. Then he seemed to snap out of it. What was extraordinary then was how he and Looms suddenly seemed to be on the same wavelength. Crises create strange alliances, I suppose. It was only later that I came to realise that from Lloyd's point of view, Bronwen dying was a godsend. Her death necessitated the conspiracy of silence which also enveloped the lesser crimes and misdemeanours, of which his was by far the most serious.

He and Looms organised it between them. The hanging was Lloyd's idea. They used my tie; I was in the ordinary evening uniform, those pants that chafed

266

like mad and a blazer with a standard school tie. The other two were in full black suits and couldn't go back into the ball without a tie, nor could Lloyd, so I had to provide the noose. There was a sturdy rail which must've been used for a curtain or drape to block off the doorway and they hung her from that. Lloyd looped the tie round her neck and stood on a chair to attach it to the rail while Looms held Bronwen off the ground. Then he let her go and she dangled there like a broken doll.

Lloyd told me to get back to the house and to go straight to bed, not to talk to anyone, and to see him the next morning. When I undressed, I found her dance card in my coat pocket. I didn't even remember picking it up. The next day Lloyd gave me a lecture about how it was a terrible accident, they hadn't meant to kill her, but what was done was done and nothing that happened now would bring her back. If the truth got out, all our lives would be ruined so it was better to forget about it, to pretend it never happened. He said I had to be really tough and tell absolutely no one even though there would be times when I'd want nothing more than to confide in someone to get it off my chest. It must've had some effect I suppose; until today, I've never told anyone. He also found me a new tie from somewhere.

I never went with Lloyd again. We did talk about Bronwen a few times; I remember asking him why it never came out that Bronwen had been drinking. He said they would've hushed it up for her parents' sake. For weeks afterwards I expected to be called down to the housemaster's study to find a policeman waiting for me but it never happened. Eventually it dawned on me that it suited everyone – except the Ticehurst family – to treat it as suicide. If the truth had come out, the scandal would've rocked Prince Albert to its foundations and there was far too much money and power and prestige tied up in the school itself and the old boy network – the old school tie syndrome – for that to be allowed to happen. Probably still is.

Perhaps you think that's cynical. Then consider this: if they knew that Bronwen had been drinking, it would've been a reasonable, if not irresistible, assumption that she wouldn't have done so on her own. Not many 16-year-old girls are solo drinkers and she'd hardly have headed off to the ball with a bottle of brandy in her handbag. That opens up all sorts of scenarios, so why didn't the police make an effort to find out who her drinking companions were?

Secondly, how was she supposed to have found her way up to the belltower? Some of the boys wouldn't have even known those rooms were up there. Thirdly, remember how we had to have a name label stitched onto every item of clothing including ties? Lloyd ripped the label off my tie; did the police think Bronwen had done it herself? And where had she got the tie from in the first place?

So there you are Victor. It hasn't salved my conscience but I feel better for knowing that I won't be taking this secret with me. Now that you know, what are you going to do with the knowledge? I'm sure you've heard the old curse – Chinese? – that may you get what you've always wanted? I find it hard to imagine that your peace of mind will be enhanced should you pursue the matter – if anything the reverse. On the other hand, I can vouch for the fact that to know and keep silent eats away at the soul like acid.

God bless you

Julian Gage

When he'd finished reading the letter, Sparks rang Tito Ihaka.

"Thanks for sending me Gage's letter."

"That's okay Reggie. Use it wisely."

"Was he right?"

"What about?"

"You know what I'm talking about – that the investigation was tanked because it suited everyone to call it suicide."

"How the fuck would I know? I was nine years old."

"Don't pretend you haven't looked at the file."

"Sparks, are you asking me as a journalist?"

"Yes."

"In that case, the answer to your question is no, Gage wasn't right. The investigation was properly conducted and thorough in every respect."

"Okay, just between the two of us."

Ihaka said, "Between the two of us, I'm surprised you have to ask," and put the phone down.

Two days later, a Wednesday, a foretaste of summer arrived unheralded in Auckland. A warm wind blew in from the north and the temperature nudged over 20 degrees for the first time in months. Reggie Sparks was driving Louise Appleyard to the airport to catch a plane to Brisbane. She was going to spend some time with her sister; an indefinite amount of time.

As they skimmed alongside the Manukau Harbour foreshore she asked, "Did you see Gage's letter in the end?"

"Yeah, Ihaka sent me a copy."

"What did you think?"

Sparks looked at Louise who looked back at him through big dark glasses. Her window was half open and the breeze whipped around her head, fluffing up her dark mane.

"I thought it was sad. Sad for Bronwen, sad for Gage, sad for Victor."

She nodded. "I've been meaning to ask," she said. "What

made you go up to Looms' farm? I mean, how did you know?"

"I didn't have to be Sherlock Holmes. Delamore knew the whole story because he'd had Gage's letter; I knew he'd gone north and when Quedley said Delamore had told him he was going to talk to someone else about the letter, the obvious conclusion was that he'd gone to see Looms."

"Where's he by the way?"

Sparks smiled. "Delamore? He went back to Sydney to get his face fixed up. He said if they could make him pretty again, he'd go back in the drag show. He's decided he's not quite devious enough to operate on the edge, plus it's too hard on his looks."

"Second question. How did you know Looms had co-murdered Victor?"

"Oh that was just an educated guess. It seemed to me all along that if Victor was murdered, whoever killed Bronwen must've done it. But I was just trying to give you a bit of motivation."

"Well you did. I needed some."

After a while he asked, "So why did you go up there?"

Louise gave him a brilliant, slightly mocking smile. "Reggie, don't tell me you haven't figured that out. You've been so clever about everything else."

He shook his head. "Sorry, you got me there."

"Because," she said, stretching out the word, "Tito thought you might be in danger."

Sparks nodded slowly. "Oh that's why? And here was I thinking you just wanted the chance to shoot someone."

He pulled up in front of the overseas terminal and carried her bags inside. She thanked him for the lift and told him not to wait around.

"Okay." He hovered awkwardly. "Well, have a nice trip."

"Thanks." She gave him a long look. It was part amusement and part fondness. He thought there might have been a part something else too but seeing she was going away and hadn't booked her return, he felt it was prudent to settle for amused and fond. "Reggie, I've been thinking that in a few weeks' time, when my sister and I are no longer on speaking terms, I might come home via New Caledonia. You speak French don't you?"

"Yeah pretty well. I used to think it was my only attribute but it's not a lot of use to me here."

"Oh it's definitely an attribute. I was wondering, perhaps you could come up and be my interpreter, you know, and introduce me to French culture and whatnot. Don't worry about the money – I'd take care of that, now that I'm rich." She tilted her head and raised her eyebrows questioningly.

"Sounds great," said Sparks hesitantly, wondering if he dared believe his ears. "But forget that stuff about paying for me – I'd feel like a kept man."

Louise nodded gravely. "Yes you're probably right. First of all I'd want to be sure you were worth keeping."

She gave him a sly smile from beneath lowered lashes that would throw his sleep patterns into disarray for several days, put one hand on his chest, and kissed him softly on the lips. "I'll be in touch."

Sparks drove home feeling slightly light-headed. He went straight to the desk he'd installed in the downstairs TV room. On the desk was a laptop computer which his brother Gavin had lent him and pages and pages of notes. Sparks studied his notes for a while, turned on the computer and stared at the illuminated screen.

Then he started to write: It was entirely appropriate that Wallace Guttle, the private investigator, should have spent the last hour of his life looking at pictures of other people having sex . . . .

# Other Vista crime titles include

**Dead Beat**  Val McDermid  0 575 60002 0
**Paint it Black**  Mark Timlin  0 575 60014 4
**Falconer's Judgement**  Ian Morson  0 575 60004 7
**Falconer's Crusade**  Ian Morson  0 575 60079 9
**The Death Prayer**  David Bowker  0 575 60028 4
**Poet in the Gutter**  John Baker  0 575 60045 4
**Significant Others**  Robert Richardson  0 575 60049 7
**Making the Cut**  Jim Lusby  0 575 60013 6
**Fast Road to Nowhere**  Joe Canzius  0 575 60104 3
**Falconer and the Face of God**  Ian Morson  0 575 60063 2
**Sharman and Other Filth**  Mark Timlin  0 575 60101 9
**Invitation to a Funeral**  Molly Brown  0 575 60036 5
**Sicken and So Die**  Simon Brett  0 575 60048 9
**Find My Way Home**  Mark Timlin  0 575 60176 0
**Flashback**  Jim Lusby  0 575 60066 7
**Ashes By Now**  Mark Timlin  0 575 60156 6
**Big Italy**  Timothy Williams  0 575 60018 7
**The Curious Eat Themselves**  John Straley  0 575 60135 3
**The Trapdoor**  Andrew Klavan  0 575 60230 9
**There Fell a Shadow**  Andrew Klavan  0 575 60229 5
**The Profiler**  Harry Asher  0 575 60163 9
**The Bath Detective**  Christopher Lee  0 575 60179 5
**The Rain**  Andrew Klavan  0 575 60228 7
**Killer**  Christopher Newman  0 575 60240 6
**Rough Justice**  Andrew Klavan  0 575 60227 9
**Murder Unprompted**  Simon Brett  0 575 60020 9

VISTA books are available from all good bookshops or from:
Cassell C.S.
Book Service By Post
PO Box 29, Douglas I-O-M
IM99  1BQ
telephone: 01624 675137,  fax: 01624 670923

**VISTA**